RALPH'S CHILDREN

RALPH'S CHILDREN

Hilary Norman

This first world edition published 2008
in Great Britain and the USA by
SEVERN HOUSE PUBLISHERS LTD of
9–15 High Street, Sutton, Surrey, England, SM1 1DF.

British Library Cataloguing in Publication Data

Norman, Hilary
  Ralph's children
  1. Children - Institutional care - Great Britain - Fiction
  2. Teacher-student relationships - Fiction 3. Suspense
  fiction
  I. Title
  823.9'14[F]

  ISBN-13: 978-0-7278-6673-8   (cased)
  ISBN-13: 978-1-84751-081-5   (trade paper)

All Severn House titles are printed on acid-free paper.

Printed and bound in Great Britain by
MPG Books Ltd., Bodmin, Cornwall.

For Jonathan

Acknowledgements

My gratitude to: Howard Barmad; Jennifer Bloch; Sheena Craig; Aisha Faruqi; Sara Fisher; Howard Green; Peter Johnston; Helmut Pesch; Helen Rose; Rainer Schumacher; Richard Spencer; Dr Jonathan Tarlow.

People speak wistfully of the innocence of childhood.
Of the still untainted honesty of child's play.
Harmless games of unspoiled imagination and open minds.
Yet some children play, from early years,
with instincts far from pure.
Some play their games with the souls of killers.
And then they grow up.

Prologue

When the lights went out in prison, most inmates longed for sleep.

But the sounds went on and on, making it impossible. The moaning and coughing and spitting and calling and headbanging and . . .

Lying on his bunk in his cell in Oakwood Prison, the teacher closed his eyes and strove for the hundredth or more time to transport himself forward to another place and time, to the day that surely had to come when they finally believed him.

Innocent, for pity's sake.

Sleep had become a double-edged sword with its nightmares, so that the teacher had come to dread night as much as day, because that was when *they* came back to him again, the faceless monsters who had done this to him, who had brought him to this place, destroyed him.

Madness, all of it.

'Beast,' they had called him, over and over again.

Beast.

One day, he told himself, one day . . .

No days left.

Now.

It came so swiftly that he had no time to prepare himself.

First, the sound. Different from all the many others.

Different.

Someone entering his cell.

'What—?'

The last word he said before the horror was stuffed into his mouth.

Last word ever, no time left.

Cloth; strips of sweat and piss-stinking material, filling his mouth, pushing over his tongue and into his throat while his jerking arms and legs were pinned down and his vomit rose up.

The worst death in the world, the devil *himself* in his cell.

'Message for you, Beast.'

The man's voice came through the roaring in his ears.

Them again, the teacher registered as he began to die.

'End game,' the voice said.

Them.

Oxford Examiner
4th August

Alan Mitcham, the Barton schoolteacher convicted last month of the Summertown newsagent's armed robbery, was found dead in his cell at Oakwood Prison yesterday morning.

Despite the massive weight of evidence against him, Mitcham, who used a replica gun to terrorize Sanjit Patel, protested his innocence throughout his trial, claiming he had been forced to commit the crime last December by a 'gang of abductors'. The jury at Oxford Crown Court failed to believe his story and Mitcham was jailed for ten years.

A spokesman for the prison said it was too early to speculate on the cause of death.

Before

The Game

On the evening of the tenth day of October, they gathered in a bedroom above the Black Rooster public house, as the woman known in the game as Ralph addressed them via the speakerphone on the bedside table.

'This time,' she said, 'we're going to do a killing.'

Outside, rain fell out of darkness on to the road and surrounding Berkshire landscape. It was a dull, characterless kind of rainfall, with no wind to lend it any dramatic sweep; the sort of weather to make one glad to be at home and draw curtains, switch on lamps and be cosy.

The room in which they sat was anything but cosy. Drab and meanly furnished, and too small to comfortably accommodate four adults at one time, but the group had met in many far worse surroundings than this over the years.

Venues always the last thing on their minds.

They were all present, which was one of the rules: every member to attend whenever a game plan meeting was called. Every member except Ralph, who did the summoning but was never there these days, yet who was, despite that, still their leader, as she had always been.

In the old, early days, they had held their meetings in the burial chamber at Wayland's Smithy. Not any more. Too much risk.

In the old days, they had seen each other all the time, but over the past ten years their reunions had become rare events and were all the more intense for that.

The most special times of their lives.

Though not as special as the games themselves.

'We've done killing before,' said the man known in the game as Pig.

He shuddered again at the memory, which was not, of course, his own recollection, but seemed to him, each time it assaulted his sensibilities, as vivid as if he had been there – haunting his dreams, too, on a regular basis. Pictures and sounds of Mitcham's gagging terror that August night as the ripped, bunched-up prison sheet had choked and suffocated him to kingdom come.

'Only because we had no choice,' Ralph's voice reminded him.

'And not really *we*, in fact,' said the woman known as Simon.

'It's all "we",' Ralph corrected her. 'All accountable. You know that.'

'Still such a fucking wuss, Sy,' said the man known as Jack.

'We all hated it, as I recall,' Ralph said.

'Not all.' The woman known in the game as Roger spoke for the first time.

'Not you,' Jack said. 'Gotta have real feelings for that.'

'It scared me shitless,' Pig said.

'Everything scares you shitless,' said Jack.

'He wasn't the only one,' Simon said, defending Pig.

'Anyone object –' Ralph's voice brought them to order – 'to us moving on?'

They all fell silent.

The thrill filling them, as it always did. Always had.

'There'll be another difference, too, this time,' Ralph said. 'If you all agree.'

This poky bedroom over the pub near Childrey had been reserved for them by Ralph. Only Simon, though, would stay the night, and that only to avoid attracting notice, since she, like the others, could easily have gone home.

Jack had bought the speakerphone with cash from the Carphone Warehouse in Didcot that afternoon, had pulled out the old phone and bedside lamp from the jack and socket in the grimy wall and plugged in the new one to be ready for the call.

Now they stayed silent, hearts beating faster, mouths dry with anticipation.

Waiting for Ralph to tell them about the next game.

And what was to be different about it.

Kate

'For the last time, Rob, why don't you just piss off and leave me *alone*.'

Kate Turner's closing words to her estranged husband last Tuesday evening, after their 'friendly' drink near the fireplace at the Shoulder of Mutton had degenerated to a point well below acrimony. She'd regretted the words almost as soon as they were out of her mouth, but regret had come too late. Rob *had* pissed off, leaving Kate wanting to cry, but staying instead like an obstinate stone in her seat.

Stupid, she was still castigating herself by Thursday.

Why had she *done* that?

She might not have minded quite so much had Rob been the only significant person she'd used her shoot-first-think-later PMS tongue on in the past few days.

Richard Fireman – the editor of her weekly column, *Diary of a Short-Fused Female*, in the *Reading Sunday News* – had summoned her to his office that morning to pass some reasoned critical comments about the Christmas draft she'd emailed him that morning, and Kate had reacted by flinging practically all her toys out of her pram – narrowly avoiding sending her job flying with them.

She'd never had much truck with the festive season. In years gone by, her mother, Bel Oliver (from whom Kate had inherited curly auburn hair, hazel eyes, small breasts and a low voice that sharpened with mood), had always drunk a great deal more than usual – 'usual' being more than enough as it was – which had inevitably led to rows with Michael Oliver, Kate's father. But family issues aside, over the years Kate had grown increasingly hacked off with the seasonal rituals and the claustrophobia of the shutdown days themselves.

It was all just so downright *depressing*, and this year, with the fragmenting bones of her own marriage following her parents'

on to the rocks, she'd been dreading Christmas more than ever
and had, it seemed, brought that spirit somewhat too gloomily
into her proposed column.

'Fuck's sake, Kate, you'll have them slitting their wrists before
they've even uncorked the bloody sherry.'

Fireman's opener.

He was a stocky man with a round, boyish face, receding
downy fair hair, and granny glasses. His office was cluttered,
but the area immediately around his computer screen and
keyboard was scrupulously tidy.

'I hoped I'd been entertainingly wry about it,' Kate had said.

'Not especially wry, and definitely not entertaining,' he'd
said. 'And no warmth, Kate, that's the worst of it. Any fool can
take the piss, but you've always been able to make us feel you
give a damn.'

'I do,' she'd said, with a sudden urge to cry.

He'd looked at her and recognized the signs. 'Oh, God.'

'Don't,' Kate had warned. 'Just don't.'

Fireman had shrugged and looked back at his screen. 'Write
it again.'

'All of it?' Indignation had replaced misery. 'Some of it's quite
funny.'

'Colonoscopies and funerals come to mind,' he'd said.

'Yours, preferably,' Kate had said.

And from there it had nosedived all the way to the moment
when Kate had pushed her way around to his side of the desk
and tried to delete her column. And *no one* touched Fireman's
computer, and she knew, when the mists had cleared, how lucky
she was that her editor was tolerant *and* still quite liked her work,
or else she'd probably have found herself seriously unemployed
with twenty-something lousy shopping days to go . . .

'You're your own worst enemy.'

Her mother's contribution on the telephone soon after.

'Not exactly what I need to hear, Mum,' Kate had said.

'The trouble with you,' Bel had started to say, 'is that—'

Kate had put down the phone.

Not in the mood for Bel Oliver right now.

In her younger days, Bel had designed jazzy party clothes for a
handful of private clients, but her craving for wine and vodka
Martinis had taken its toll, since when too many of Bel's designs

had been tailored to make Kate's father, Michael Oliver, feel guilty and as miserable as she was.

When the marriage had at last broken down, most of their mutual friends had gravitated towards her husband, leaving Bel's life horribly empty but for her friend Sandra West, a widow from Goring she'd met at a depression self-help-group meeting; a mousy looking but pushy, frequently spiteful woman whom Kate greatly disliked.

Her mother considered Sandi West something of a saviour.

'She believes in me,' Bel had told Kate more than once. 'In my talent.'

'Why not?' Kate had replied. 'You are talented.'

Sandi also pronounced Michael a fool to have left Bel, and Kate cold not to have invited her mother to move in with her; and, according to Bel, despite chronic back pain and money problems, Sandi always seemed to manage to make time for her.

'A cross between a fan and a bully,' Kate had described her once to Rob.

'Your mum's hardly the oppressed type,' he'd pointed out.

Which was true enough, though Kate had wondered now and again about the timing of Mrs West's arrival in Bel's life such a brief while before the final crashing of the marriage. Had wondered, too, if Sandi might not be in love with her mother, and frankly Kate didn't think she'd mind if Bel swung herself around sexually, so long as she could finally become truly happy.

Preferably with anyone *except* Sandi West.

More than a fair share of the blame for the break-up of Kate's parents' marriage lay at her father's door, and Michael Oliver was the first to admit it.

'I'm just not the man Bel signed up to marry,' he said once.

Which was also true, Kate supposed. An attractive, long-legged man with friendly grey eyes, matched these days by greying hair, Michael had been a criminal lawyer who'd suddenly decided he no longer wanted to practice law because the wrong people kept getting punished.

'For God's sake,' Bel had said at the time, 'you've always known that.'

'But suddenly it seems to matter to me a great deal,' Michael had explained.

'Bollocks,' Bel had said.

And with his wife's failure to back him up at that pivotal moment seeming like one disillusionment too many, Michael had decided after a while that he didn't really want to be her husband any more either. In fact the only thing he really, passionately, wanted to continue being – of all the relationships and occupations that had shaped his identity till then – was Kate's father.

'I couldn't stand to think,' he'd told her, 'that you might never forgive me.'

'It's not me,' Kate had replied, 'who has to do the forgiving.'

'But I know how tough it's been on you,' Michael had said.

'Obviously,' Kate had told him. 'Because I love you both.'

'Love,' her father said wryly. 'Blessing or curse.'

'Bit of both, I suppose,' Kate had said, and had promptly gone away to use that as the opening gambit of that week's column.

However much she did love both her parents and – for better or worse – Rob, Kate often spun into monthly denial of that with her dark plunge into PMS, blowing their smallest shortcomings out of all proportion, carping, bitching and generally doing her best to drive loved ones away. Ending up despising herself most of all.

'I'm such a lucky cow,' she remembered saying once to Rob, 'that you put up with me. With *this*.'

Only a year since she'd said that, while they'd still been happy.

She *had* felt so lucky then, knew just how sweet life had been to her, how comfortable her upbringing in Henley-upon-Thames, how easy her years in Sheffield studying journalism, how convenient her return after landing a trainee job at the *Sunday News* – and lucky too that Richard Fireman had warmed to her chatty style and eclectic palette of topics, and that she'd found a studio flat off Church Street in Reading just around the corner to the newspaper's offices in Prospect Street.

'Why not London?' Abby Wells, a friend from university, had asked when Kate had accepted the job.

'Not sure,' Kate had said. 'Lack of confidence, I think.'

'You?' Abby was surprised. 'You can write, you know how to make people listen to you, how to make them *let* you write.'

'Only at uni,' Kate said. 'And maybe in Reading, too, if I'm lucky.'

The old theory about fewer tiny fish in small ponds.

All her blessings had culminated in the preparation of a feature on Reading Park School, where she had been allocated, as her guide, their modern foreign languages teacher. Rob Turner had seen the young woman with russet hair and earnest eyes and fallen for her instantly, and Kate had crashed in much the same way. Rob was tall, chestnut-haired and blue-eyed, with a warm smile and quick mind. In less than twenty-four hours Kate had learned that he loved children and horse riding, and that his heart had been pretty much smashed to shrapnel when his ex-wife Penny had walked out four years earlier, taking with her to Manchester their nine-month-old daughter.

'How could she do that?' Kate had been appalled. '*Why* did she do it?' She felt a need to know, to find out the worst before she lost her heart entirely.

Rob took a moment. 'Penny says she only married me to have a child. Not that there was anything so special about me – she just wanted to have a child by someone comparatively "normal".' His grin was self-deprecating. 'Her word, not mine.'

Kate had said nothing, let him go on.

'Apparently she always planned on leaving when the time was right, because as it turns out she doesn't particularly like men and was never keen on living with one.'

'When did you find this out?'

'The day she told me they were leaving.'

'God,' Kate said.

'She was painfully honest about it that day,' Rob had said wryly. 'But I suppose if she'd been that frank at the outset, we wouldn't have had Emily, and I'd rather have my daughter in my life on my ex-wife's screwed-up terms than not have her at all.'

'She sounds like a monster,' Kate had said.

'She's a good mother,' Rob said.

'Depriving Emily of her father,' Kate had said.

'I do my best to make sure Emmie knows I'm here for her.'

'But that's not enough, is it?'

'Of course not.'

Kate had put her arms around him then, and Rob had said that if she wanted to, she could speak to Penny, who'd promised to confirm the truth to any woman who became important to him.

'Like a job reference,' Kate had said.

'In a way,' Rob had said.
'I don't need to ask her,' Kate said.

She had really believed they were solid.
For keeps.
They were so good together. Sharing their home – a pretty gabled cottage between the south Oxfordshire villages of Sonning Common and Kidmore End – confident that they were enriching each other's lives. For several days each month, Rob sympathized with her darkness and put up with her bitching, and Kate sometimes wished he had some semi-awful habit to match, but there was no *side* to Rob.
Life with him was simply good.
And then it was over.

Laurie

L aurie Moon surveyed her best work of the month.
The most important work, at least. Her gift for Sam. A portrait in vivid acrylic paint of mother and son at the funfair, complete with candyfloss, cuddly bear prize and plastic bag with pitiful goldfish. Happy memories of the 'best day out ever'. Sam had told her it was the best, so it must have been.
What Sam said *went*. What Sam asked for, Laurie did her damnedest to give him. And he asked for so little. Love, mostly. Cuddles. And more time with his mum.
The one thing she couldn't give him.
When it came to her painting, Sam was so easily pleased, her greatest fan. Not so impressed, Laurie was painfully aware, when it came to her role as his mother. There she came about fifth or sixth best, depending on whether, prior to her arrival, his carers and teachers had made him eat sprouts or cabbage or carrots or look at maps. Sam hated green and orange vegetables, but maps really alarmed him. If Laurie arrived on a map or bad veggie day, Sam's greeting was more fervent than usual, though when

she looked into his warm, slightly slanted eyes on those occasions, she saw a touch of desperation that spoke more of relief than love.

Not that Sam needed saving from anyone at Rudolf Mann House, where he lived and was educated. His care was magnificent, his schooling as fine as it could be. Bought and paid for by his grandparents, Peter and Michele Moon. Pete and Shelly to their friends, who thought them salt of the earth people. And even if Pete's money had come from a chain of Essex garages, the Moons had moved up in the world long enough ago for few people to hark back to when they had not lived in their handsome red brick house off the Henley–Wallingford road between Nuffield and Nettlebed and run their excellent riding stables less than a mile away.

They were philanthropic, too, Pete and Shelly, always happy to stick their hands in their pockets or work for charity. Good neighbours with a love for their animals and respect for the beautiful part of the country they lived in.

'We know how lucky we've been, simple as that,' Pete had said many times.

Everyone agreed. They were a lucky, good-looking couple with a clever son, Andrew, married to Sara, a local girl and qualified accountant, living with their kids over in Moulsford; Andrew in the horse business, too, having brought in a few promising racers as well as Sara, who did the books for the Moons these days. And then there was Laurie, their pretty fair-haired daughter still living at home, and working at the stables too now – though she'd studied art and wasn't too bad at it according to the locals whose homes she'd painted.

Laurie had left home for a while some years ago, had gone to stay with relatives in France, painting and – according to Pete and Shelly – doing 'her own thing', though there had been a bit of gossip at the time. People had thought she might have got herself pregnant or maybe just involved with a chap the Moons couldn't approve of – and if *they* didn't approve, there had to have been a good reason, because you couldn't find more tolerant people or better parents.

'You have to know when you're beaten, sweetheart,' Peter Moon had said to Laurie at the time.

Over the breakfast table on a Sunday, both her parents looking uncomfortable but determined, her mother's bobbed hair shiny as ever, but tension in her eyes and around her mouth, her father's rimless spectacles part-way down his nose as his brown eyes fixed on Laurie.

'Some things are just too much to cope with,' Michele Moon had agreed.

She usually agreed with her husband, not because she was a doormat, but because he was a clever, good man who'd steered their path skilfully through life.

'And that's why we're doing this,' Pete went on, 'because we love you so much and want the best for you.'

'That's all we've ever wanted for you, baby,' said Shelly. 'You know that.'

'*Baby.*'

Laurie must have heard her mother use that throwaway endearment a thousand times, but hearing it from her lips at that moment had made her feel as if ground glass was churning deep inside her.

Throwaway.

Baby.

She had fought them, raged and pleaded until her throat felt like sandpaper and her insides like taut-stretched rusting wire, and she'd walked out because she had nothing left to fight with. And then she'd regrouped, sure that if she steadied herself she'd find a way to make them understand and be her kind, loving parents again rather than these new, alien parent-forms that she hardly seemed to recognize. But it had all been to no avail, because she was too young and inexperienced.

No excuse.

Too weak.

More like it.

Too pathetic.

A pathetic excuse for a woman.

A mother-to-be.

Of a baby. Her own baby. Precious to her from the first shock of pregnancy. She'd hardly been able to believe that release of incredible warmth, of that never-till-then experienced *love*. The kind her own mum had described to her in the past, the kind Laurie knew, therefore, that Shelly would comprehend in time. And her dad, too. Once he'd got over the understandable disappointment in his no longer perfect little girl, Pete Moon, her adoring daddy, would see how amazing and beautiful it was that she was going to be a mum and make him a granddad.

But instead, they had wanted her to throw it away.

It.

Sam.

He was eight years old now and living at the Mann Children's Home because that was where Peter and Michele had decreed he should live, because Rudolf Mann House was like a friendly version of a stately home with acres of land, including a petting farm and sporting facilities and gardens, all safely laid out so that children like Sam Moon could play without too much supervision and still not endanger themselves.

The Mann was the only home Sam had ever known. Hospital visits, organized outings and Laurie's days aside, he had spent his entire life there. It was his world, and there was absolutely nothing wrong with it; it was a remarkable place, run by good people. The Mann had its own school and ran workshops and training courses for its older residents when they were ready to either leave the Mann altogether or move into one of its 'satellite' flats or shared houses.

They did not all survive, depending upon the condition that had qualified them for residence in the first place. Down's syndrome in Sam's case. The most common kind, Standard Trisomy 21, with no additional health burdens; a tendency to chest infections when he was small, but no heart issues, which Laurie knew was a great blessing since the ratio for heart problems in Down's syndrome children was about one in two or three.

'He's a lucky little chap,' her dad had said to her once, when Sam was three.

Laurie had never imagined she could ever want to physically attack her father, but at that moment she could have beaten him with her fists for his sheer stupidity. It had to be stupidity, she clung to that, because both her parents *were* kind, even if the Down's had made them denser than beasts, blinding them to what mattered.

Sam being Laurie's son. Her beloved child.

'You can't really think we don't know that,' Shelly had said in an early battle.

'If you do know it,' Laurie had said, 'that means you're wicked, and I don't want to believe that.'

* * *

Her first battle of any substance with her parents had been over her passionate wish to go to art school. Laurie's only real interest in horses had been painting them, which disappointed Pete and Shelly. They'd have been happy enough if Laurie had wanted to become a lawyer or doctor or, better yet, a vet, but studying art struck them as a total waste of time and money. Still, her teachers felt she had talent, and the Nettlebed School of Art was close to home, so they'd given in.

Laurie thought she'd put all her strength of character into that fight, and then she'd slept with Mike Gilliam, a fellow student, just after a twenty-four-hour stomach bug which had screwed up the effects of her pill. And Mike had told her very nicely three days after he'd made love to her that he was getting back with his ex, and Laurie was a really great girl, and he hoped she didn't mind too much, but he couldn't see her again.

'Of course not,' Laurie had told him, though she had minded deeply because Mike was sexy and amazingly talented and she'd wanted him for ages, but he was never going to know that, which was the only thing that made it bearable.

Maybe if she'd got pregnant by someone less special, she might have found it easier to contemplate the idea of abortion, but she doubted that, because she thought it both wicked and cruel. Besides which, that extraordinary warmth, that *love*, had already taken her over.

'We're on your side,' her parents had both said.

Which was precisely why, they had added, there was only one solution.

'No,' Laurie had told them. '*No!*'

Some strength of character left, after all. Enough to make them see that she would die rather than have an abortion.

'I presume this means I'm banished forever,' she told them when they arranged for her to go away, 'since if no one's to be allowed to see me getting fat, then they obviously won't be allowed to see my baby.'

'Not necessarily,' Pete had said.

'What does that mean?' Laurie had asked, then realized it meant they were hoping that either she would change her mind, or that nature might intervene and she would lose the baby.

'God forgive you,' she had said.

Her father's cheeks had grown hot and her mother's eyes had filled with shame, and Laurie had decided that she had won another battle, because if they did send her to Provence to stay with her Aunt Angela – her mother's sister – she would take such great care of herself and her baby that nature would not dream of intervening.

The Game

The group of four had been drawn to each other even before the book had slipped into their lives and bonded them. Tentative friends until then, faintly suspicious of each other, almost in the manner of warily sniffing dogs, sensing that trust without question was unsafe, unwise.

Trust, like good faith, was at a premium at Challow Hall Children's Home, where many of the more troubled children aged between seven and sixteen wielded private agendas and axes to grind, having been brought to the home by a variety of local authorities and courts and feeling dumped, abandoned and generally shat upon.

Once the residence of a wealthy landowner, Challow Hall stood, a large, grey, weather-battered slab of a stone mansion, in the midst of rolling countryside near the village of Bartlet in Oxfordshire, two miles south of the Ridgeway, the ancient pathway that wound some eighty-five miles over chalk downs from Ivinghoe Beacon in the east of England south-west towards Avebury.

Living so close to an area of officially designated 'outstanding beauty' and historical interest, but without so much as a cinema, let alone an arcade, within miles, meant that the majority of the young inhabitants of the home were constantly yearning for some-thing *decent* to occupy themselves with.

Bartlet itself had nothing but a village shop and a church. Swindon, over the Wiltshire border, was the only town worth visiting from the kids' points-of-view, the only place where a person could play machines and buy a decent burger or bag of chips, where the shops had stuff worth nicking. But that happy hunting ground was six endless miles from Challow Hall as the crows flew – and if you weren't a bird and had no wheels at your disposal, then you had to trek up and down hills and over bumpy, often muddy paths through acres of wheat and long grass before you even reached a proper road.

Going to school was, therefore, the best chance of escape for many of them, since the authority saw to it that they were transported to and from their primary and secondary schools, and so, once delivered, they were at least close to a *real* bus route and could, if they were unafraid of punishment, make a break for temporary freedom.

Almost any punishment was worth risking when you were bored to death.

The book had changed everything for the four.

A dog-eared old paperback found by one of them on the 47 bus and brought back to the home. Finders keepers, especially in a place like Challow Hall.

In a sheltered corner of what had once upon a time been a thriving vegetable garden, but was now a trampled, brownish grass play area, the finder had read the dedication out loud to her three closest friends.

'For my mother and father,' she said.

One of them, a red-haired boy, had snorted rudely.

'If I wrote a book,' said the other boy in the group, a thin, freckled lad, 'they'd be the last people I'd thingy it to.'

'Dedicate.' The finder, mixed-race and tall for her age, supplied the word.

'That's OK, I suppose,' said the other girl, who was fair-haired and pretty, 'if you got a nice mum and dad.'

'Or if they're dead,' the thin boy said, and flushed.

'Gotta *have* parents,' the red-haired lad said, 'to feel like that.'

'Is it sci-fi?' The fair girl leaned across and scrutinized the cover. '*Lord of the Flies*. Sounds like that film where all the people went blind and the plants ate them.'

'Triffids.' The finder shook her head, turned the book over, looked at the back. 'This is supposed to be a really *good* book.'

'Do me a favour,' the red-haired boy said disgustedly.

'It's OK, I think,' the finder said. 'It's about kids and murder.'

And then she started reading it out loud.

*   *   *

The thing that surprised them most was that the book was more fun than they'd thought any book could be, and that none of them had any urge to walk away or even yawn. All they wanted to do, right there and then, was go on listening to their friend reading them this tale about a bunch of school kids whose plane had crashed in the middle of some war, leaving them on a desert island without any grown-ups to boss them about.

'Cool,' one of them said.

'Shut it,' another told him.

So the girl who'd nicked the book from the bus and was doing the reading, and who was particularly gifted at doing different voices, went on with it. And though none of them ever read *any* books if they could help it, this story seemed to fire up something inside them, and when the time came for them to have to stop, they found they were all looking forward to getting back to it again.

Escaping from their real lives.

'We need a better place to do this,' one of them said, after two more sessions.

'Somewhere *they* can't spoil it,' another said.

'What about the Smithy?' the reader suggested.

That was another thing that had turned it into something special.

Wayland's Smithy was a Neolithic burial chamber close to the Ridgeway, guarded by enormous sarsen stones, nearly five thousand years old, yet part of the chamber itself and a passage leading to it still surviving. The children had been taken there earlier that year, groaning through a talk about ancient remains, with some dopey legend about horseshoes they were supposed to get excited about.

'Fucking pathetic,' had been the consensus.

Still, the fact remained that it had once been a place filled with dead bodies, which did make it sort of interesting, plus it was in the middle of nowhere, which meant away from the home.

Going outside Challow Hall's boundaries after dark was strictly forbidden.

Wayland's Smithy itself, therefore, massively out of bounds.

And seriously spooky.

They'd gone after lights out, leaving rolled-up towels in their beds (though bed checks were mostly cursory affairs, staff keen to get back to TV and supper) and making their way silently, armed with torches – two bought, two pinched – along the chalky paths and grassy tracks, waiting until they'd reached their destination before lighting candles nicked from the kitchens.

'I don't like it,' the fair-haired girl had said the first time, down in the darker-than-dark passage.

'Don't be scared,' the thin, freckled boy had reassured her.

'It's fucking brilliant,' the other girl had said.

'The dog's fucking bollocks,' said the red-haired boy.

They'd all laughed then, and heard their laughter bouncing off the ancient stones, the sound seeming to shimmer past the boulders at the entrance, and float on up through the beech trees into the black sky.

'Let's do it,' said the tall girl.

It became their own private ritual. Walkers and cyclists might visit the Smithy in daylight, sometimes even camp nearby in season, but the burial chamber was *their* place now for what they called 'doing' the book. A kind of alternative world for them as they journeyed the two hundred and something pages, taking it in turns now to read, swapping characters as if trying them out for size, growing ever more excited as they neared the end.

And then, when they had done with the book itself, they set it aside.

Which was when it *really* began.

The game.

Kate

Even now, almost a year later, looking back on the dark, painful period leading to their separation, it was still hard for Kate to make complete sense of what had gone so horribly wrong between her and Rob.

A positive pregnancy test had brought joy in early January,

sent crashing down in April with the news that a routine blood-screening test had shown abnormal levels of alphafetoprotein in Kate's blood.

She'd gone to her appointment alone, though it was the Easter break and she'd been advised to come with Rob, but he had a meeting that morning, so she hadn't mentioned it to him. At the time, she'd told herself she'd hoped to spare him unnecessary anxiety, but later she realized it had been more a case of burying her own head in the sand, because if Rob wasn't beside her listening to any bad news, then maybe it wasn't real.

Except that after he'd come home, kissing her first, then stacking up his paperwork on the light oak dining table in their living room (where he usually worked, though they'd turned one room into an office) she'd had to shatter his normality and tell him herself.

'What does it mean?' Rob had asked. 'What does this protein do?'

'It means there might be something wrong,' Kate said.

She was fighting to remain relatively composed, had made up her mind that the only way through this for her was to at least *feign* calm.

'Wrong with you?' Rob asked quickly, alarm in his eyes.

'Not with me,' Kate reassured him.

He didn't say anything, sat down at the table and looked at his work.

'It means,' she pushed herself on, 'that our baby might have—'

'"Might",' he interrupted, 'always seems a bit of a pointless word to me.'

She knew right away how odd that remark was, yet felt a surge of compassion, and understood that it was his way of trying to fend off brutal reality.

'That's all we have right now, Rob,' she said. 'We need to be aware that our child might have spina bifida or—'

'Don't,' he cut in again.

Kate pulled out the chair beside his, sat down quickly. 'You need to talk to the doctor with me, to ask questions.' She laid her left hand on the table, waited for him to touch her, but he didn't move. 'Though we won't know any more till after my next ultrasound.'

That was when she'd seen the strange expression on his face: a kind of obtuse shutting down.

'I need to get on with this work,' Rob had said.

As if he had not heard the potentially shattering words she'd spoken.

Bewildered, needing to know that he had taken it in, needing comfort, needing him to be *Rob* again, Kate had made another attempt. 'We have to—'

'*No.*' Sharper this time.

She stared at him.

'I'm sorry,' he said, 'but I don't want to talk about it.'

'But I do.' She had stood up. 'We *have* to.'

'No,' Rob said, definitely. 'We do not.'

'Not yet, perhaps, if you can't—' She broke off, confused. 'But if—'

'Stop,' he had said. 'Please just *stop.*'

She'd told herself it had been nothing more than a blip, a refusal to face the possibilities; and though she knew it might have helped her to share her fears with him, she remembered the shock he'd had at losing Emmie and resolved to give him more time.

Nothing had changed. The intelligent, loving man she'd been married to for two years seemed to have disappeared, hidden behind a frustrating fog of obduracy. When Kate begged him to talk over prospects and options, Rob let her talk, but seemed hardly to be listening and offered no response.

'This is so stupid,' she had told him. 'And horribly unfair to me.'

'I see no point in talking about something that's not going to happen.'

'But what if it does?' Kate was growing desperate. 'What if the ultrasound shows something badly wrong with our baby.'

'That's not what I mean,' Rob said.

'But you just said—'

'I mean termination,' Rob said. 'There's no point talking about that.'

'I'm hoping – praying – we won't have to,' Kate said. 'God knows it's the last thing in the world I want to even think about, but if the very worst happens, and they tell us our child is going to suffer in some dreadful way or . . .'

His eyes stopped her. They'd always been a bright, but gentle blue, but now their softness was gone, leaving them hard as gemstones.

'You need to understand,' Rob said. 'No matter what anyone

tells us *might* be wrong with our baby, I will never, under any circumstances, agree to an abortion.'

For an instant, she felt a bubble of hysteria rise inside her. 'That's not you talking,' she said. 'You sound like a Victorian, or—'

'What?' Rob asked. 'Like a father?'

'For God's sake,' Kate had retaliated. 'What do you think this is doing to me? I'm the one carrying this baby, I'm its *mother*.'

'You're talking about killing our child, Kate.' Rob had been implacable. 'Which makes me realize that maybe I don't really know you at all.'

It had been to all intents and purposes an ultimatum which Kate, already overwhelmed by fear and the possible prospect of all kinds of grief, had felt unable to cope with. Which had made it almost a relief when, that same night, Rob had packed a bag and left the cottage, heading for Manchester.

'I need to be with Emmie,' he'd told her at the door.

'And to hell with me,' Kate had said.

'Don't be stupid,' he said. 'At least try to understand that much.'

She had suppressed an impulse to hit him.

'When will you be back?' she'd asked, instead.

'I'm not sure.'

'The ultrasound's scheduled for Wednesday,' Kate said. 'I assumed you'd want to come with me.'

'I don't think that's a good idea,' Rob had said.

Kate had shut the door in his face.

Ralph's Journal

Those four children didn't care that William Golding's novel was a modern classic. They came upon it by pure accident and became tantalized by it because Lord of the Flies *is a terrific adventure yarn about children turning into savages, complete with heroes and villains – all of them kids – and a mysterious beast needing to be slain.*

The story plucked them, for a while, out of their own miserable, boring lives, simple as that. And when they'd finished reading it, they took from it just what they needed, nothing more.

What they took were four characters named Jack, Roger, Simon and Piggy (all boys because there were no girls in the story) – and, of course, the 'Beast' – and they created a game of pretend. A role-playing fantasy game which became the focal point of their lives. Which became so real and vital to them that they carried it with them into their adult world.

Four characters plus one other, who invited herself along for the ride, and who was lucky enough to be allowed to stay, and become their 'chief'.

Laurie

During one of her scans at the Clinique Saint Joseph-Martin
– situated just outside Avignon, three miles from where
her Aunt Angela lived – they had told Laurie that she was
expecting a son. Neither of her parents had been present, but
her aunt had observed the joy in her young niece's face and had
phoned Shelly later to say that she was only sorry they hadn't
seen it for themselves, because if they had, any doubts they
might have about Laurie's fitness for motherhood would have
melted away.

'She's born to it,' Angie had said.

'We're all born to it,' Shelly had replied.

'This was really special,' her sister had insisted. 'And even if
most mums-to-be do look like that,' she'd added, 'they haven't
usually been sent into exile because their parents are still trying
to stick their heads up their own backsides.'

At twelve weeks, a Combined Ultrasound and Biochemical
screening had been undertaken. This and the Triple Test – a
blood screening to establish risk factors for spina bifida and
Down's syndrome and the less common Trisomy 18 – had estab-
lished Laurie's baby as being in the low risk group. Not that
anyone had been concerned, the mother being young and healthy
and an earlier scan having shown no structural abnormality.

'Thank God,' Angela said to Shelly, who'd come to stay.

'Yes,' Shelly had said. 'Of course.'

Her sister had stared deep into her eyes, blue as her daughter's
and her own. 'You do mean that, don't you, Shelly?'

'Of course I do.' Shelly had shaken her head, tossed her blonde
bob like a pony shaking off insects. 'Don't be stupid, Angie.'

They had known as soon as he was born.

Laurie had seen it in their eyes, first the obstetrician's and nurses' and then, a little later, after they had taken him away, in her parents' and her aunt's.

'What's wrong with my baby?' she had asked.

The question had been trapped in her mind till that moment, packed in ice, not emerging because she'd been too afraid of hearing the answer. Yet she had held her son, had scanned him from head to toe, and he had looked to her eyes utterly *perfect*, and suddenly it occurred to her that maybe this reaction was some kind of ploy, a trick. Maybe now was when they had planned to play their endgame, to try to keep her baby from her, maybe to . . .

'They're not sure yet.' Her father's clumsy answer broke into her thoughts.

'What of? Where is he?' Laurie had felt fretful, afraid. 'I want him back.'

They had said when they'd taken him away that there was nothing to be concerned about, that they were just doing routine checks.

'Try not to worry,' her mother had told her. 'It'll be OK.'

'Not it,' Laurie had said, quickly. 'He. Sam. His name is Sam.'

'That's a lovely name,' her Aunt Angela had said, warmly. 'He's gorgeous.'

'I know he is,' Laurie had said.

They had reached their decision swiftly. No talk of adoption, nothing as savage and pointless as that, because they knew she would never agree, but only three days later, while Laurie and Sam were still at the clinic, Pete and Shelly had arrived fully armed for their sales pitch on the Mann Home. Brochures, letters of praise, glowing results and tributes from families, doctors and even Members of Parliament.

'Nowhere else that comes close,' Pete had told her.

'Nowhere else *like* it, is what we've heard,' Shelly had backed him up.

'No way,' Laurie had said, her whole body rigid. 'He's my son. I'm going to take care of him.'

'I wish, my darling,' Shelly said, 'that was possible.'

'The fact is,' Pete said, 'you just don't know what you're talking about.'

They had taken their time, speaking patiently to her, kindly and, worst of all, sensibly, telling her she had very little choice.

Even though it appeared, so far, that her son was one of the lucky ones, in that he had no immediately apparent heart problems, Sam was still going to need special attention, they said, if he was going to have the best possible chance in life. Which was, of course, what they all wanted.

'You've wanted me to get rid of him from the beginning,' Laurie said.

'At the beginning, that was true,' Pete admitted. 'But not any more.'

There were tears in his eyes, and Laurie couldn't imagine he was that good an actor, had not wanted, even after such a long period of embattlement, to think him capable of that.

She had waited for him to say that it might have been better if she had gone through with an abortion, had waited, wound up like a killer creature with claws and teeth ready to rip out his throat, for him to say it might have been better for Sam. But he didn't say anything of the kind. He and Shelly had just continued on their magnificent sales pitch, giving her time to hear them out, mull it over.

Not too much time, though. Just enough to get it right.

'See if you can look at it as the best possible start for Sam,' Pete said. 'Nothing more than that, sweetheart.'

'The best possible start for Sam, same as any baby,' Laurie told them, 'is with me, his *mother*.'

At least that was what she had tried telling them, but there was something wrong with her; she felt too weak and drained, not up to competing on what felt more like a negotiation with people vastly more experienced.

And of course, they were right, weren't they? He did deserve to have the best start available to him. And if all these people – mothers and fathers, grandparents, siblings, doctors, psychologists and the rest who'd written those letters of praise – if *they* all felt that being in a place as fine as the Mann Home was more important for children like Sam than being with their own mothers, then who was she to argue with them?

There. She had already used one of their phrases. 'Children like Sam.'

No one else *like* Sam on earth. Unique as his DNA and fingerprints.

Remember that, Laurie had told herself. Remember it for ever.

If she forgot that, he was as good as lost.

Kate

After Rob had left, Kate had stayed alone for a time, keeping away from her parents and the paper – telling her friend Abby, who'd been coming to visit, that she and Rob both had flu – putting all her energies into what she was best at: researching what their child might face if one of the disorders thrown up speculatively by the blood screening was confirmed by the next stage of testing.

She could have gone to the hospital, spoken to specialists there, had a talk with Mary Kennet, their GP – and she knew, of course, that she might well have to do all that in time, but she knew too that the only thing keeping her sane for now was the pretence that this research was work, was not about her and certainly not about her own unborn child.

Except, of course, it *was* her baby, which meant that even if Rob had walked away, she was not alone because their child was growing inside her – and *there* was the clincher, finally, for her. And she was almost certain that she would have arrived at the same decision even if Rob had not refused to talk things through, had not cut and run.

Their child *was* growing inside her, and had a right to live.

In sickness or in health.

She had asked her parents, finally, if she could meet them together, deliver all the news to date in one hit, rather than having to endure two painful encounters.

'And please,' she had told Michael on the phone, 'can we keep this to just us?'

Meaning could he please not tell Delia.

The new woman in his life. Delia Price, a website designer from Melbourne. A clever, attractive brunette, taller, younger and steelier than Bel – and, according to Kate's besotted dad, courageous into the bargain, bearing scars on her back from an old

riding accident yet still getting back on horses at every opportunity.

'Which pretty much sums Delia up,' Michael had said a while
ago.

Kate had never quite managed to get past her dislike of Delia,
who was always charming to her when Michael was around, but
cool if they were alone. Not to mention the way she had of trying
to score points with Rob, inviting him to go with her on Sunday
morning horse rides, knowing Kate wouldn't come because she'd
been badly thrown as a child and had been nervous of horses
ever since.

'If she had any sensitivity,' Kate had told Rob, 'she wouldn't
rub my nose in it.'

'But she isn't asking you to ride,' Rob had pointed out.

'Quite,' Kate had said, knowing she was being unreasonable,
but Delia had made her hackles rise from the first.

She certainly wasn't about to share this most private, sensi-
tive matter with her.

'I'm not keen on keeping secrets from Delia,' Michael said.

'Fair enough,' Kate agreed. 'Except then I won't be able to
tell you what's happening to me, and I really could use your
support, Dad.'

'Emotional blackmail,' her father said. 'Bit beneath you.'

'Sometimes,' Kate said, 'that just can't be helped.'

'Rob must be very relieved about your decision,' Michael said
after she'd told them. It was warm for April, and they were sitting
out in the cottage's back garden, using the teak table and chairs
that Kate and Rob had bought last summer, sitting beneath an
apple tree on the grass that, in growing season, Rob liked to
mow once a fortnight.

'He doesn't know,' Kate had said.

'When are you going to tell him?' Bel had asked.

'I'm not certain that I'm going to,' Kate answered.

'You're not serious?' Her father had been shocked.

'I'm not sure I blame her,' Bel said, 'in the circumstances.'

'It's just so unlike him,' Michael said.

'Are you implying any of this is Kate's fault?' Bel demanded.

'Of course not,' Michael said. 'But I think Rob's probably
grieving right now because he may believe your child's already
gone. His, too, remember?' He took in Kate's pale, weary face,

wanted to stop, but pushed on. 'I just can't imagine you think it's fair to punish him by keeping the truth from him.'

Kate had telephoned Rob as soon as they'd left.
    Before she had time to change her mind.
    The relief in his voice was plain to hear.
    'How's Emmie?' Kate had asked.
    'Beautiful.' Rob had paused. 'Kate, I want to come home.'
    She felt suddenly unable to respond.
    'If it's all right with you,' Rob said.
    Kate heard the uncertainty and neediness in his voice.
    Yet he had emotionally abandoned her at exactly the moment when she had most needed him, had totally shut down on her. She remembered his obduracy, the hardness of his eyes. Remembered him packing. Leaving.
    'I'm not sure,' she said, surprising herself.
    'I see,' Rob said.
    A world of disappointment in his voice.
    'No,' Kate had said. 'I don't think you really do.'

The miscarriage had happened swiftly and agonizingly a fortnight later, and she had gone through the nightmare alone, refusing to let the hospital call anyone. And afterwards, when she had told her parents and they'd come together to the Royal Berkshire, she had made them promise not to telephone Rob.
    'But you have to tell him,' Michael said.
    'And have him feel obligated to come and see me?'
    She'd felt so vulnerable in her hospital gown, emptied out, her thoughts muddled, grief ebbing and flowing, half submerged by medication, corrosive anger seeming to surface more readily, its first target the husband who had wanted their child more than his wife.
    'He'll want to come,' Michael had said. 'Of course he will.'
    'Maybe,' Kate said. 'I'm not sure I want him.'
    'You're going to need each other, Kate,' Bel had told her gently.
    'I'll tell him when I'm ready,' she said.

Sandi West, her mother's friend, came to see her two days later, at the cottage.
    The last person in the world Kate wanted to see.

She wore a limp-looking raincoat, carried her walking stick and a brown paper bag, which she thrust into Kate's hand.

'Grapes,' she said. 'People sneer, I know, but healthy all the same.'

Rage filled Kate, at her mother for confiding in this woman, of all people.

'You look tired.' Sandi took a critical look. 'But not too bad, considering.'

'I wish,' Kate said, 'Mum hadn't told you.'

'Your mother tells me most things.' Sandi leant on her walking stick. 'Would you like me to make you a cup of tea?'

'I'm actually very tired,' Kate said. 'I was about to have a sleep.'

'You're not an easy person to help, Kate, are you?' said Sandi.

'I don't recall asking you for help,' Kate said.

Sandi gave a sigh, began to turn to the front door, then stopped. 'I just wanted to say what I expect you'll be too raw to believe right now.'

'Time,' Kate said, harshly. 'Healing. All that.'

'And true, I expect,' Sandi said. 'Mine's another cliché, really. God moving in mysterious ways.'

Kate froze. 'Meaning what exactly?'

'That perhaps, awful as this must be for you, it might, in the circumstances, be for the best.' Sandi paused again. 'For you and the child.'

Kate stared at her in disbelief.

'Get out,' she said, her voice shaking.

'I'm sorry,' Sandi said. 'I don't want to upset you!'

Kate pushed past her, opened the door, stood back.

'Please,' she said. 'While I still have enough self-control not to slap you.'

She shut and bolted the door, then went to the phone and called Bel.

'How the hell could you do that to me, Mother?'

'God,' Bel said, 'what have I done now?'

'Sandi just paid me a visit.'

'Oh.' Bel took a breath. 'I'm so sorry. It was a moment of weakness.'

Kate held on to herself.

'Can I at least take it that you haven't told Rob?'

'We promised we wouldn't,' Bel said.

'Sandi thinks my baby dying was for the *best*,' Kate said acidly. 'She says you tell her everything.'

'That's not true,' Bel protested.

'Good to know, Mother,' Kate said, and she put down the phone and tossed the bag of grapes into the bin.

When Rob arrived two days after that, without a word of warning, carrying flowers, for an instant Kate's anger at her parents resurfaced – but then she saw the soft teddy bear tucked under his arm, and burst into tears again because plainly he did not know.

'God, Kate,' Rob said. 'I'm so sorry.'

He had grown a small beard, something he'd never done when they were together because she hated the prickle of stubble, and whether it had been encouraged to sprout out of independence or misery, she disliked it because it seemed to emphasize his unfamiliarity.

'You'd better come in,' she said, and stepped back.

She took the flowers from him, but not the stuffed toy, and then she told him, without any more delay, right there in the hallway.

And saw, instantly, shockingly, that he did not believe her.

'How can you do that?' His face had grown ashen. 'How can you stand there and tell me such a *lie*, about our own child?'

Kate had stared at him for a long moment, and then she'd turned and gone up the narrow staircase to their bedroom and shut the door behind her.

Moments had passed.

And then the sound of the front door closing again.

Ending them.

He had returned again, two days later, having spoken to Michael.

'I'm so sorry,' he said. 'For everything.'

Kate saw that his remorse was real, that he was filled with self-recrimination, but somehow none of that helped, and this time she let him into the living room, asked him to sit down. And told him that he was too late.

'I'm not saying,' she said, 'that it's all your fault, because I expect it isn't.'

'I left you,' Rob said. 'I wouldn't even let you talk.'

'You found it too hard to contemplate what I felt we needed to.'

'I did,' he agreed. 'And I was wrong, and I'm sorrier than I can say.'

'All the same,' Kate said, 'right or wrong, it all seems ruined to me.'

'It needn't be.' Rob looked aghast. 'Surely not.'

'I'm afraid,' Kate said, 'I really think it is.'

A hormone and grief-fuelled catalogue of mistakes, of idiocy, by both of them.

'You're so stubborn,' Michael told her, some time later.

'They're both stubborn,' Bel – by then almost forgiven – affirmed.

They had gone on telling Kate that, after Rob had moved into a rented flat in Coley Hill, after the initial anger and pain had dulled, after she had begun to become fully and horribly aware of how much she missed him, how empty the cottage felt without him, how dead.

Like their son.

'It's plain as day you still love each other,' Bel had tried one more time, 'so why can't you both just swallow your pride?'

Fair question, Kate knew.

With only one answer.

Idiocy.

Ralph

It was Wayland's Smithy and the children's ritual of creeping out of the home after dark that had first brought Ralph to them.

Not, of course, that she had *been* Ralph – which was the name of the children's leader in the book – or their '*chief*' – right away. And anyway, none of the group had believed back then that she would not make trouble for them, get them into shit.

She was one of *them*, after all. A grown-up, old, and one of *them*.

From the home.

*   *   *

She could remember even now, many years later, what she had felt that first time, standing in the dark just outside the chamber, concealed from them by one of the great standing boulders, watching and listening.

Mesmerized.

Her heart pounding, her palms perspiring.

Something being tapped deep within. Some kind of emotional wellspring blocked off since her own adolescence, when her father had made it necessary for her to shut down sensibility in order to survive.

Rape, impregnation and the killing of her firstborn.

Not born.

Barren ever since, in body and mind.

Till that moment.

She had been at the time a residential support worker at Challow Hall, assisting with the care and general welfare of the children; a position of responsibility of which she was not particularly proud, conscious that with the intelligence inherited from both her parents – she came from educated stock, her mother a teacher, *he* a librarian – she might have gone further academically. Yet she had not, had merely travelled as far as she felt she needed, and then stopped, decided that was as far as she would bother to progress.

She could not, back then, recall ever being proud of anything. She had been a hollowed out shell of a human, with no capacity for pride or any other strong emotion.

A woman who had taught herself not to feel.

She had happened upon them by chance, when she was leaving the home early one winter evening, had stopped her car to check that she had brought out a particular file, and had seen strange flickering lights in the dark distance.

She had opened her window and heard a curious sound.

Silvery on the evening air.

The laughter of a girl and boy, she thought, the joyful sound cut off, perhaps suppressed, then escaping again like bubbles into the atmosphere.

The lights were from torches, she realized after a moment, moving steadily away from the home along the pathways that led through wheat and tall grass up towards the inky black Ridgeway Path.

She had parked her car, switched off the engine and lights, and taken her own torch from the glove compartment.

And followed them.

It was hard, afterwards, to be sure of her initial motives for pursuing them: children bent, she had assumed, on some kind of mischief. Whatever they were up to, they were certainly endangering themselves, but at the moment when she'd made the decision to follow, she had done so neither for discipline's sake nor even because she cared about what happened to them.

She had not cared about them at all then, had not cared about anyone in those days, not even herself. She had simply been curious, especially once she had become aware – as they headed straight across the Ridgeway Path itself and passed through the gate directly ahead – that their final destination had to be the ancient long barrow known as Wayland's Smithy.

She hung back close to the gate, shielded by trees, watching them walk, single file, along the path. She could see now in the moonlight that they were four quite young children, judging from their shapes and sizes and the pitch of their voices which were still hushed even now they were two or more miles from the home.

Shivering a little, not having anticipated a cross-country night walk, she waited, impatient to follow again. She knew what lay around the corner, had come here alone last spring and been moved by the peace of the site, remembered sunlight streaking down through tall, sheltering beech trees, birdsong lifting her spirits.

It occurred to her suddenly that they might be planning vandalism, felt an intense hope that they were not; not because she cared for the stones, but because a good part of her intrigue, following them this evening, had come from the fact that these, clearly, were adventurous children, interesting children – not, she hoped, mindless thugs.

She waited until they'd turned under the trees ahead and disappeared, and then, masking all but a pinpoint of light from her torch, she trod carefully along the narrow grassy verge between the path and barbed wire fence, her rubber-soled footsteps silent.

At the corner, she paused again, saw the glade and the English Heritage sign before it and the mound up ahead.

The children had vanished, their torchlight with them.

She held her breath, not daring to move.

Not that there was any fear in her. This might, she supposed, have been an eerie, even frightening place at night, yet the moon's light, dispersed in constantly shifting glimmers by the swaying branches of the tall trees, lent it serenity.

In any case, she was too intrigued to be afraid.

She heard a new sound, of scraping.

Matches being struck.

A glow came from the left, below the mound.

She recalled the construction of the place and what remained of the tomb, and realized that the children had walked between the two great guarding stones to the left of the mound and gone down into the passage beneath.

She crept closer, aided in her silent approach by creaking branches and shuffling creatures and the calls of night birds, and . . .

They were speaking.

She stepped closer still, until she was standing right up against one of the huge sarsen stones.

Not speaking, but *reading*, she realized. Reading aloud.

From a novel she recognized. One she'd read in her own schooldays, a famous book, she knew it immediately.

That was the instant in which it had all begun for her, with a curious thrill that was so physical it felt like a note being struck deep within her, seeming almost to reverberate, to shimmer through her.

She trod another two small steps to her left, peered through the darkness into the passage and saw them.

They were standing in a semicircle, their young faces illuminated by their candles, their exhaled breath vaporizing in the cold air.

Familiar faces, from Challow Hall. Two boys and two girls, all about ten years old, all intent and wholly absorbed.

Not vandals at all. Just children.

Reading from a book being held by one of the girls.

That was the thing, of course. It was not *what* they were reading – the effect on herself at that moment would probably have been similar if they had been reading Mark Twain or Shakespeare – perhaps even Enid Blyton. It was the sheer, unexpected oddness of the fact that they were reading *anything* at night in such an extraordinarily atmospheric location.

It was the intensity of their focus.

She felt that something extraordinary was unfolding.

Something remarkable.

They were remarkable, she thought.

And in that instant of awakening, she had felt something she had no memory of ever having experienced before, not even in the years when her mother had still been alive.

A most profound sense of connection.

She had to make a crucial decision, whether to turn away and leave them, or to speak.

She knew right away that she could not leave them.

'Hello,' she said, and added swiftly: 'Please don't be alarmed.'

They all jolted and stared into the night, eyes adjusting, finding her, their expressions hostile and afraid, yet she had a sense that her own heartbeat was racing even more wildly than theirs.

'You're not in any trouble,' she said.

None of them spoke. Two of them – the taller girl and a boy with hair that seemed burnished gold in the candlelight, but was in fact, as she recalled, fiery red – went on staring past her into the darkness, and she realized that their impulse was to run and scatter into the night, but she was blocking their exit.

They could have pushed her aside, but they did not.

'Truly.' She felt an urgent need to make them believe her. 'You don't have to worry about me.'

Still they said nothing.

'In fact, I'm pretty impressed,' she went on. 'That's quite a book you're reading.'

'And?' The first word spoken to her, by the lad with red-gold hair, who looked and sounded belligerent, still waiting for trouble.

She felt as she imagined a wildlife student might, coming upon a rare species and wary of snapping a twig and losing them forever.

'Have any of you seen *"Dead Poets"*?' she asked, knowing instantly that it was a foolish question because they were ten and at Challow Hall and of course they hadn't seen it.

'Huh?' the second boy said.

'She means the bloke who wrote the book,' said the tall girl. 'Cos he's dead.'

'He's not, actually.' Having embarked on it, she felt she had to stick with it, went on lightly. 'But I meant a film called *Dead*

Poets' Society about some schoolboys who meet up secretly to read poetry and escape rules.' Their expressions glazed, and she made a swift amendment. 'Though mostly,' she said, 'they're escaping too much control. A bit like you, maybe.' She paused. 'Have you done this before?'

'Are you going to tell?' the belligerent boy asked after a moment.

'No,' she said. 'So long as you mind how you go.'

It was, she knew, a strange and irresponsible decision, but a sense of something at stake much greater than rules had gripped her, was moving in tandem with her own just awoken emotional response.

'And so long as you let me drop in again,' she had added.

A touch of blackmail, she supposed.

Seconds passed. They looked at one another, uncertainly.

'OK,' the boy said.

'You were reading Simon's character last time, weren't you?' she asked the pretty, fair-haired girl the second time she came.

'A bit,' the girl said, cagily.

'He suited you,' she said.

The girl said nothing.

'I've been wondering,' she went on, 'if you'd let me join in.'

'In what?' the thin, less hostile boy asked.

'Reading,' the tall girl said. 'She means reading the book.'

They had got about halfway through the novel at that stage.

'Why?' the red-haired boy asked.

'I'd just like to,' she answered. 'It'd be more fun for me, if you wouldn't mind.'

'I suppose –' the same boy shrugged – 'she could read the bits that aren't people speaking.'

'Narration,' the tall girl said.

'I'd rather be Ralph,' she had said then, quickly, decisively, needing to be clear.

She had thought of little else since the first time. Of her desire to play the part of their leader.

'I wanted to be Ralph,' the red-haired boy said.

'You said you wanted to be Jack,' the thin, freckled boy said.

'You're a perfect Jack,' the fair-haired girl said.

'Don't forget,' the tall girl reminded them, 'she's one of them.'

'I just want to join in,' she said.

And then she held back, waiting, because it was the only way, not wanting them to realize quite how inexplicably violently she wanted it.

They looked from one to the other.

'OK,' the red-haired boy said.

She knew they were uncertain. Still waiting for her to bring them trouble. Which she did not.

Not, at least, in any way they might have anticipated in those days of innocence.

Kate

However she felt about Delia, Kate reflected on Friday – the day after her near-debacle with Fireman – while steering her red Mini out of a pay and display space in Maidenhead, it was hard to deny, in retrospect, that her parents' divorce had probably been right for them both. Her father's love affair with Delia had shocked Bel, but it had also been a turning point. Not that she'd actually given up drink, but she had cut back with impressive self-discipline, gone on attending her self-help group, finding – and keeping – a job selling pretty clothes in a Henley boutique.

As for her father, Kate had to admit he seemed positively in bloom, had found fulfilment in his new life, even helping Delia run her website design company – using his own freshly gleaned IT skills – from their riverside flat.

To which Kate was now headed, bearing a spur-of-the-moment Thai takeaway for three because even though it was a business day, she knew they were home, having phoned briefly to say she was on her way and bringing a lunch.

'Not the best time, darling,' Michael had said.

'You need to eat, however busy you are,' Kate had said and put down the phone.

A burst of goodwill, she decided, at the close of what seemed to her an almost irredeemably vile week – like crocus shoots, she thought, battling up through frost.

Not to mention a sudden great need for her dad's sympathetic ear.

The apartment overlooking the Thames had smooth beech floors and crisp white walls, relieved by vivid Aboriginal landscapes and tall green plants. More Delia than Michael, Kate felt, but it clearly made him happy, and perhaps if Bel were to move out of their old home in Henley, she might have a greater chance of happiness too, or at least be freer of the past, good and bad.

Goes for you, too.

Nothing upbeat about Kate's own separation.

She was still living in the cottage she'd shared with Rob, surrounded by memories – the emptiness of the bed so painful some nights that Kate slept downstairs on the fawn-coloured sofa with its old coffee stain created when they'd been necking like kids one evening and Rob had knocked over his mug and they'd been too into each other to bother wiping it up. The gaps left by his personal things made her ache with longing, and of course she could easily have filled them . . .

But he might come back.

You'd have to ask him first.

They'd begun meeting up for the odd drink or coffee about four months after their parting, and almost as soon as that first layer of ice had been cracked, they'd realized that they both felt much the same. Sad and ashamed of having failed one another, bewildered by that shocking breakdown of communication and their inability to overcome their differences.

Kate still, deep down, feeling betrayed, wary of trusting Rob again.

'I need to take this slowly,' she'd told him in August.

'I need to be with you now,' he'd said. 'I'm afraid if we wait too long, we may never find each other again.'

'I think we already have,' Kate had said. 'At least, we're on the way.'

She had really believed they might be getting close to talking about real reconciliation on Tuesday, but then her *bloody* PMS had collaborated with her angst and still lingering anger, and blown it out of the water again.

Now, this chilly Friday afternoon, she arrived at her father's flat determined to make a real effort with Delia, for her dad's sake mostly, but also because maybe this was her chance to turn a miserable week around, and if she could get through one at least lukewarm hour with Delia Price, then all things might be possible.

The Christmas decorations started it.

'It all looks wonderful,' Kate managed, standing on the unblemished floor gazing ahead into the open plan living and dining area.

Which was a true enough statement, if one wanted to live in a showplace. Not a bauble out of place – nothing, come to that, that could reasonably *be* described as a bauble. Plenty of style, but not a scrap of real warmth.

'Delia did the whole thing,' Michael said.

'I don't doubt it,' Kate said.

Her father and Delia shot each other a look of unity. Against her scepticism, against *her*.

'I brought Thai,' Kate said, holding up the box.

'Darling, I wish you hadn't,' Michael said. 'I was trying to tell you when you phoned, but you hung up.'

'If you've eaten,' Kate said, 'you can probably heat it up for dinner.'

'Except,' Delia said, 'we're going to be in Amsterdam.'

'We're in the middle of packing,' her father said.

Another look passed between them. Lovers, packing to go away.

'We're really sorry,' Delia said.

Yeah, Kate thought.

'I'll go,' she said.

'Why don't you at least dish up for yourself?' Michael suggested. 'Then we can come in and out, and pick at bits while we pack.'

'Not the greatest idea,' Delia said, 'getting pad thai on your shirts.'

Kate tried to remind herself that this was the woman who had turned Michael's life downside up.

Who'd also put the kibosh on any hopes of her parents getting back together.

'Couldn't we just sit down together for a little while?' Kate directed the question at her father. 'You don't have to touch the food.'

'Why don't you do that, Mike,' Delia said. 'I'll finish the packing.'

Kate hated it when she called him that.

'Really?' Michael looked pleased.

'So long as you don't mind my choosing all the wrong things,' Delia said.

'What time's your flight?' Kate asked.

'Not till six,' Michael said.

'Oceans of time,' Kate said.

'Not really,' Delia said. 'Not if we want to look in on those people.'

'Oh, God,' Michael said. 'I forgot.'

'New client,' Delia said.

'Got the picture,' Kate said. 'No time for me, right.'

The dark, hormonal, selfish mood was steaming back up to the surface.

'Darling, don't be—'

'And what's with all this *"darling"* business, Dad?' He'd hardly ever called her that in the past, pre-Delia, not that way, at least, like some actor.

'Is that a sin too now?' Delia enquired. 'Along with daring to go away for a weekend?'

'It might have been nice to know, yes?'

Which was nonsense, and Kate knew it, but she couldn't stop herself now.

'Are you OK?' her father asked.

'Do you care?' Kate asked back.

'Jeez,' Delia said.

'And you can just butt out,' Kate said.

'Kate, stop it,' Michael told her.

'It's all right,' Delia said.

'Of course it isn't,' he said.

'Times like this,' Kate said, 'I understand why Mum turned to drink.'

Neither original, nor the first time she'd said it.

No retaliation from her father, just disappointment in his eyes.

'She says she never drank to escape till she married you, and I believe her.'

No stopping her once she'd begun.

Much like Bel in the past.

'What's all this about, Kate?' Michael asked wearily.

'Oh, sod off to Amsterdam and have a great time,' she said. *Very* adult.

'I hope we will,' Delia said, and put an arm around her father.

Kate headed for the door.

'Don't forget your lunch,' Delia said.

Kate banged the white front door behind her so hard it made the sleek brass knocker clang, raging not at them but at herself for her appalling display, so *exactly* the kind she despised in others.

Shit, shit, *shit*.

No one left to piss off now, because she hadn't called her mother back since putting the phone down on her yesterday, and she didn't want Bel to find out that Delia and *Mike* were going to Amsterdam, because she'd always wanted to go there with him.

End of a perfect week then. Nothing to do now but sod off herself. Get right away and make it harder for anyone to find her – not that anyone would want to, and who could blame them?

She made the decision as she was getting back into the Mini.

Time out needed for her too.

Just her car and the open road and, at journey's end, a bottle of wine, something seriously fattening to eat and, finally, a peaceful night or two's sleep at Caisleán, the old barn that she and Rob had converted together as a weekend retreat in the section of south Oxfordshire that formed part of the Berkshire Downs.

God, she missed him, but there was nothing she could do about it today.

All she wanted, all she *needed*, right now, was to be left alone.

Laurie

Eight years had passed since Sam's birth. Since when Laurie had completed her degree course at art college, collecting her useless qualifications while Sam got his 'start'.

She'd gone to Reading this time, in case people remembered her and asked questions, her parents said, so better to study somewhere no one knew her. And meantime, Sam was doing well and living contentedly at the Mann Children's Home without her. Happy when she visited, knowing perfectly well who she was, as loving and full of hugs with her as he was with most people.

They loved Sam at Rudolf Mann House, and Sam was easy to love; a sweet-natured boy with considerable learning difficulties but with little tendency towards tantrums. Compliant for the most part, like his mother, who worked now, when bidden, at his grandparents' stables (not that Sam knew who his grandparents were), who painted more or less to order, seldom for pleasure, unless it was a gift for Sam.

Laurie knew by now, had known for a long time, that her parents had lied, that of course Sam could have come to live with them, the way thousands of children with Down's syndrome were taken care of by their families even if it was harder teaching them simple skills, even if their lives could be a battle. But all the fight had gone out of Laurie long ago, and she supposed they probably thought of her with contempt at the home – she knew that one of them did, at least; a woman who had come out to speak to her one Saturday afternoon when she was bringing her son back after their day together.

'You mustn't worry,' she had told Laurie. 'He never frets after you've left him.'

Bitch, Laurie had thought, though she knew she ought to be glad, because she never wanted Sam to be unhappy for a second, and this woman – who had to be extra worthy because she had a disability herself, which meant that she'd not only overcome, but was giving of herself to God knew *how* many children, while Laurie, who had nothing wrong with her, couldn't manage to give her own son more than one day a fortnight – was surely right to think badly of her.

Bitch.

Laurie supposed her fight would come back if someone were ever to want to hurt Sam in any way. But that was never going to happen so long as he lived in his safe haven.

Safe and sound near the hamlet of Barford St John, south-west of Banbury. Far enough away from his mother's home to be virtually sure that no one from *their* world would ever spot Laurie coming to call at Rudolf Mann House, let alone identify Sam as anything to do with the Moon family.

Laurie didn't hate them any more.

Just herself.

'At least,' Shelly had said to her when Sam was about five and Laurie was showing her a photograph of his smiling face, 'you'll always know you've done right by him.'

The photographs Laurie used to give her parents were never displayed in frames like Andrew and Sara's children's photos. Sam's pictures always disappeared, and Laurie had once decided that her parents either cut them up or burned them in case someone went through their rubbish.

She had stopped giving them his photos a long time ago.

That was not important. *They* were not really important any more. Except that they paid Sam's bills because she could not, because she had not listened to them when they wanted her to become a lawyer or doctor, which meant that the time would never come when she could begin to take on what they did for her son.

But Sam was alive and well, and Laurie was able to see him once a fortnight.

That had been laid down in the ground rules made after Provence, along with the law of 'absolute secrecy'. They had negotiated a little, had suggested at first that Laurie see Sam only once monthly, but with what was left of her will she had dug in her heels, and they had given way.

After that it was take it or leave it. So she took it.

She was pleased with the picture she'd completed in time for her next visit. She couldn't wait to see the look on Sam's face when he realized it was the memory of their day out at the funfair in Banbury. Couldn't wait for one of his wonderful hugs.

'They're so loving,' people often said about children with Down's syndrome. Most of them knowing so very little about the realities of their everyday problems.

Just like Laurie.

The Game

In the beginning, the group's pretend games were always set in their imaginary, greatly restricted version of Golding's wild, fictitious island, the two boys and two girls continuing to swap characters till they felt they had the right fit. When that much had become clear to them – who was playing who – they'd junked the rest of the characters and plot, but each of them had held tight to their own role as if they really needed it, almost in the way that younger children sometimes needed battered stuffed bears or a night light.

I find it remarkable – Ralph had written in the private journal in which she'd begun to set down her observations on the children and their metamorphoses – *how snugly their characters do seem to fit them. And where they didn't exactly fit, the manner in which they've adapted to their new alternative selves.*

Easy enough to see why they needed imaginary identities, since anything was likely to be happier than their own, real lives, and though Ralph had not been officially privy to their files, she had found opportunities to read them.

Sad stories. Their collective pasts even worse than their present.

Since beginning her friendship with the children, she had found herself wishing for the first time in her life that she had persisted with her studies, perhaps become a psychologist, a person really up to *helping* these extraordinary children.

Though if she had, of course, she would probably not have come to Challow Hall at the right time. Would not have been able to follow their lights and find them.

She began to write her journal in a manner she felt a trained psychologist might; told herself this was a kind of personal further education, that she was conducting a sociological exercise. She tried to analyse her motives in befriending the children, and concluded that there was nothing at all reprehensible in it. She simply wanted to be their friend; wanted to be among them and playing their games, partly because it was the most fun she had ever known, but mostly because she hoped she might be the kind of person they needed on their side. An adult as much on their wavelength as it was possible to be.

From the beginning of her notes, she used their adopted names for anonymity's sake, in case anyone else found the journal; but as time passed, she realized she had actually begun to think of them by those names, found it interesting how little the gender of the names mattered – girls renaming themselves Roger and Simon.

Even beginning to think of herself as Ralph.

'JACK'. Our boy, with his red hair, sharp green eyes and straight, too grim mouth, unlucky from the off, dumped as a newborn in a Bristol shopping centre car park without so much as a note from his presumably desperate mother. In care from the start. No adoption for Jack, just a string of foster homes, his behavioural problems reportedly ending each attempt. Deep abiding anger described by families and social workers, along with an inability to love or be loved. Supposed *inability. I am not convinced about that.*

'SIMON'. Our girl is soft and fair, but they say she's prey to depression. Her early history was dire, even pre-birth. Her teenage mum, terrified that her own violent parents would find out if she sought abortion, punched herself repeatedly in the hope that she might kill her foetus. But it survived – Simon survived – born with internal injuries, needing surgery, after which her wretched mother committed suicide and left a note of confession. Simon's scars are invisible, but her inheritance weighs upon her. She fears, according to Dr Lindo, that she may be a wicked person.

'PIG'. When our boy was three, his parents were jailed for child cruelty and his baby sister adopted, but he was placed into care. Described as generally placid, with peri-odic flashes of temper, always followed by acute shame. If there is blame to be apportioned, Pig usually takes it

on himself. He's rake-thin, freckled, not special looking perhaps, but certainly not unattractive. He has a kind heart.

'ROGER'. She came into the care system aged seven, while single mum was having chemo and unable to cope with her two kids. Her half-brother went to live with his dad, but there was no one to take Roger. Her mum was afraid a foster family might give her more than she could match when she recovered, so Roger came to Challow Hall. According to her file, Roger showed no emotion when told her mother had died, though another note refers to 'a display of apparent grief' at the funeral home – as if this was disbelieved. It's true to say that our Roger is a fine actress.

Over time, as Ralph had observed and participated in their evolving games, she had come to understand more about the bond that had formed between the four even before role-playing had reinforced their mutual trust and interdependence. Much of what they had in common, they shared with many children at Challow Hall and other homes; kids who nurtured feelings of intense bitterness against authority figures, do-gooders and parents who had, for whatever reasons, caused them to be placed in care. Ralph wrote:

These four, however, all appear to have particularly powerful feelings either for or against mothers. *Whether their own, or foster mums, or bad mothers in general, or beloved lost mums. Fathers, it seems, don't really count in their experience; their own either weren't there to begin with, or pissed off, or got sent down – and face it, no one expects much of dads, but mums are meant to be different. Better.*

And two years later, by which time they were all inextricably bound together, she had added to her theme:

They have developed strong feelings about the 'glory' of motherhood or, conversely, the Philip Larkin approach: 'They fuck you up . . .'

Ralph never wrote a word about her own parents. About her father.

Still shut away, closed off, that part of her life.

Better things – at last – to occupy her now.

Their games always revolved around 'the Beast'.

They were children, after all, taking the parts of other children in an adventure setting, with a beast that had to be slain if they were to survive. The kind of metaphor commonly employed by children in pretend games all over the world. Yet these children had swiftly developed a more sophisticated slant to their games, nominating actual people whom they disliked as Beast.

A certain harshness in their play even then.

Innocent, though, at heart – Ralph wrote.

'Shirley's the Beast today,' Jack nominated one week.

Meaning Matt Shirley, a kid who had brought him down in a football game the previous day.

They didn't attack the *real* Shirley in their game, because Ralph discouraged violence. Pig was chosen by Jack to play the part of Shirley, and that was the way the games all went; each one in turn chose a Beast and which member of the group was to act him or her.

Harmless back then, but undoubtedly complex and unusual. A springboard to mental and physical freedom, as Ralph saw it, enabling, even empowering them and increasing her urge to protect what she saw as a healthy outlet for their fantasies.

She was well aware, in those early days, that they had tolerated her because they felt they had little choice, yet still she felt honoured that they had let her stay amongst them, on the outer edges of their play – though it had always, if she was truthful, been more intense than child's play.

She had been, at the time, thirty and alone. No siblings, her mother long dead of an embolism, her father remarried and vanished from her life, wholly indifferent to her by then. Her own flawed psychology buried deep along with her past sufferings, leaving her, she felt, as a blank canvas on which these children – *her* children, as she had begun to think of them – could paint with personal creativity, gradually bringing her, as Ralph, to life alongside them.

A secret life, of course. One which would, had it been discovered, have brought her dismissal, perhaps worse. But the fact

was, she had felt truly alive and filled with potential for the first
time in her own sad existence, and nothing could have made her
want to give that up.

There seemed a purity about it all then which she had no idea
would change.

She never expected to lose herself in her new identity as their
leader.

Chief.

Never expected to guide them into the mire, to taint their
souls, ruin their lives.

Not to mention her own.

Kate

Caisleán – Gaelic for castle, so Rob had told her when he'd
chosen the name for their converted barn – was less than
an hour's drive from home but small and isolated enough for
tranquillity.

All Kate had wanted, on leaving her father and Delia's place
in Maidenhead, was to reach the retreat as rapidly as possible.
But by the time she'd got back to the cottage to pack a weekend
bag and her laptop, it was after three; and then she'd had to go
back to Reading to pick up some notes at the *News* – and luckily,
Fireman was in his Friday afternoon meeting, so there was little
risk of an encounter, though she had mustered the common sense
to shoot off a swift email telling him she was going to the barn
to rewrite her Christmas column – and Lord knew she needed
a few brownie points after her awful tantrum.

After that, she'd stocked up at Waitrose in Church Street –
more than enough ready meals and bread, cheese and wine for
the weekend, plus some Belgian chocs and mince pies *and* cream
– but by then it was ten past four, which was a pity because
winter darkness meant she'd be deprived of the beauty of her
journey – half the pleasure of going up there – and also because
if she was on her own, she preferred arriving at Caisleán in

daylight, being settled and cosy, with a nice fire lit, before dusk fell on the Downs.

Leaving that message for Fireman meant – she reflected, leaving behind Reading's built-up area and bright lights – that she was now committed to working for at least part of the weekend, but she'd remembered to stick her new Anne Tyler in her bag, and a couple of classic DVDs, too, in case there was nothing that appealed to her on TV, and the Radio Berkshire weekend forecast was colder, which suited Kate too, because there were few things she liked better than walking in the wind over the Downs before snuggling in front of the fireplace.

Few things, of course, except doing that with Rob.

'So stupid,' she said to herself, regretting yet again her own idiotic temper.

Missing him more than ever.

Darkness was already straining her eyes and creasing her fore-head, though traffic was unusually light for a Friday afternoon as Kate, still on the A329 nearing Streatley, allowed her concen-tration to wander into a swift fantasy in which Rob arrived at Caisleán determined to win her back.

'Grow up,' she told herself sharply.

Even if Rob did want to see her, it wouldn't be possible this weekend, because he'd told her that Penny had asked him to have Emily, and that hadn't happened in a long time, and since there was, quite rightly, no one more important to Rob than Emmie, Kate would not dream of disturbing their—

The bang as her car's front offside tyre burst was as loud as a gunshot.

'Jesus!'

The Mini veered lethally into the oncoming lane, terrifying the driver of the small Mercedes coming the other way, then zigzagging for what felt to Kate like hundreds of yards, and the steering wheel seemed to be juddering in her hands, and she only just avoided a van looming out of a narrow road to the left, and she was conscious of flashing lights and furious hooting from somewhere behind her, but finally, mercifully, the little car came to a halt on the edge of the grass verge.

'Jesus,' Kate said again, blood roaring in her ears.

And then another bang, almost an *explosion* of sounds,

reverberated through her as two – no, three – cars behind her skidded and collided with each other.

Time passed as Kate sat, shaking.

Too afraid to turn around and see the havoc she had caused.

Praying silently for no one to be hurt.

Please.

The Game

'Game on.'

The word had gone out within minutes.

Jack's wife was used to being dumped with their kids at a moment's notice.

Pig was ready to call in sick.

Neither Simon nor Roger had anyone to answer to.

'Take care,' Ralph had told them all.

She had never felt more bereft than now at being left behind.

Laurie

The day before she visited Sam always brought a mix of happiness and fear to Laurie because she so longed to see him but was desperately afraid that something might happen to prevent her from going. And heaven knew there'd been no shortage of times when her parents had done their best to achieve that, though not even Shelly's flu last summer and Pete's broken wrist the previous winter had prevented Laurie from arriving at Rudolf Mann House on the dot of 8 a.m. on Saturday morning.

Not that her anxieties ended there.

Would Sam be happy to see her? Would he look fit and well? Would he enjoy their time together? How would he be when they had to part?

Laurie knew how she would be.

She remembered one visit that had begun badly because Sam had been taken ill at breakfast time, but Laurie had spent the day sitting with him, and in a way, it had turned into one of her happiest memories because Sam had really needed a mother that day and she had actually *been* there for him, aware that there were others at the home who could have helped him just as well, probably better, than she could, amateur that she was.

But they were not his mother.

The bitch had been there that day, had almost managed to sour it for her.

'Enjoyed that, didn't you?' she said to Laurie as she was leaving.

'I certainly didn't enjoy my son being ill,' Laurie had said, managing to find the right words, 'but yes, I'm glad I've been able to be here with him.'

And the bitch had just smiled, given a shrug, and turned away.

Only thirteen hours and fifty minutes to go till she saw him.

Dinner time soon in the Moon house.

The atmosphere between them the evening before visiting days was always strained. No questions were asked about Laurie's plans for the weekend. More than eight years since Sam's birth and they were still the same.

At some levels, Laurie still loved her parents, but on these particular Friday evenings, she hated them as much as the bitch. More so, if she was honest about it.

Thirteen and three-quarter hours to go.

The Game

Ralph sat in her winter garden, decaying leaves whirling around her, circling and enclosing her, whipped up by a sudden squall. Seen from a distance, she might have been at the core of a vortex, the base of a small tornado, but she was utterly still.

Thinking about them.

About the new game.

About that other, early game that had kept her from being with them – *fully* – ever again.

Some of the leaves landed on her head, stalks catching in her hair. The wind dropped and they remained there, like a twisty golden crown.

The Chief.

It had happened during their third year together, when the children had been about thirteen and she had been thirty-three.

The games had long since ceased to be childlike, their edges too razor sharp for that. They still took turns to nominate a Beast and punish him or her, but whenever possible, they no longer role-played the Beast, but used the *real* targets instead.

It had been Roger's idea to move the game up that notch.

'It's too dangerous,' had been Pig's reaction.

'We might get caught,' Simon had agreed.

'We won't,' Roger had said.

'Not if we plan it right,' Jack had backed her up.

Planning it *right*, they decided, meant isolating the Beast from outsiders, playing under cover of darkness and using war paint – as the children had in the novel that had first inspired them – faces smeared with black and layers of brilliant colour to confuse and alarm their target and, most important, to make them unrecognizable.

They were wary of getting caught, though it was not

authority of which they were wary, but the awful spectre of being split up.

'I couldn't bear it,' Pig had said.

'It would be rough,' the girl called Roger agreed.

'It would be piss-horrible,' Jack said.

'We mustn't let it happen,' said the girl called Simon, 'not ever.'

'We won't,' Jack said. 'Not with Ralph to help us.'

'If she will,' Pig said.

'She always does,' Roger said.

It was true. Ralph knew that somewhere along the way she had become their creature, rather than simply their protector. And if her relationship with them had begun out of fascination, it had long since become something of an addiction.

'I'm not sure,' she had said, when they'd first broached the new idea – knowing that by not stamping wholeheartedly on it, she had as good as given it her blessing.

'Whoever we punish,' Simon said earnestly, 'would have to be a true Beast.'

'Obviously,' Jack said.

'We're not brutes,' Pig said.

There was no shortage of potential Beasts, but the children were practical, realistic about degrees of risk. If they were to take action against, say, one of the more detested teachers at school, they knew they'd be unlikely to get away with it; and the same could be said for the skinny old battleaxe who ran the Bartlet village shop, and who mistrusted every kid who stepped out of Challow Hall.

They had fewer misgivings about the cleaner.

Rose Miller, a pinch-faced woman with meaty arms, worked five days a week in the home, lived in a terraced cottage just outside the village, was always loving to the smelly mongrel dog she called Billy, but was a nasty piece of work when it came to her little girl and boy, always yelling at and smacking them in the shops and in the road. *Real* slaps, too, not just taps on the bum or arm, bestowed with a force that left the kids in little doubt of what probably went on once she got them indoors.

And since *nothing* was worse, in their eyes, than mothers who were cruel to their children, the group had unanimously agreed that Rose Miller deserved whatever they could manage to give her.

Intimidation, mostly.

'And pain,' Jack had urged one evening at Wayland's Smithy.

'Not pain,' Ralph had intervened. 'I won't be a party to thuggery.'

'Not even if it's deserved?' Pig asked.

Ralph had heard longing in his tone, aware that while Pig was in most ways a gentle soul, his own parents' savagery had made child abuse anathema to him.

'Not even then,' she had answered firmly.

'So what's the point,' Jack had wanted to know, 'if we can't hurt the cow?'

'We can make her afraid,' Roger said. 'Show her that if she can't take better care of her kids, she'll pay for it.'

They'd all looked back at Ralph, waiting to see if she objected to that.

It would, she knew, have been the moment to call a halt, but she was too fascinated to know how the new game might unfold, and so she had said neither no nor yes, and knew that she might as well have given them an A for effort.

They were all quiet for a minute.

'What if it goes wrong?' Simon had asked. 'What if she recognizes us and tells?'

'She won't,' Roger said. 'And if she does . . .'

'Worst comes to worst,' Jack said with a shrug, 'they'll lock us up.'

'Separately,' Pig said, grimly.

'They might not believe her,' Ralph said, quietly, and explained that she thought Rose Miller might be fiddling social security, because she'd been keeping an eye on the cleaner herself, had tracked her as she went to jobs in three other villages in the district, had even stood behind her in the post office in Ashbury one afternoon when she'd been collecting her benefit.

'So we could blackmail her,' Jack had said with relish.

'No,' Ralph said. 'But if worst did come to worst, she might not be believed.'

'I wish,' she had said to them, on the morning itself, 'you wouldn't do this.'

They were not in the Smithy at that hour, but in the former

vegetable garden at Challow Hall, plenty of kids around, Ralph having walked past the four carrying her battered attaché case, casually stooping to pick up the dented football they'd been kicking aimlessly around.

'You're not going to tell, are you?' Pig had asked her anxiously.

'Of course not,' she'd said. 'I just want you to think about it one more time.'

'We've thought about it,' Roger said.

'You need to understand –' Ralph spoke quietly – 'that however rotten she is, it doesn't make what you're planning to do right.'

Right and wrong, good and evil, still separated in her mind back then.

'We,' Roger said, quite sharply. 'You've helped us, remember.'

'Of course,' Ralph said, and saw Simon glance uneasily around.

'Are you going to stop us?' Jack asked.

'Without reporting you,' Ralph answered him, 'I don't see how I can.'

She bounced the football, caught it, scanned the garden, saw that no one was remotely interested in her or them, and handed the ball to Jack.

Simon looked at the others. 'I'm not quite sure about it.'

'I am,' Roger said. 'I'm looking forward to it.'

'You just want to do the acting,' Simon said.

'It's not,' Jack said, 'as if we're going to really hurt her.'

Ralph looked from one to the other, all in their uniform grey, and felt a pang of something like loss.

'You do remember,' she said, 'that I can't join in this one at all, don't you?'

'We know,' Roger said. 'You've said.'

'Just as long as you don't shop us,' Jack said.

Ralph felt the threat underlying his words, and was suddenly afraid, not for herself, but for him, the boy-thug.

'She never would,' said Simon, tenderly.

No active participation, but she had been there nonetheless, could not keep away.

Had to watch from a distance, just in case.

Their Chief, after all. Guardian, more like.

It had started well enough, according to plan.

They took the cleaner's dog, which was called Billy, while his mistress was at one of her jobs and the children were at school – and there was no husband or live-in boyfriend, which had made things less complicated – and after dusk, Roger had made an anonymous call from a public phone to say that the dog had been spotted tied to a fence on Bartlet Down.

'Who is this?' Rose Miller asked, but Roger had already hung up.

She came, as they'd expected, though they were all relieved she came alone, had been afraid she might have brought the children, but it was cold and dark and she had done just what Simon had guessed she would; left the kids on their own and walked up towards Bartlet Down, bundled up in an anorak and woolly hat, shining a torch in front of her.

The dog was there all right, its muzzle tied with a scarf – a long green woollen thing pinched by Jack out of a woman's shopping basket on the bus – to stop it barking, though his whines were more than piercing enough, and there was no time to lose.

'Billy boy,' Miller said, shock in her voice. 'My poor—'

She began to stoop, and they were all on her.

Ralph, hidden behind a tree but close enough to see the action, felt suddenly and violently sick, because Miller's torch and the half-moon lit up the children's monstrous war paint and the cleaner's face, and her terror in those first moments were a part of what made Ralph nauseous.

She had done this.

She clapped a hand over her mouth, afraid she might vomit.

And right away, saw it begin to go wrong.

'You bastards!'

Miller's fear seemed to fill her, transformed swiftly into a fury, endowing her with a strength none of them had bargained on.

'You *shits!*' she screamed when Jack seized hold of her thick arms, fought back, kicking and striking out with her gloved hands, while Billy whined piteously into the night air.

Do something.

If she didn't intervene now, Ralph realized, something worse would happen.

Her mind shot through one scenario even as she moved. If she was quick, then Miller might believe she'd come to help her, and the group could get away while . . .

But Rose Miller saw her coming out of the dark, and felt, in the heat of her battle, that Ralph was another threat.

'*No!*' she cried out.

'Let me—'

The cleaner tucked down her head and butted Ralph hard in the chest, and Ralph stumbled on the grassy slope, began to slip and then to slide. And what began as a fall from which she might easily have got up, became something else entirely, something *dreadful*, as she crashed into the trunk of a beech tree.

And knew no more.

Kate

For as long as they were still checking to see that Kate had not been injured, the people who had emerged, a few at a time, out of the darkness – police, farm workers, paramedics and other drivers – were quite kind to her, but as soon as they saw that she could walk unaided, it seemed to her that everyone began to shout at her.

'Stupid, bloody women drivers.'

'Shouldn't be allowed on the road.'

'Can't control their cars.'

Kate ignored them, appalled enough already by the chaos that her burst tyre had created, seeing the long line of headlights snaking back along miles of curving road as the police began ordering the onlookers away and organizing traffic controls around the cars still blocking the two-way road. More than anything, she was profoundly grateful that no one seemed to have been badly hurt, though she had seen in the lights of an ambulance that the driver of one car was bleeding from a gash in his head.

'Can I go wherever he's taken to make sure he's OK?' she asked a paramedic at the roadside. 'I mean, I know it wasn't really my fault, but it was my tyre that caused all this, so—'

'Not going anywhere –' another policeman came from behind her – 'until we're finished here.'

Which turned into a string of questions, a checking of her licence and insurance, and a long blow into the gizmo that

declared Kate sober – and she thanked her lucky stars that she
hadn't drunk so much as a sip of wine while packing her bag
earlier, then promptly had to thank them again as her spare tyre
was declared sound – more luck than judgement, since she didn't
think she'd ever checked it since buying the Mini.

It was almost an hour before she was ready to drive on – except
that the injured man had been taken to the Royal Berkshire,
which meant driving all the way back to Reading. But since she
hadn't learned his name, unless she did go there and make certain
he was all right, Kate knew she might not be able to properly
relax when she did finally make it to Caisleán.

No fractures, no concussion, just a few stitches, as it turned
out – none of which good fortune stopped the man from
haranguing Kate.

'They should make you take your test again,' he told her. 'You
obviously feel guilty, or you wouldn't be here.' And after a breath:
'There are courses for people like you.'

Kate sat politely, aware he was probably shocked, waiting for
him to finish.

'There really was nothing I could do about it,' she said finally,
mildly, wondering why she seldom managed to react so calmly
with people she loved.

She experienced another great longing to speak to Rob, but
she didn't want to sound needy, nor did she want him to think
she was trying to muscle in on his time with Emmie, so having
downed a machine-bought can of Coke and a packet of crisps
and used the loo, she went back to the hospital car park and
settled for calling up her messages at home, in case Rob might
have had a similar urge.

Only one message, from Bel.

Kate sighed, got into the Mini and returned the call.

'Hello?' a voice answered.

Not Bel.

Sandi West.

She was usually somewhere around her mother's life these
days, which Kate had just about come to accept was, for Bel's
sake, perhaps not entirely a bad thing.

'Hello, Sandi,' she said now, willing her hackles not to rise.
'It's Kate.'

'How nice,' the other woman said.

The sarcasm made Kate grit her teeth. 'Is Mum there?'

'You really upset your mother the other day,' Sandi told her. 'Putting the phone down on her instead of listening to her good advice.'

'Nevertheless,' Kate said, 'I'd like to speak to her, please.'

'You can't,' Sandi West told her. 'She's gone to the chemist's.'

'Is she ill?' Kate waited for Sandi to lay some extra guilt.

'She's gone to fill a prescription for me,' Sandi said. 'I have to go away for the weekend, but my pain's worse than usual and she was kind enough to offer.'

Kate managed to end the call without resorting to rudeness.

The phone rang again, startling her. She peered at the display, saw it was her father calling.

'Dad?'

'Are you all right?' he asked.

Kate was startled, wondering how he could possibly know what had happened.

'Only you weren't yourself earlier,' Michael said.

Just coincidence then.

'Too much myself.' Kate remembered her awful behaviour. 'I'm so sorry, Dad, I was a real bitch. And will you tell Delia?'

'No problem, sweetheart.'

She blessed him, as she had many times before, for his forgiving nature.

'Are you guys at Heathrow?' she asked.

'I'm home,' Michael told her. 'Alone. Delia had a crisis.'

'What kind of crisis?'

'Family.'

'In Oz?'

A vision of Delia boarding a Qantas jet gave her a swift rush of pleasure, which she promptly squashed because her father would miss her.

'No,' Michael said. 'Cumbria.'

If Kate had previously known about Delia's UK relatives, she'd forgotten.

'I just wanted to tell you I love you, Kate,' Michael told her. 'And that if you need to talk, I'm always here for you.'

The warmth she felt was a reviving force.

'Thank you, Dad,' Kate said. 'Though I'm on the way to Caisleán for the weekend.'

'Just what you need,' Michael told her.

'Hope so,' Kate said.

'Drive carefully, my darling,' her father said.

Kate promised she would.

'Don't worry about me,' she said.

'I'm your dad,' Michael said. 'Goes with the territory.'

Laurie

Not one, but two spanners in the works as Laurie's count-down continued.

First, a pipe had burst beneath the first floor, resulting in half the kitchen ceiling crashing down on the Moons' beautiful granite worktops and maple floor, electrics shorting out and Shelly Moon pleading with her daughter to stay home and help out.

'I am helping,' Laurie said, sweeping up broken glass. 'And I'll go on helping as soon as I come back tomorrow evening.'

'You'll have to put off your visit till next week.' Shelly was feeling desperate, though Pete was busy marshalling troops, and Dave and Frank from the stables were already on their way.

'I can't put it off, Mum,' Laurie told her.

'It's not as if it makes any real difference to him,' her mother said.

'Perhaps –' Laurie straightened up – 'if you hadn't said that, I might have postponed.'

'But now you won't,' Shelly said.

'No,' Laurie confirmed.

'You wouldn't have anyway,' her mother added, dislike in her eyes.

'Probably not,' Laurie agreed.

The second spanner struck as she was about to leave the house to pick up some takeaway pizzas and extra bottled water for the troops, and her car broke down.

The VW Polo had never let her down before, and it had started first time this evening, too – so she knew it was not as simple as her battery – but then, still in the driveway, the engine died and refused to be resuscitated.

'Please,' Laurie said to the car. 'Don't do this to me.'

Even before she got out, Laurie could predict her parents' reaction. She had no AA membership of her own, and her father would refuse to call them or the local garage for her (and she could forget any hope of borrowing Shelly's BMW), and since it would be double time for an evening call-out, Laurie couldn't afford to pay herself, because she'd maxed her credit card two days ago when she'd seen a gorgeous red scarf in a shop in the Oracle and had known that Sam would love it, and it was too expensive, but she'd had a great urge to get him something gorgeous and overpriced.

No choice then but to crawl to her father.

He was in the kitchen with the men, one of them – Frank – up a ladder, calling to the plumber who was somewhere above.

'I'm sorry, Laurie,' Pete said, 'but I've got more important problems.'

'I just thought maybe Dave or—'

Her father cut her off. 'I hope you're joking.'

Laurie saw Dave – who was holding a torch for Frank – glance first at Pete Moon, then at her, and she thought, but wasn't sure, that he'd just winked at her, and if he had, she wasn't sure what that might mean.

What it meant, as it turned out, was that after Dave and Frank had finished clearing up for the night as well as they could, Dave came to Laurie for her car keys, and in less than half an hour the Polo was going again.

'You've totally saved me, Dave,' Laurie told him.

'My pleasure,' he said, and gave her a really lovely, kind and conspiratorial smile as he left, making her wonder for a moment if he might know where she was going in the morning.

But of course he couldn't know that, because Sam was a secret.

An instant, foolish fantasy flew through her mind: Dave – who was tall and dark and good-looking, with a not-too-big tattoo on one arm – knowing about her son, asking if he could come with her one Saturday and visit him; Sam adoring him instantly, and Dave telling Laurie he was in love with her and

if she wanted to get Sam out of Rudolf Mann House, he'd like
nothing more than to be his father, and . . .

Silly cow, Laurie told herself.

Eight and a half hours till she saw Sam.

The Game

T he games, as they had previously been, had ceased after the
accident, the group's infrastructure forever altered because
of what had happened to Ralph.

She'd stayed in hospital for a long time, had not returned to
Challow Hall.

They had come to her whenever and however they could.

She had remained their creature, yet after that the group had
belonged to her in a new way, because the four children owed
her their freedom and futures, and each member had understood
that.

The night on Bartlet Down had changed everything.

Regaining consciousness and finding Simon leaning over her
shining a torch into her face, Ralph had remembered everything
instantly.

'Where's Miller?' she had asked.

'Gone.' Simon saw that the torchlight was dazzling Ralph,
turned it away. Ralph blinked, looked around, saw the others a
few feet away, their obvious terror not masked by their war paint,
saw, too, Billy, the cleaner's dog, still tethered and muzzled,
whining and growling.

'She ran off,' Pig informed Ralph.

'How long?'

'Not long,' Simon said.

'You've only been out of it for a few moments,' said Roger.

'You all right?' Jack was still feet away, focusing on the dog,
not quite able to look at Ralph who was lying on the ground so
awkwardly that it was obvious she was far from all right.

'Don't worry about me,' she told him.

Later, Ralph felt amazed by her clarity at the scene, but she had, remarkably, been able to issue directions, to instruct them to remove the lead and scarf from the dog and take them away.

'Make sure you burn them, along with whatever you use to clean your faces.' She paused. 'And scrub your nails.'

'Right,' said Roger.

'Then get back to Challow Hall and into bed.'

'We can't leave you,' Simon said.

'You have to,' Ralph had told her. 'Miller's bound to be phoning the police, but she can't have recognized you, and if she does make trouble, it'll be my word against hers, so you won't have to worry as long as you do what I tell you.'

Jack untied the scarf, and the dog snarled, tried to bite him, began to bark, then ran off into the night and disappeared.

'Now go,' Ralph had told them. 'Quickly.'

They had hesitated a moment longer, then melted into the darkness, and she had tried counting minutes to work out if they'd had long enough to get away before someone came, but then clarity had disintegrated, and consciousness with it.

When kindly voices and helping hands had roused her again, she'd been ready with her story, ready to accuse Rose Miller and save her children. And she had not realized until later that she'd been so occupied thinking about them, that she had scarcely given a thought to the extent of her injuries.

Jack had visited her in Princess Margaret Hospital in Swindon.

'You shouldn't have come,' Ralph had told him quietly.

'The others wanted to come,' Jack said. 'But I knew you wouldn't want us all.'

'I want you all right,' Ralph said. 'But it's a bad idea.' She paused. 'They've charged Miller. With grievous bodily harm.'

'GBH.' His green eyes glittered with power. 'Blimey.'

'So you need to stay away, right?' she said. 'Until after it's all over.'

'Right,' he had said. 'Won't you have to thingy, in court?'

'Testify.' Ralph had nodded. 'I should think so.'

'Fucking hell,' he said.

And then, moments later, after eating a handful of her grapes, he told her that he had killed Billy, Miller's mongrel, had hit it with a brick.

'Why?' Ralph asked in a horrified whisper. 'None of it was the poor dog's fault.'

'I had to,' Jack said. 'To punish *her*.'

'But she's going to be put on trial.' Still, Ralph kept her voice down. 'Isn't that more than enough?'

'No one's going to know what I did,' he said. 'I dumped it, and it didn't feel anything, if that's what you're worrying about, but they're not going to find it, they'll just think it's missing.'

'That's not the point,' Ralph said.

Jack had looked at her for a moment. 'D'you hate me now?'

'Of course not,' Ralph said, feeling ill. 'But I still wish you hadn't done it.'

'I did it for you,' he said.

When the case came to court, Ralph had testified, confirming what she had already told the police. That she had been out walking on Bartlet Down, had heard a dog whining and gone to see if it needed help, and that Rose Miller – who she'd recognized from the home – had shoved her without any grounds to do so.

'Though I think now that she might have been disoriented,' Ralph had said in the witness box, 'and maybe quite scared, in the dark with her dog all tied up like that, and I don't think she meant to hurt me so badly.' She had looked at the woman in the dock then, had felt real pity for her, and not a little shame. 'So even though I'm going to have to live with my injuries for life, I'm prepared to try and forgive her.'

Miller's word against Ralph's. Ralph the injured, but generous party.

The cleaner was found guilty, her sentence suspended.

Ralph's life had been altered forever, not just physically. She had committed perjury, had irrevocably committed herself to the group. Had almost certainly lost any remaining chance of having her own children – her injuries aside, no bloke would want her even if she was interested in him, which she wouldn't be.

Only one chance of motherhood, really, once upon a time, created and wiped out by her father.

Her own poor mother still alive then.

'If you tell her, it'll kill her,' he had said.

So she had kept silent about what he was doing to her.

And then she had kept silent, too, about the baby he'd slipped into her.

Then had taken out of her.

'If you have it, it'll kill her.'

Only then her mother had died anyway, of her embolism.

He had stopped after that, but too late for her.

And no more chances after Miller, just these children.

She was nothing without them.

Linked to them, then, for life.

She had continued, as the years passed, Challow Hall receding further into her past, to maintain the journal, recording the children's progress and her responses.

Not children any more.

Roger – based in Reading – has become the actress we predicted, doing well in radio plays and voice-overs, though she hasn't broken into telly. She says she prefers radio and likes having time for her other work as an official prison visitor. She receives no payment for this, but listens to these people's troubles and provides a kind of friendship, and I feel very proud of her – even if she does claim there's a prurient element to her good deeds, has told me she experiences a sexual thrill when the prison gates shut and she's free to walk through those dreadful places. Though nothing, she tells me, compares with the thrill of the games we still play.

Simon is a teaching assistant at an Oxford primary school, which suits her sweet, soft nature. She has an urge to make a difference – like me, she said once, which made me so proud – but is still burdened by bouts of depression. Like Roger and Pig, Simon remains single. She confided in me long ago that Roger told her Pig was in love with her, which makes our girl extra gentle with Pig to make up for the fact that she can't reciprocate. I believe she is afraid of intimate involvement – most of all terrified of pregnancy, in case she is a bad mother. I find this deeply sad. I think Simon would make a wonderful mother.

Pig is a BT engineer in Swindon, and doing very well at it, though nothing much eases his abiding sense of inferiority, which is one reason, I believe, for his refusal to attempt to contact his sister. Better off without him, I once heard Pig say. It made me sad for him too. It's true that he is in love with Simon, and perfectly aware that she does not feel the same. Of all of them, I believe that if Pig had the good fortune to meet a nice woman and allow himself a good relationship, he could transform his life. But only by leaving the rest of us behind. Which will not happen in the foreseeable future, since he needs the group as much as ever.

Jack is, in a way, the most straightforward. Living in Newbury, married with two children, kind to the boy and girl but awful, he says (even cruel, I suspect) to his poor wife. He makes a good living as a burglar, spends much of his profit at the bookies. No hint of shame in Jack, no obvious complex behind his decision to make stealing his career. He feels superior to those who work for their living, appears to have no conscience about it. If they're stupid enough to make it easy for him to enter their homes, he says, that's their lookout. He claims he could turn his back on the group any time he chose. I don't believe that. I think he likes being needed by the others as their hard man.

I need them all. I accepted that a long time ago. Analysing my relationship with them has never been easy for me; my feelings for Jack are perhaps the hardest to try to reconcile with what I used to hope was my fundamental decency. He is the closest to bad of them, yet we all love him. I certainly do.

No doubt about one thing now. If Jack is bad, I am worse.

Her life remained full enough, despite Rose Miller. Ralph had always found ways and means to earn money, had even tried her hand at telephone counselling, thought she had helped a handful of people; but even after all those years, the highest points in her life came through her continuing leadership of the group.

The games, as they had evolved, appalled and thrilled her in equal measure. They occurred infrequently now, their magnetism all the more powerful for that.

What had begun in innocence – Ralph still believed that to be true – had long since transmuted into wickedness.

For which she, of all of them, was most definitely responsible.

If she were ever to have confided in a counsellor or therapist, Ralph knew that they would have told her to stop.

The truth was, that if anyone was to try to cut her off from her children now, Ralph thought that she might want to kill them.

Kate

B ack on the road again, Kate felt a little more content than she had before the accident, on better terms, at least, with her father, if no one else.

She was glad, all things considered, that she'd suppressed her urge to speak to Rob, felt it was wiser, certainly less selfish, not to interrupt his time with Emmie. Much better to drink in the solitary pleasures of Caisleán and rest up, maybe write a really decent *Short-Fuse* for the first time in some weeks, then head back early Monday more equipped to mend fences with Rob, Bel and Fireman.

A creature – perhaps a fox, though it was too inky dark to be sure – ran across the road ahead of her, forcing Kate to slam on the brakes, and she managed to miss it and was thankful of that, but the new small shock had set her heart pounding again, her eyes darting to the rear-view mirror, relieved to see only blackness behind her, unable to face another pile-up.

Arrival and a large glass of red could not come soon enough.

The Game

Over the last several years, the four had each brought one Beast to their new, more daring arena. Their aim now, where possible, was to have their target held responsible for some misdeed of the group's own making, though they had come to realize that getting their victims actually prosecuted was seldom going to be as successful as it had been in the case of Rose Miller.

'That's just the nature of the game,' Simon had said at one of their meetings. 'There's only so much we can do.'

They had come together on that occasion in the Boathouse in Wallingford. The pubs they tended to choose these days woefully lacked the mystique of the Smithy, but were more practical in every other way. Sometimes they booked a room, other times they sat outside and, if they were out of earshot – and on that particular chilly November afternoon they had been entirely alone at their table near the river – they placed a mobile phone on the table and spoke to Ralph via its speaker.

'You don't mind them not getting done,' Jack told Simon, 'cos you're a wimp.'

'Sy's just nicer than the rest of us,' Pig had defended her.

'Kiss-arse,' Jack had scoffed, fondly.

Between game plan meetings they lived in separate worlds, not communicating with each other, but if one of them uncovered a Beast, they contacted Ralph to consult her about their possible candidate for a new game, making her feel fully alive again because they still *needed* her to take charge. She listened, conducted her own research, considered, then summoned them all to a meeting.

She seldom attended now in person, Rose Miller having put paid to so much for her, but she arranged the location and chaired the meetings via a telephone connection.

Still the Chief.

'We could not –' they had all told her – 'do it without you.'
Special dispensation, splendid isolation.
Loneliness.
She told them, once, how much she missed seeing them.
'You love us,' Jack said, 'cos we're a bunch of fucked-up weirdos.'
'Can't argue with that,' she said, and smiled.
She had tried to instil in them her belief in simplicity and minimal risk-taking, though the two adventurers of the group, Jack and Roger, sometimes objected when she turned down their more ambitious projects.
'Simple means safe,' Ralph told them once, after an argument. 'That way we get to keep on playing.'
She knew, even as she said it, that it would not always stay that way.
That it had never, in truth, been either simple or safe.

When, almost three years ago, Pig had telephoned her about a new Beast, Ralph had heard a level of distress and anger in his voice that she had never detected before. His parents had both been out of prison for some years, and Pig had learned that they had remained apart, but neither had tried to contact their son. Recently though, he had received a phone call from his mother's neighbour, a woman named June Norton, informing him that his mother was seriously ill and wanted to see him.
'No,' Pig had said. 'I don't think so.'
'But she's dying,' the woman had told Pig. 'She really needs you.'
It had taken considerable strength of will to go through with the visit, his motives for agreeing to go unclear in his own mind. Pig knew it was not for his mother's sake – he felt nothing but loathing for the woman who had so badly abused him and his baby sister – but he wondered if his visit was simply for closure, or if, perhaps, he wanted to see his mother suffer.
He had driven from Swindon on a Saturday afternoon to the address in Wokingham, had walked rather shakily into a drab flat off the high road and been let in by June Norton, a large bosomed, middle-aged, cloyingly perfumed blonde.
'She's through here,' Norton said, showing him into the dimly lit bedroom in which his mother lay.

The room smelt rancid. Of illness, or perhaps dying, blended with the other woman's perfume.

Pig felt sick.

His mother was so shrunken that she was unrecognizable.

'How are you?' he asked at last, feeling obliged to speak.

'Finished,' she said.

He compelled himself to look into her emaciated face and still found no point of recognition, not even in the fading eyes which once had glinted brightly enough to inspire terror in her small son. The hands that had slapped and punched him and his baby sister, that had stubbed out her Silk Cut cigarettes on his thighs, were withered and bruised-looking, fingering an unclean sheet.

'I'm glad to see you at last,' she said.

'Are you?' said Pig, with irony.

The visit had been mercifully brief. At no point had Pig's mother told him that she was sorry for the past, nor had she asked him for forgiveness, as he had expected she might. June Norton had not offered him tea, had appeared reluctant to leave them alone, standing vigil in the doorway as if she thought either that Pig might try to escape, or that the ailing woman needed protection from him.

'My life has been very hard,' his mother had said, in a voice that was weak and as unfamiliar as the rest of her. 'I wanted to see you before I died, to know that you're all right.'

'I am,' Pig had told her. 'All things considered.'

'Do you want to ask me anything?' his mother asked.

'No, thank you,' Pig had answered.

There was no point asking her what had made her so wicked, or what two little children had done to merit such evil from both their parents.

'Not even about your dad?' she said.

'Is he still alive?' Pig asked.

'Far as I know,' she said.

Pity, he thought, but did not lower himself to say it.

When the moment came for him to leave, she startled him by holding out both her spindly arms as if she wanted to embrace him, and Pig took a step back, knowing he could not bear to be touched by her.

'I'll see you out.' June Norton's lips were taut with disapproval.

'Thank you,' Pig said, almost inarticulate with his longing to be gone.

She opened the door, and he stepped quickly over the threshold.

'I don't know –' she followed him out on to the landing, speaking quietly – 'how you could be so cruel.'

Pig turned around, shaken, saw accusation in hard blue eyes.

'To refuse to kiss her,' the woman said.

'You know nothing,' Pig said softly.

'She's your *mother*,' June Norton said. 'And she's dying.'

As if her death, or even the misery of her life, were Pig's fault.

'You should be ashamed,' she said.

And then she had gathered saliva in her mouth and spat on him.

'I just can't seem to get over that,' he had told Ralph after he'd phoned her to nominate June Norton as his Beast. 'Or to forgive it.'

'No wonder.' Ralph had wished she was with him, could hold him.

'I know it wasn't her who did those things to me and my sister, but I mean –' Pig's voice had trembled – '*spitting* on me like that.'

There was no question, Ralph had said, that Norton qualified more than most as a target, and had summoned the others to a meeting.

'I'd like to bash the bitch,' Jack had said.

Ralph said no.

'Why not?' Jack asked. 'Bashing is simple.'

'Things go wrong when there's blood,' Ralph had said.

They had all remembered her falling against the tree on Bartlet Down, and had given way to her greater wisdom.

Norton, Ralph had learned, worked for an insurance company in Bracknell, which was pleasing in itself, Ralph decided, since it seemed more likely that if their plan worked, Mrs Norton would at least lose her job.

She placed Jack in charge of surveillance, and having observed her shopping habits for a fortnight, he'd followed Norton one day during her lunch break to a small chemist's shop with no CCTV, but with an alarm system and a sign in the window declaring: ALL SHOPLIFTERS WILL BE PROSECUTED.

It was the simplest, most basic of strategies. While Simon – her appearance subtly disguised, like the others, in case of witnesses or hidden cameras – occupied the sales assistant and pharmacist with questions about the side effects of a pain relief tablet, Roger attracted the Beast's attention for long enough to allow Jack to steal some lavender toilet water – its package tagged with an alarm activator – and slip it into her shopping bag.

Moments later, out in the street, they'd all watched as Norton passed through the detectors at the exit, setting off the alarm, and seconds later, the sales assistant and pharmacist had rushed out and nabbed her.

'This is outrageous,' Simon heard Norton protest as the toilet water was retrieved from her bag. 'I don't even *use* that rubbish.'

She'd gone on to object violently as they'd escorted her back inside, had even kicked at the pharmacist's legs, adding a possible assault charge, the group had decided hopefully, though they'd all realized that a halfway decent brief might get her off, if charges were actually brought.

They'd hung around until the police had arrived.

'Better than a poke in the eye,' Pig had said afterwards.

'I don't think so,' said Jack.

Roger had brought them the next candidate: a male officer at Hurstpark, a women's prison in Gloucestershire that was on her voluntary visiting list – a man with a reputation among inmates for cruelty to pregnant prisoners.

'This isn't personal, like Pig's bitch,' she'd said, proposing the screw to Ralph. 'But he seems to be what the game's supposed to be about these days, don't you agree?'

Ralph had. They all had.

Given his expert skills, Jack could probably have carried out their plan for the prison officer single-handed, but having them all involved, whenever possible, had always been part of the game. So one evening while the new Beast and his wife were out at their local in Dursley, Pig had cut off the phones at the screw's house and at his next-door-neighbour's, before Roger (wearing a cropped wig and blue contacts) had rung the neigh-bour's front door bell.

I'm from the Dursley Residents' Association,' she began. 'We're getting up a petition because of this plan to buy up houses in your road for a drug rehab centre.'

'You're joking,' the other woman said.

'I wish,' Roger said.

Which conversation kept them both occupied while Simon sat in her car outside, keeping watch and ready to act as getaway driver, and Jack entered the back of the house, removing a VCR, Play Station and silver framed photograph, before departing again, leaving no trace of his entry or exit.

Right after which he'd gone, smooth as silk, into the screw's house and planted the stolen items in his upstairs spare room. Pig had reconnected the phones soon after, and next morning Roger had made an anonymous call to the victim of the burglary to tip her off about her tea-leaf screw neighbour.

Still simple.

Still bloodless.

Laurie

'I'm going to bed,' Laurie had told her parents an hour ago. She had reminded them that she would be leaving early, had wished them luck with the clearing up, said she'd be back as soon as she could manage tomorrow evening and would help all she could then.

'After the worst is over,' her father had said.

Her mother had said nothing at all.

Laurie knew she probably wouldn't sleep. Excitement did that to her every time, and the only reason it mattered was because she wanted to be feeling bright and energetic in order to give her son the best possible day out.

She lay on top of her bed, closed her eyes and pictured him.

Some people thought that all children with Down's syndrome looked alike. She supposed she might have thought that too, once upon a time, if, that was, she'd ever thought about it at all.

Sam Moon did not look like anyone else on earth.

His photographs lay in a box in her locked wardrobe. One was brought out most nights before she went to sleep and put away again when she woke because that was one of the rules. In case Josie – her mother's cleaner – was to wonder who the boy in the picture might be.

Heaven forbid.

Laurie had long since given up pointing out that no one ever needed to come into her bedroom to clean, that she preferred doing it herself.

'Even if you do,' Shelly said, 'it doesn't mean they might not come in.'

'I could lock my door,' Laurie said.

'That would look strange,' her mother said.

Rules of the Moon house.

Sam was not photogenic. In photographs, he looked happy, but quite ordinary. In real life, however, he was spectacular, and Laurie didn't really need photos to conjure him up, could just shut her eyes anytime and whisk him up at will.

She smiled now at the prospect of seeing him in the morning, then returned her thoughts again to that brief, foolish fantasy about Dave, wondering what exactly that had been about, before pushing it away again.

She plumped up her two pillows and lay back.

Closed her eyes firmly.

'See you soon, Sam Moon,' she said.

The Game

Jack's contribution had taken the game back to the level of physical roughness that had been absent since their assault on Rose Miller. His chosen Beast was a woman he had seen at Kennet Shopping Centre abusing her frail, elderly mother, swearing at her and dragging her along, almost pulling her off her feet.

'This one really deserves a taste of her own,' Jack had insisted to Ralph. 'And I'll tell you straight, if you don't let us handle this the way I want, I'll take care of her on my own, and it'll be a bloody sight worse.'

They had all talked it over for a while, Simon wondering if this might have been a one-off event, if this woman really was a Beast.

'We need to be certain,' she had said.

'I know an abusing bitch when I see one.' Jack had been blunt. 'But if you don't want to take my word for it . . .'

'I know what Sy means,' Pig had said. 'June Norton thought I was a rotten son for not kissing my mother goodbye.'

'Appearances can be deceiving,' Ralph agreed.

'Jack knows what he saw,' Roger said.

All together for once at a restaurant opposite Swindon Station because it was Ralph's birthday and she'd been missing them so badly and wished for no present more than a real reunion.

So she'd been there to observe the hardness in Jack's eyes when he talked about 'taking care of her' himself, had caught a responding flicker of excitement in Roger's, and had realized that they were both out of her control.

Had recognized, too, that this was yet another opportunity to detach herself.

An opportunity she had not, of course, taken.

They had talked through the plan carefully, then left it to Ralph to work out the details and dovetail them with the Beast's movements.

The daughter, she learned, travelled each weekday by train to work in Reading, which meant there was nothing more complex to take care of than choosing the right place, rehearsing split-second timing and – with witnesses and CCTV on site – paying careful attention to their own disguises.

They decided to play the game on a Thursday afternoon, just after the daughter had alighted from her train at Newbury Station. Three of them moving into position as she and her fellow passengers crossed over the stepped footbridge and started down to the opposite side and station exit. As the Beast began her descent of the final twelve steps, Jack slipped into place beside the young man just in front of her, gave him a furtive but hard shove, then stepped neatly away as the man fell with a cry to the stone platform below.

'*She* pushed him!' Pig had shouted, pointing to the Beast. 'Stop her!'

'I didn't *touch* him!' the young woman protested in shock.

'Call the police,' Roger yelled, knowing that Simon – just outside the station – was already doing exactly that; then, as Pig melted into the throng on the platform, made a grab for the woman's arm. 'Someone help me *hold* her!'

An elderly man, cheeks rosy with outrage, and a young female backpacker hurried forward to lend a hand, while a cluster of passengers gathered around the fallen man.

'This is *ridiculous*,' the Beast told the official. 'I didn't do anything.'

Out of the corner of her eye, Roger saw a uniformed official moving quickly towards the steps.

Releasing the Beast, she stepped back, passed unhindered through the small crowd, and went quietly on her way.

'Was the young man all right?' Ralph had asked later.

None of the four knew for sure, had been too focused, they said, on the Beast.

Ralph had scoured the *Reading Evening Post* every day for the next week and the *Newbury Weekly News* after that, certain that if he had been badly injured it would have merited mention. It pained her to think of an innocent man's suffering, brought back her own grim times after her accident, pricked at her conscience.

It relieved her just a little to find that she still had a conscience.

She wondered sometimes if the others ever thought about the novel that had sparked off their games, if any of them were aware that there were certain points of comparison between the evolving nastiness of their own adult games and that old tale of children becoming savages. She supposed they did not dwell on it any more and was, she thought, glad of that.

Bad enough that she noted similarities and was chilled by them.

And exhilarated too, of course.

She had, by then, come to accept that sickness in herself.

*   *   *

The great and irrevocable change had come with the Mitcham game.

More complicated and, ultimately, much more violent than any of them, even Jack, had intended it to be.

Alan Mitcham had been Simon's beast. A teacher at the primary school where she worked as a teaching assistant.

'He has no business being a teacher,' she'd said, fiery tears in her eyes as she proposed him to Ralph. 'Or working with children at all.'

Mitcham, a single man, appeared, Simon said, to dislike children and to have scant respect for their parents. The incident that had helped turn him into a candidate had begun when Simon had witnessed him being unkind to a six-year-old with learning difficulties. The child's mother had come to school next morning to complain to the head, but had encountered the teacher first, and Mitcham had retaliated by humiliating both mother and child.

'Right there, in front of everyone,' Simon had said. 'Made her feel completely inadequate. Poor woman turned tail.'

'Why didn't you report him to the head?' Ralph asked.

'I might have,' Simon had answered, 'if that had been the only thing.'

It had, in fact, been the least of it, because a few days earlier Simon had caught sight of something in Mitcham's locker just before he'd slammed the door.

A photograph of a naked child, unmistakably pornographic.

'I only caught a glimpse,' she said. 'But I know what I saw.'

She had felt shocked, sickened.

True Beast.

Two days later, Jack had confirmed Simon's suspicions, breaking into Mitcham's flat in Barton and finding photographs so revolting to him that his first impulse had been to lie in wait and give the scumbag a beating he'd never forget.

The group met the following week in a private room over a Didcot pub.

'I've been thinking,' Jack said, 'that it's time to rev up the game.' He was having trouble blotting out the images of the children in Mitcham's collection. 'We have to make this filth really *do* a crime,' he said. 'Like a robbery, something heavy.'

'That sounds complicated,' Ralph said, on speaker phone.

'Not really,' Jack disagreed, 'because we'd be making sure he *didn't* pull off the job, wouldn't we?' He paused. 'But it's gotta be something big enough so we'd know he'd get seriously banged up.'

'Maybe we should just shop him, after all?' Simon was growing doubtful. 'I mean, we're not vigilantes, are we?'

'No, we're fucking not,' said Jack.

'We're a lot smarter than that,' Roger said.

'And shopping him wouldn't be the *game*, would it?' Jack pointed out.

'But how can we possibly make anyone do a robbery?' Pig had asked.

'Blackmail,' Roger said flatly. 'Make him realize he either does what we tell him, or he ends up doing ten years as a nonce.'

'Maybe that'd be the right punishment,' Simon said.

'Maybe it would,' said Ralph, from the speaker.

'And what if he found himself a good brief who got him off?' asked Roger.

'At least he'd be finished as a teacher,' Simon said.

'You can't be certain of that,' Roger argued. 'Anyway, it wouldn't be nearly enough.'

'He's your Beast,' Jack reminded Simon. 'The biggest dirtbag we've had.'

'Jack's right,' Pig agreed.

'Biggest dirtbag,' said Roger, 'biggest game.'

'It'd have to be armed robbery,' Jack said. 'I can get a gun, no sweat.'

'No guns,' Ralph's voice said promptly.

'But nothing less would really do it, would it?' Roger backed Jack up. 'Not if we want to make sure Mitcham gets a long stretch.'

'Couldn't we use a replica gun?' Simon asked.

Ralph wondered why she hadn't thought of that, was glad Simon had.

'Yeah, OK,' Jack said. 'If it makes you feel better.'

'It would,' Ralph had said.

Doubt had gnawed at her that Jack might say one thing and do another, which meant the only way to be certain would be to insist on inspecting the gun when the time came. Except she wouldn't be there, and anyway, it would be insulting to Jack and unsettling for the group.

Guilty as charged, and locked up in HM Prison Oakwood.

Innocent Beast, though only of *that* crime. Guilty as all sin in their eyes.

What had followed though, a month later, had not been in the original plan. And yet it had become necessary, Ralph had been forced to accept, because after Roger had called in a favour from a contact at Oakwood, she found out that Mitcham was claiming to have remembered new and 'significant' details about the gang.

'It might be bluff,' Roger told Ralph on the phone, 'but what's scaring me is that most of what we had on him came from Simon.'

'And you think he's linked it to her?' Ralph felt ill at the thought.

'With all that time to think, I suppose the penny could have dropped,' Roger said. 'And Sy was the one sitting outside, so someone might have noticed her.'

Ralph was silent.

'He needs shutting up, Chief,' Roger said. 'Fast.'

'How much have you told your contact?' Ralph was alarmed.

'Not a thing,' Roger had assured her. 'It's on the grapevine.'

'We need a meeting,' Ralph said.

'I don't think there's time.'

'We have to at least tell the others,' Ralph insisted.

'Of course.' Roger paused. 'I gather it can be arranged. For the right sum.'

'*It* being shutting him up?'

'Permanently.'

Ralph felt a shudder go through her. 'Dear God.'

'I know,' Roger said. 'Not simple or safe any more, is it, Chief?'

'Couldn't we just arrange a reminder of how it would go for him in there if they knew about the photographs?' Ralph felt suddenly on the end of a hook, struggling for her immortal soul. 'It worked in the first place.'

'Trust me, Chief, it's because of the photos that this *can* be arranged, no questions asked,' Roger told her. 'That's how much his sort are hated.'

'But mightn't a beating be enough to keep him quiet?' Ralph was still hanging on.

'How long for?' Roger said. 'Do you really think we can take that chance?'

Ralph took another moment, thought about Simon, who'd
wanted to change her mind and shop the teacher rather than play
the game; who was, of all of them, still the most innocent.

'How much?' she asked.

And knew, right away, that she was lost.

She spoke to the others one at a time.

It was, they all knew, a massive step into the abyss, and yet
they all agreed to take it, making Ralph feel, with a sense of
quiet, clamping bleakness, that it was as if they had always
known this would happen.

Jack had been shocked at first, but had swiftly seen the point,
and Pig had been more afraid for Simon than about what it meant
to him, had therefore not argued as much as he might have.

'I don't want this,' Simon had said. 'This is wrong.'

'None of us wants it,' Ralph had told her.

'But you've more or less said it's for *my* sake.'

Ralph heard her desperation. 'It's for all of us,' she told her.
'Like always.'

'But surely,' Simon went on, 'if something happens to him,
they're even more likely to go back and look at what happened
before.'

'But he won't be around to give evidence,' Ralph said.

Simon had been silent for a moment.

'We're really going to do this, aren't we, Chief?' she said at
last.

'I don't see,' Ralph told her, 'that we have any real choice.'

All of them trying to block out the truth: that they were about
to be party to the greatest of sins, and no part of it a game. Their
abiding awareness of Mitcham's wickedness had helped, of
course, and their desire to protect Simon had enabled them to
believe they had no alternative. They were, Ralph thought, all
afraid of breaking ranks, of smashing the group, ruining the
friendships which had become everything to them. So they had
stood together and agreed to it.

To murder.

The hit had been costly in more ways than moral. Neither Simon
nor Roger could afford much, but Jack had accumulated some
ready cash, Pig had badly wanted to contribute, and Ralph had
known it was her duty to pay the lion's share.

Immortal souls *all* down the Swanee then, she supposed.
Hers first in line.

Mitcham's game had indeed changed everything. There was
no going back from there, and they all knew it.

Nothing but a trial run, as things had turned out, for the ultimate game.

The Game

Kate

All this, and now fog too.

Not a pea-souper, but bad enough, and driving the last mile to Caisleán in the dark was always a strain on the eyes, but anything more than a slight mist was enough to disorient, to blot out the familiar and give the illusion of shifting landscape.

The relief when Kate saw in her headlights the signpost that she and Rob had erected at the junction with the long track leading to the barn over open grassy land, was considerable. Another memory, of Rob hammering that post into the ground while she had held a glass of champagne for them to share . . .

Not that Caisleán looked in the least welcoming this evening as the Mini jolted over the last section of bumpy track and stopped.

A black slab with a pitched roof in a grey blanketed world.

For just a moment, Kate felt oddly unnerved.

'Daft,' she told herself out loud.

She switched off the engine, leaving the headlamps on to light her path to the barn, fished the keys out of her bag and went to unlock the front door.

It opened with a creak.

Kate leaned in to flick the switch on the wall inside, and Caisleán came alive.

'Thank you, Mr Edison,' said Kate.

She walked back to the Mini, pulled out her weekend bag and shopping, then turned off the headlights, shut and locked the doors, slipped that key into her bag and went inside.

Kicked the front door shut behind her.

Everything looked as it should.

Lovely. Just as she and Rob had intended.

Soft caramel-coloured sofa with burgundy cushions and throws, two warm kilim rugs on the stone floor that Rob had bought without her at an Istanbul market. The heavy, rustic oak dining table, chairs and old oak chest they'd found together in an Oxford auction. The tiny kitchen off to the right, the bathroom to the left. The spiral staircase up to the galleried first floor that had once been a hayloft – some of its original timbers and iron lamp hooks retained for atmosphere – where they had made their bedroom.

Where they used to sleep together and make love and watch the stars and the dawn through the skylight over their bed.

Kate set her bags on the floor and walked into the centre of the room.

'Hello, Caisleán,' she said softly.

Awash, suddenly, with loneliness for Rob.

She thought of the wine bottles in with her shopping.

A glass would help.

She started to turn.

Heard them, *saw* them, as they emerged, moving swiftly out of the bathroom and kitchen, from the cupboard by the front door and from the back of the little house.

'Hello to you, Kate,' one of them said.

Four terrifying figures in red overalls with black stocking masks over their heads, flattening and obscuring their faces.

Kate opened her mouth to scream.

'Please don't,' one of them said.

A woman, her voice only slightly muffled by her stocking.

'All right.' Kate's heart pounded like a jackhammer. 'I won't.' Shock made her hoarse. 'Take what you want, then please go, I won't stop you.'

'What we want,' a second figure – a man – said, 'is you.'

'Oh, God,' Kate said.

'Better sit down,' the third – another woman – told her.

Kate did so.

Laurie

It was almost one a.m. when Laurie – who'd given up on sleep and was flipping through that week's copy of *Heat* – heard a quiet knocking on her door, which startled her since neither of her parents ever came into her room at night.

'Come in.'

It was her father, in dressing gown and slippers.

'What's wrong, Dad?' Laurie closed the magazine.

'Nothing's wrong,' Pete Moon answered.

He asked if she minded if he sat on the edge of her bed.

'Course not.'

'I just want to say –' he spoke slowly as he sat, like someone groping his way forward, which was not a bit like him – 'that I sometimes think you've forgotten how much your mum and I love you.'

Laurie said nothing, wondering where this was going.

'You're so busy hating us . . . '

'I don't hate you, Dad.'

Which was only half a lie, since much of the hate she'd undoubtedly often felt since conceiving Sam had been more disappointment than real hatred. Plenty of that.

'I hope you know,' Pete went on, 'that if we thought Sam wasn't happy, wasn't fulfilling his potential—'

'How can you know if he's happy or not when you never see him?' Her retort came sharply, almost automatically.

'We get reports,' her father said, 'as you know. Which all tell us about his happy nature. Which you do too, Laurie.'

'And if he wasn't?' she asked. 'Happy?'

There was a silence.

'Then I imagine we'd have to think about something else.'

'Such as?'

'That would be up to you,' Pete said.

'Since when has anything about Sam been up to me?' Laurie asked.

'It's all been up to you,' said her dad. 'Your mother and I have always gone along with your decisions.'

She was staggered. 'How can you say that?'

'It's true,' Pete insisted. 'Fundamentally. We may not have handled things the way you would have.'

Laurie was silent again, new imaginings clanging in her brain. Was this a new trick, perhaps, to stop her visits to Sam? Or maybe they were going to say they couldn't afford Rudolf Mann any more, and where would they want to send him then?

'But we've always done what we thought was best,' her father continued, 'for you and your son.'

Sam's lovely open face came into her mind, pushing away everything else.

'What are you telling me, Dad?' Laurie asked at last.

'Nothing.' Pete shrugged. 'Except your mum and I hate the way things get between us because you think we don't care about Sam.'

'Me too,' Laurie said, with an effort. 'I hate it too.'

'OK.' Her father reached for her hand and squeezed it, and they used to hug all the time before Sam, though it was hard for Laurie to remember the sweetness of those days, because being a mum herself had changed everything, even if wasn't the way being a mother was meant to be. 'Shall we try a bit harder then, baby?'

She found, with surprise, that the endearment did not offend her, simply because her father had just extended what felt like a real hand of friendship, maybe even of respect.

And after he left the room, she turned off her lamp and lay in the dark again, a new set of possibilities – happier, this time, almost *golden* – rushing in. Because maybe they were going to let Sam come home with her, *live* with them, with *her*.

A picture of her son playing at the Mann came to her.

If Sam came to the Moon house, he would miss that place, wouldn't he? The only real home he'd ever known. And his friends, too, not to mention all the stand-in mothers who knew just how to take care of his needs.

Special needs.

Laurie stopped herself before the thoughts got out of hand. Her father hadn't said a word about anything having to change,

either for better or worse; he'd only said they should all try a
little harder to be kinder to each other. He certainly hadn't said
there was the slightest possibility that Sam should come home
to this house.

Nor would he.

At least the sad resignation settling back over her was a feeling
to which she was all too accustomed, and she wondered suddenly,
in one of her moments of franker self-appraisal, how well she
might cope with the challenges of real change.

Given that she was, after all, a coward.

Laurie glanced at her clock.

Just over six and a half hours.

The Game

They had removed Kate's parka but not her gloves, and then
they had bound her ankles together with a triple length of
crêpe bandage over her jeans above her old Todds loafers, had
strapped her wrists behind her, stuck wide adhesive parcel tape
over her mouth and had forced her down on to the sofa.

A flurry of brief directions before that from the men and
women in their creepy, stocking-deformed faces, red overalls,
latex gloves and trainers.

'Sit still.'

'Feet together.'

'Hands behind your back.'

'Shut up.'

But then, for a long time, they had spoken neither to her nor
to each other, had given her no indication of what exactly they
wanted from her.

'What we want is you.'

One of the men had said that, hadn't he, in the first minute
– the bigger, brawnier-built of the two – but what had he meant?
And were they waiting for someone else or some*thing*, or were
they just using silence now to freak her more?

Succeeding.

They'd drawn the curtains so that no one could see in, leaving just enough of a break between them, Kate hazarded, to be able to see outside.

She was sitting in the centre of the sofa, her feet on the kilim rug before it. One of the males was now seated beside her to her left, one of the females to her right, their proximity making Kate's flesh crawl.

For the first time in her life, she knew the meaning of terror. Of helplessness, too, and bewilderment.

'So . . .' the second female, standing a few feet away, addressed her suddenly. 'I suppose you feel really defenceless, right, Kate?'

Kate stared up at her.

'That's how they feel.'

They?

'By the end of the second month –' the female beside Kate had a low, mellifluous voice – 'they only measure about one and a quarter inches, but they already have arms and legs.'

'And a beating heart,' said the standing woman.

Babies.

Embryos.

Kate's mind floundered, fumbled, came up with nothing better than more fear.

She looked from one to the other, took in the mobile phones clipped to the waistbands of their overalls, looked up at their dark impenetrable faces, unable to stop herself from trying to seek out features, some identification point, aware as she did so that it might be the worst possible thing to do, that *not* seeing these people's faces might ultimately be what gave her the best chance of getting out of this.

'What are you looking at?' The male now standing near the front door, the tougher-built one, spoke with what might possibly have been a Bristol accent, though more significantly, he sounded aggressive. 'Just listen, right?'

Kate nodded, made a sound of appeal behind her gag.

'Quiet.' The man on the sofa to her right seemed a little less hostile.

She looked straight ahead at the TV she had expected to have switched on by now; dinner in the oven, glass of red in her hand.

'That's better,' the male beside her said.

Kate wondered if they were playing 'good captor, bad captor'.

'By the end of the third month –' the female beside her started again – 'they respond to touch, and nerve fibres transmitting pain are present.'

'Though the fibres that will inhibit pain are not,' the standing woman said.

A regular double act.

Kate recognized, even through her fear haze, a mixing of different studies of the subject she'd had good cause to research in the past.

The standing female was holding stapled papers in her right hand.

'If abortion is carried out early enough, they call it *suction*.' She emphasized the word, her voice quivering a little. 'A powerful suction tube is introduced into the womb –' she was reading now – 'and the suction pulls the embryo's body apart, drags it and the placenta off the wall of the uterus and deposits them into a bottle as *waste*.'

Pro-lifers, then.

Fanatical pro-lifers.

Kate felt as if her insides were shrivelling.

'If they wait a little longer –' the seated female was not reading, was either better informed or rehearsed – 'or if they've left a little of the *foetus* behind, they use a curette to scrape it away.'

Kate turned her head to look at her.

'Keep your head down,' the male near the door ordered.

Terrorists, Kate decided, described them better than captors.

It was hard to say how that made her feel, except even more numb.

Numb was probably the only way through this.

The male beside her shifted a little, and now he, too, was holding papers. Kate chanced a glance, saw printed text but could make out no words.

'The first thing you learn when it happens to you,' he read, 'is that every preconceived idea – even when it's been founded in good faith and sincerity – flies straight out of the window.'

Oh, dear God.

They were her *own* words, from one of her columns.

'Nothing, when it comes to this ultimate life or death decision –' his voice was higher than the other man's, his reading stilted, like a schoolboy's, and even through the stocking his breath smelt sour, and Kate had a sense that he was nervous

– 'is black and white, nor is it grey. If we're talking colours, it's the blazing reds of hell versus the gentle nursery pastels of hope or the drabness of earth and ashes.'

Was this why they were here then, in Caisleán? Because she had written in *Short-Fuse* about abortion?

That first glimmer of comprehension brought Kate no comfort.

Ralph

Everything about this game was different, had been since its inception.

Two Beasts instead of one.

Both of them brought to the group by Ralph.

A first.

And perhaps, Ralph suspected – had felt this from the start – the last.

Kate Turner, of course, had come to her attention long before Laurie Moon.

Clamouring for attention, spilling her opinions and feelings over a whole page of the *Reading Sunday News* every single week. One of life's true coincidences taking care of any doubts after that, proving that Turner really was a bitch and a killer.

A Beast.

A temporary assignment at the Rudolf Mann School had brought her Laurie Moon. This selfish, self-obsessed, *weak* young woman. Unfit, unworthy, to be called a mother.

It had taken time, more investigation and vastly more organization than any game they had ever played, most of it undertaken by Ralph herself, before and since bringing it to the group that evening at the Black Rooster pub.

It had taken a long time for her to be sure that it was right, for *them*.

That taking them to this kind of level was right, to such heights. Such depths.

She had already forced herself to face the possibility that, having presided over one death, there seemed an inevitability about this deeper descent.

Ultimate sin already committed, after all. Not by her hand or theirs exactly, but still their sin, done and dusted and ready for judgement.

The swiftness with which they had all accepted her proposal had surprised Ralph somewhat, coming so soon after their initial doubts over the decision to have Mitcham killed. Jack and Roger had agreed to the new game so readily, she realized, partly because they genuinely shared her sense of outrage about Turner and Moon, but also because they were both naturally attracted to violence. Simon had accepted the plan because, though Ralph believed she remained fundamentally gentle, the group had always come first with her, and both these female Beasts represented everything that set her personal anger flowing like lava. Pig had gone along with it because the same things made him rage, and because he loved Simon.

Yet for all that, and for all that she wanted this game with the most startling passion, Ralph knew that their readiness to agree meant they'd come to accept the use of brutality to further their aims. Which saddened her.

And thrilled her, yet again.

They had argued for a time about where the main event should take place, batting possibilities back and forth. Turner's cottage was not, they'd all agreed, sufficiently isolated; there might be watchful neighbours, random callers, there were too many unnecessary risks and unknown quantities attached to it. They'd considered taking over an unoccupied rural property, anything from a vacant holiday cottage to a farm outhouse, but Caisleán had seemed like a gift.

'Perfect,' Roger had said.

The planning of the game had, at times, almost overwhelmed them.

'Lucky we've got Jack,' Pig had said at that first meeting. 'A real pro.'

'I'm a burglar, right,' Jack had reminded him. 'Not a murderer.'

'*We're* not doing a murder,' Pig said.

'Don't pick nits,' Roger told him.

Super-vigilant was what they were going to have to be, Ralph said.

'And *then* some,' said Jack.

Surgical gloves to be worn every second, no matter what. Littlewoods trainers on their feet, same as thousands of other men and women in the country.

'Most important thing,' Ralph had said during a later planning meeting, 'is not to let the Beasts claw or bite.'

'No releasing them –' Jack again – 'for peeing or crapping or drinking.'

'Not even if they say they're about to choke to death,' Roger said.

Simon was pale, Pig not much better.

'What if the husband shows up?' he'd asked.

'He hasn't gone near the place since they split up,' Ralph said, 'so far as I know.'

'There's always a first time,' Simon had said.

'If he comes,' said Jack, 'he'll wish he hadn't.'

The jury had still been out on whether or not Rob Turner – whose first wife had taken their daughter so far away from him – might be a Beast in his own right, but for the time being they were wavering *against*, since his break-up with Kate suggested to them that he couldn't be all bad.

They had been relying on general surveillance and Pig's monitoring of Turner's phone calls to find out when she was next going up to Caisleán.

'Only half the story, though, of course,' Roger had said, 'if we can't get our second beast at the same time.'

'Patience,' Ralph had told them. 'We'll have a chance with Miss Moon every fortnight.'

Just a matter of time.

Ψ

'I think it's time,' the sitting female said after a while, 'we introduced ourselves.'

Kate shivered involuntarily.

'I'm Roger,' the woman said.

'I'm Simon,' said the standing female.

'I'm Jack,' the male near the front door said.

'And I'm Pig,' said the man beside her.

Messed up as her head was, Kate still instantly put the names together, the strangeness of the last one – Pig – leaving little room for doubt. Characters out of a book she'd read at school, she thought.

She chased her memory now for any obvious pro-life connections in that old novel, gave that up quickly – then remembered an old film in which a gang who hijacked a subway train had called each other by different *colours*, which meant, she supposed, there was probably no real significance to these names either.

If she got out of this, she thought she might never watch another thriller.

'You paying attention, Turner?' the man by the door asked.

Jack. The most obviously nasty of the four.

'Want a drink of water?' the sitting male, whose breath smelt – Pig – asked her.

She hesitated.

'She doesn't trust us,' the sitting female – Roger – said.

'Just plain water,' Pig said.

'From your own tap,' the standing female – Simon – added.

Kate nodded.

'I'll get it.'

Simon walked around the sofa, her rubber soles padding almost noiselessly on the uncarpeted areas of stone floor. In the kitchen, Kate heard water running first into the sink, then into a cup or mug, then the tap being turned off.

Simon came back into her line of vision, a red mug in her gloved right hand, one of the Habitat stoneware mugs Kate and Rob had chosen together.

Kate watched her hand it to Jack.

The move seemed rehearsed to her, planned.

'Peel off the tape,' Jack told the woman named Roger.

The tape came away easily, painlessly.

'Make any noise –' Jack looked down at her – 'and I'll punch you so hard you may never wake up.'

Kate believed him, *meant* to be still and silent, but then, as he bent over her, she suddenly became certain there was more in the mug than just water, and instinct made her turn her face away.

Jack hit her hard on the side of her head.

'Careful,' Simon said to him.

Kate's left temple throbbed, her senses reeling.

'I warned her.' Jack held the red mug back, close to her face.

'You want it or not?' He shrugged. 'Far as I'm concerned, you don't ever have to drink again.'

Kate managed a nod. 'Please.'

He was rough about it, the rim of the mug striking her upper front teeth, water sloshing out, running down her chin and over the blue roll-neck sweater she'd pulled on at home what seemed like a year ago. But at least the water seemed untainted, as far as she could tell, and she swallowed what she could, not knowing when she might next get the chance to drink.

'Right,' Jack said and straightened up.

Roger turned, the adhesive tape in her hands.

'I need to pee,' Kate said quickly.

'Tough,' Roger told her.

'I really need to,' Kate said.

'So pee.' Jack set down the mug on the oak chest. 'It's your sofa.'

Kate flushed. 'What is it you want from me?'

'It's simple,' said the woman called Roger.

'We want to punish you,' said the man called Pig.

'But what *for*?' Kate asked.

'Don't you know yet?' asked the woman called Simon.

Kate shook her head, trying to remember the complete text of those columns she'd written after she and Rob had faced their time of trial over their baby.

'For supporting the murder of innocents,' Roger said.

She stood up, stretched her legs, slipped the piece of used tape into one of several pockets in her overalls.

'You want to punish me –' Kate spoke slowly, trying to follow, needing to make sense of what was happening, knowing that if her writing was, in some insane way, what had brought this nightmare to her, then understanding might be the first step of getting her out of it – 'because I wrote some pieces about abortion?'

'Only you did more than write about it, didn't you?' said Simon.

Kate realized suddenly what they had assumed about her.

Which was not so surprising, given that even Rob had made the same assumption at the time.

'I didn't have a termination,' she told them. 'If that's what this is about.'

'We know you did.' Simon's conviction was unshakable, for Ralph had given them the facts, and the Chief never lied to them.

Till then Kate had felt Simon to be softer than the other female, but now this woman's gloved hands were clenched into fists and the underlying intensity in her voice was alarming.

'I had a miscarriage,' Kate said, fighting for calm.

'Shut up, bitch,' Jack said.

'Shut up, Beast,' said Pig.

There had been something about a *beast* in that novel, and what in God's name could that have to do with her, with *anything*, and what suddenly frightened her most was a sense that there was no purpose in telling these people the truth, because they would not, did not *want* to, believe her. And if she could have seen their eyes, Kate suspected they would be glinting with the light of inextinguishable belief.

The kind you could not argue with.

Ralph

Even now, with the game under way, I find it hard to decide which of my two Beasts I despise more. The woman who brags about killing unborn children and her other sins, or the woman who keeps her son shut away in a home while she lives under the protection of her wealthy parents.

The *home*, of course, had been the clincher for the group, making Laurie Moon the worse of the two for them.

'No contest' – Jack's words.

So very different from the word go, this game.

Not only because it was her very own, not just to oversee as in the past, but to devise completely.

They were playing it to her 'script'. Improvising, of course, as the situation developed – and if there was one thing they'd all learned, it was that circumstances had a knack of intervening, changing plans, often dramatically. Which could be a good thing at times, could be fascinating, creating the need for the group to work to their full potential, raising the stakes.

Raising the risks.

Her game, her chosen Beasts, but they were the ones out there, taking those risks.

'This one's for you, Chief,' Roger had said last week, sounding as if she was raising a glass of wine, as if this was to be a performance dedicated to her.

Ralph supposed, in a way, that was what this had become.

If you could say such a thing about a double kidnapping.

About murder.

> *Now that it has begun, I have to sit and wait. We have agreed to communicate as little as possible for safety's sake, so I am, for now, at the mercy of my imagination. An armchair general, having sent out my troops – my children – to play the most dangerous game of their lives. At my instigation.*
>
> *It occurs to me, for the very first time, that I may be the Beast.*

The Game

'Sleep well, did you, while they did that to your baby?' Roger asked.

Kate shook her head wearily. 'They didn't *do* anything.'

'Not to you.' Simon's voice trembled.

Pig got to his feet and peered at the papers in his hand because looking at the words through the black stocking was almost like reading in the dark.

'After about twenty weeks, the legs of the foetus—'

'Baby,' Jack interrupted. 'It's a *baby*.'

'The legs of the baby –' Pig read like a stilted schoolboy again – 'are drawn through the birth canal with forceps, after which scissors are used to puncture the back of the head, so—'

'The *base* of the back of the head.' Simon interrupted this time. 'The soft bit.'

'Please,' Pig protested. 'This is bad enough without.'

'Sorry,' Simon apologized.

Kate was afraid she was going to vomit.

Pig went on: 'So that they can use suction to remove the brains, which causes the skull to collapse, making it easier to remove the entire foetus.'

'Is that what they did to your baby?' Roger asked Kate.

'No.' Kate's answer was inaudible, her face parchment pale and sick.

'Answer her, Beast,' Jack ordered.

'I did answer,' Kate said. 'No.'

'Bet they did,' Jack said. 'Bet they fucking *did*.'

'They might have done it with salt,' Roger said. 'They stick in a long needle and put concentrated salt into the amniotic fluid so the baby breathes it in and swallows it and dies of poisoning.'

'Enough,' Simon said softly. 'Please.'

'All right,' Roger agreed. 'But I think she ought to tell us which they used on her baby.'

'They didn't use *anything*.' Rage was rising in Kate, toughening her up.

'Your baby never had any choice, though, did it?' Jack said.

'No,' Kate said, for that, after all, was true. 'But—'

'I learned so much –' Pig was reading *her* words again now – 'during that short, interminable time—' He paused, seeming to find the words difficult. 'About abortion procedures, both therapeutic and illegal, in different countries. I learned much more than I wanted to know, details of nightmare methods and their repercussions that are now engraved on my mind.'

'Poor you,' said Roger scathingly.

Kate's eyes hardened. 'Not my best writing, I'll admit.'

Simon moved so quickly that she startled everyone, her slap rocking Kate, leaving the mark of her latex-covered fingers vividly on her cheek.

'Slow to anger, our Sy.' Jack sounded pleased.

'Sorry,' Simon said, to him and the others.

'I did not have an abortion.' Kate's eyes were stinging as well as her face. 'I did not have a fucking *abortion*.'

Though if she had, she went on in her head, it would have been her *right*.

Not brave enough, stupid enough, to say that out loud.

'They told you your baby had spina bifida, didn't they?' Roger asked.

How did they know *that* when she'd never written about it?

'*Didn't* they?' Jack made her jump.

'Yes, they did, but—'

'And you wanted a termination, but your husband did not.' Roger again.

Kate stared up at her. 'How do you know that?'

'Invasion of privacy,' Simon said.

Jack laughed. 'She doesn't like that.'

'Your baby didn't like it much either,' Roger said.

'For God's sake,' Kate said, 'I lost my baby.'

'You wanted an abortion, didn't you?' Jack badgered. 'Tell the truth, Beast.'

'What's the point –' Kate felt her cheeks flaring – 'of my saying anything if you're not prepared to even *listen* to me?'

He moved towards her so rapidly that she flinched, anticipating another slap, but instead he pulled out a roll of adhesive tape from one of his pockets, ripped off a length and smacked it over her mouth.

'No point at all,' he said.

'My mum came to call this week –' Roger took up the reading again – 'which means, of course, I've been gnawing my fingernails and ripping out my hair.'

'Not just a baby killer then,' said Jack.

'Cruelty to mothers, too,' said Simon.

'Almost as bad in our book,' said Roger.

'Worse, I'd say,' said Jack.

'What would you say, bitch?' asked Roger.

'What *would* you say, Beast, if you could?' Jack's smirk was clear in his tone.

'If I had a mum like yours –' Pig hadn't spoken in several minutes – 'I'd be the happiest man in the world.'

Kate's senses were reeling again, further confused by the new slant, and was there any chance that they knew Bel, or—

'If I'd ever had a mum at all,' Jack said, 'I'd have shown her some respect.'

Kate fought a new wave of panic, tried to ride it. None of this could possibly have any connection with her mother, who'd been so totally supportive when she'd lost the baby. And she could remember the column that the last snippet had come from, too, knew that in fact, she'd gone on to take herself to task for being unfair to Bel, had ended up being hardest on herself instead, after which it had turned into a mini-treatise on guilt. As many of her columns tended to.

The tape over her mouth was more tightly stretched than before.

Not the first journalist to be gagged.

She wondered, abruptly, if she would ever write another column.

Laurie

L aurie had been up for a while, was drinking coffee in the semi-wreckage of her parents' kitchen while Pete and Shelly slept upstairs, presumably exhausted.

Laurie thought about her dad's late night visit to her room, the unexpected warmth of it, and one of her self-damning attacks of shame engulfed her.

The fact that Sam was so well cared for was all down to them.

Not living with me, though, she batted straight back.

She pushed the argument away. Same old thoughts, with no point to them. The only sensible way forward, the only valid purpose to her existence for the foreseeable future, was to go on living for her visits to Sam – even if they were more for her own sake than his.

An old weakness had resurfaced last night, she realized. The awareness that she still, despite everything, needed her parents. She still missed the old days, the warmth and love that she had, once upon a time in her naivety, believed unconditional; the comfort of hugs and of the belief that her parents were the *best*.

Sam would never feel that way about her.

Whoever's fault that was, it was a sad, true fact.

Laurie drained her coffee and went upstairs to get dressed.

Not long now.

The Game

A nother wave of panic was just subsiding as a new one began to rise.

Jack had begun to pace, striding back and forth across the room, something brewing, something bad, worse than this.

He stopped, suddenly, right in front of Kate, and pulled something out of another of his pockets. Something square and small.

She stared at it.

A condom packet.

'What is it they say women like you – stupid bitches who get yourselves knocked up, who don't deserve babies – what is it you need most? In school, in our stupid fucking nanny state, what are they always banging on about?' Jack held the packet up. 'Safe sex, right?'

Kate felt her mind shrivel up, burrow into itself.

'*This* is what I wanted to do to you,' Jack said. 'I wanted to *educate* you, teach you a fucking lesson with *this*—'

He leaned forward suddenly, thrust the packet up against her face, and Kate could smell its plastic wrapper, and she thought again that she was going to be sick, turned her head away, but Jack grabbed her hair, turned her back to face him again.

'But the others wouldn't let me,' he said, 'so you're in luck, aren't you?'

Kate was trembling violently.

'*Aren't* you?' He yanked at her hair again, dragging at the roots.

Her eyes were wet, and she loathed him, despised him, but she nodded, had to, *had* to, because if she did not, God only knew what this man might do.

'Right,' he said. 'Fucking right.'

Ralph

Not long now until the next stage.

Till Jack, Simon and Pig left the barn and Turner.

They had discussed at length who would stay with her, had settled on Roger for a number of reasons. First, because two men would be needed for strength. Second, because Simon was, they all agreed, potentially the softest touch, and there was no knowing what tricks the first Beast might try to play if left alone with her. Lastly, because not only was Roger much tougher than she looked, but also because if anyone did turn up at Caisleán while the others were gone, Roger would be the best equipped to whip off her mask and act out whatever role seemed right at the time.

Ralph wanted to phone them now so badly it was making her teeth ache, but if anything were wrong, they would be phoning her.

Their protector. Their Chief.

She found it so hard to contemplate disaster: the kids being stopped, arrested.

'I'll always protect you,' she had once told them.

But as the years had passed and the games had grown rarer and riskier, she had amended that to: 'I'll always do my best to protect you.'

The thought of them incarcerated and, worse, unreachable, was unbearable.

Ralph turned her thoughts to Caisleán, pictured the scene.

Turner trussed up and helpless, being forced to listen to her crimes.

Such basic crimes against humanity. Against the unborn and mothers.

Ralph closed her eyes and imagined her children, faces all but invisible beneath their scary masks.

Scary grown-ups now.

She felt such pride.

The Game

S omething was changing.
  They were getting ready.
For what?
Kate was trying not to think about that.
But they had stopped haranguing her a long while back, had stopped talking to her altogether.
She could hear and smell someone making coffee in the kitchen, and yes, they were definitely getting themselves prepared for something.
'Come on,' she heard Jack say.
'Plenty of time yet,' Pig said.
'Better early,' said Simon.
'Not too early,' said Roger.

Laurie

O n her way, at last.
  Laurie's car had started first time, thanks to Dave.
No last-minute reproaches or pleas from her parents. Nothing at all from them, in fact, her mother still dead to the world when she'd left the house, her father already at the stables, where he loved to be in time for dawn.
It was still dark now, but last night's fog had already almost gone, and Laurie found herself anticipating the beauty of the sunrise before her arrival, the rosy fringes of the outer rims of fields and trees and hilltops, and perhaps when she was back

home again after the visit and needing to occupy herself, she would try to recreate that loveliness for her next gift to Sam.

'Good morning, darling,' she said to him out loud, as if he could hear her. 'Get up and dressed and have a good brekkie.'

She wasn't sure where they would go today, since she liked letting Sam choose what he wanted to do, and they were very kind at the Mann about things like that, encouraging the children to anticipate and enjoy every minute of their outings. If Sam had nothing in mind, Laurie would take him either to Legoland or to the Cotswold Wildlife Park, both great successes in the past, and wasn't that the *best* thing about her beautiful son: his infectious joy and enthusiasm, his easily won-over heart.

'Never frets after you've left him.'

Laurie doubted she'd ever get the bitch's words out of her memory.

'I'm on my way, son,' she said now, softly.

Driving on into the morning.

The Game

B efore they left, they made her lie on the sofa, face down into the cushions, and for several long minutes Kate believed she was going to die, that they were going to shoot her *now* or stab her in the back, or maybe smother her, and she fought to keep her nose clear of the soft, suffocating fabric and foam beneath her face.

'Keep still.' Roger was crouching, maybe kneeling – Kate couldn't *see* – beside the sofa, keeping pressure on her, one hand in the centre of her back, the other on the back of her head, and she was a strong woman, Kate knew that now.

God help me.

There was a tiny cavity between her nose and the cushioning, just enough to allow a little air through her nostrils, but with her wrists and ankles still bound she was helpless and waiting for *worse*, her mind flying through time and space from Rob to Bel to Michael and back to Rob again and, most desolately of all, to their lost, unborn son, and maybe if—

She heard the front door open, felt cold air.

Stopped preparing to die and started listening instead.

Roger's hand was still on her back, but the one on her head had been lifted, so the intent was not, after all, to kill her now, Kate thought, just to keep her from moving, from turning, and she realized suddenly that the reason she was face down might be because they had taken off their masks and didn't want her to see them.

If they don't want me to see, that means I'm not going to die.

And if they were *going*, then any second now that hand would lift off her back, too, and she would hear the door close and would be alone, still bound and gagged, but alone and *alive*, with a future in which to get over this . . .

They were speaking softly, she couldn't hear them.

'Take care.' Roger's low voice came from just above her, not moving away.

Why didn't they *go*?

She heard movement, rubber soles squishing on stone, the faint swishing of material, perhaps their overalls brushing against furniture . . .

The door closed.

But the hand was still there, had moved up a little, was pressing against her shoulder blades, and the suspense was worse now than the pressure.

It lifted, at last.

'You can sit up,' Roger's voice told her.

Kate turned her face first, inhaled air greedily, then tried to get up, but it was hard with her hands behind her, she was rolling clumsily.

'Wait.' The other woman pulled her to a sitting position.

Kate looked up at her, realized for the first time how tall and slim she was, almost elegant despite the overalls and mask.

Stocking still in place.

The others gone.

Kate felt torn between gratitude for the scrap of help, for not having been *killed*, and massive disappointment because Roger was still here, still guarding her.

Which meant that it was not over.

Roger stooped again and pulled off the tape.

Kate gulped in more oxygen.

'Anything to say?' Roger asked.

'Thank you.' The first words into Kate's head.

The masked woman bent again, stuck the tape straight back over her mouth.

'Personally, I'd have said something a little more worthwhile.'

The sound Kate made was of pleading, frustration and anger.

'Yeah,' said the terrorist named Roger.

Ralph

E yes glued to the clock on her wall.

They'd be on their way again by now.

Ralph imagined the tension building in their vehicle as Simon drove.

Positive tension in Jack's case, she guessed, itching for the next stage. Less conviction and more angst for the other two, though Simon's head and heart were well into this, she knew that. And where Simon's heart went, Pig's tended to follow.

She thought about Roger.

Alone now with the first Beast.

No calls, unless absolutely necessary – the deal they'd agreed on.

Did her sanity count as a necessity?

Ralph picked up her phone and keyed in Roger's number.

The Game

It was the first time a phone had rung since the start of Kate's ordeal.

Roger took the mobile from her waistband, looked at the display, pressed a button. 'Anything?' she asked curtly.

Kate strained to hear a voice from the other end, something that might help when this was over, but though the stocking-masked woman was less than three feet from the sofa, not even the faintest whisper of sound reached her.

'All to plan.' Roger listened for a moment. 'No problems, Chief.'

Less brisk now, a touch of warmth in her tone, Kate thought, and of respect.

'*Chief*' took her back to the novel again. Even if these names were just covers, these people must have had some reason to choose the book, if only because they – or perhaps their 'chief' – liked it. Had been inspired by it, maybe, by the horror of the story, by its violence.

'Much later,' Roger said, and ended her call.

Kate made a sound, attempting to communicate, to make the best of this time with only one of the gang present, a woman, strong though she knew she was.

'Want to talk to me?' Roger asked.

Kate nodded.

'Tough.'

Kate made another sound, of appeal.

'Still want to pee?' Roger shrugged. 'Guess I could live without having to smell your stink.'

Instant plans leapt into Kate's mind: if her ankles were freed, she would *do* something, kick out, and what should she aim for, what would be the most vulnerable, the most reachable part of this woman's body? Her legs, she supposed, and they hadn't taken her Todds, so she could kick hard.

'You'll have to shuffle,' the terrorist told her, wrecking that hope.

God, it hurt getting back on her feet because her legs had stiffened up and the bandages and immobility had restricted her circulation.

Her mind, at least, was still on the move. If Roger did not free her hands, either, then the other woman would have to help pull down her jeans, which meant she'd have to bend down, and then Kate could—

Nothing, Kate realized. There was not a damn thing she could do with her hands trussed behind her, nothing she could do except pee and be grateful for that.

Like hell. The only thing she would be grateful for to this bitch was if she untied her and let her go, let her leave.

Let her *live*.

And after that, Kate would stop being truly grateful again until the police had locked her and the rest of her scum friends behind bars.

Ralph

'**M**uch later.'
Ralph knew she ought not to have telephoned.

Anxious parent unable to let go.

Not their parent.

Not really their *chief* either, not any more. Fit to make plans, but not to join in; more of an encumbrance were she to try.

She wondered again how they were coping with the strain. Not so much Jack, but the others.

Jack, too, perhaps, when it came to the finish.

He was just a burglar, after all, as he had himself pointed out.

A baby dumped in a car park.

Not so hard beneath the tough shell he'd built up over the years. Feeling by now that it was expected of him, probably expecting it of himself too.

Ralph worried about Jack. About them all.

Still her children, after all.

Laurie

There was a lane that curved between the road and the long driveway at the Rudolf Mann estate, a stretch of road with, even at first light, the sweetest of vistas beyond it. The kind that instantly lifted the heart – before the lane twisted into an always darker, tree-shadowed semicircle where the vista eluded for a while, to be recaptured again in slivers of light through the surrounding woodland.

Laurie had painted both these views for herself, finding that they rekindled the thump of excitement and tension she always felt just before arrival, just before seeing her son again. Wondering how he would look, what changes the last fortnight might have brought, if his brown eyes would still brighten when he saw her, or if he might seem as if he'd rather be doing something else – which had never yet happened, but Laurie knew he was growing up and that it might happen some day, perhaps even today . . .

Not today.

She saw the vehicle blocking the lane: a white van stopped sideways on, taking up the whole of the width of the lane, making it impossible to pass or to see the driver.

Laurie slowed the Polo to a crawl, then halted.

She felt no agitation because she was early, and Sam might not be ready for her, so it was no trouble to sit in the dark green shadows, having a few moments longer to enjoy the anticipation of seeing her son.

But the van still wasn't moving, nor was there any sign of life, and no one could possibly be unloading here, in the middle of the woods, which meant that although the bonnet wasn't up, it had probably broken down, and so maybe after all she ought to do something. There must be another entrance to the Mann estate, but she didn't know where, and suddenly she was growing a little anxious in case Sam was early too, because she'd never kept him waiting, not once in eight years.

She hooted. Just once, politely, to let the driver know she was here.

Nothing.

Perhaps he'd gone for help, in which case . . .

She opened her door, got out of the car.

'Hello?'

She glanced back down the lane, saw no other cars, but she seldom saw any traffic at this time because visiting started at nine, and her eight o'clock arrangement had been made years ago because of the restrictions on her visiting.

'Hello?' she called again.

'Round here,' a woman's voice called back. 'Spot of bother with the van, sorry.'

'Anything I can do,' Laurie asked.

'Can't hear you,' the woman called. 'Can you come round?'

'OK.' Laurie remembered her phone in the VW. 'I could call someone for you.'

This time the woman didn't answer, so Laurie walked towards and around the front of the van, glancing in the direction of the estate, estimating that there was only a half mile or so separating her and Sam now, so if necessary she'd have to walk it.

'Hello, Laurie.'

Another voice – male – came from behind, startling her.

She began to turn.

The arm around her waist was strong, another grabbed her around her neck and a gloved hand covered her mouth before she could get out a scream as she was pulled off her feet and dragged to the back of the van.

She saw two figures – *terrifying* figures– and they hauled her up inside the van, into the dark, slammed her down on the hard floor on her back, the sound of her body colliding with the metal beneath booming. For a second her mouth was free of the hand, and she began screaming, but then something wet and awful-smelling was shoved back over her nose and mouth, and her head started to spin and she felt the worst sickness, and . . .

Sam would be waiting.

Her last thought.

The Game

If anyone had ever told Kate that it was possible to be in her present situation and be *bored*, she'd probably have told them to get a brain.

But this woman, this tall, slim, faceless creature with her surprisingly beautiful voice, had not spoken to her once since half dragging her to the bathroom and allowing her the humiliation of peeing in front of her. She had sat beside Kate on the sofa, an example of complete composure, bringing her captive close to screaming pitch, ready for *anything* rather than this.

Almost anything.

Then, about fifteen minutes ago, that had changed.

Roger had stood up, gone over to the front window, peered through the still-drawn curtains for a moment into the daylight – and the fog had gone, Kate could see that much, at least – then returned to the sofa, sitting again.

Composure cracking, just a little.

Expecting someone, Kate realized. Or something.

Her boredom had gone. Fear back in place and building.

She would have given a great deal to have the boredom back.

Ralph

Ralph had observed both her Beasts for long enough to have some sense of how they might react to their ordeals.

Turner, complacent in her self-belief, incredibly fortunate yet tossing away blessings like a rich woman who thought there would always be more to buy. And little Laurie Moon, holding up her chicken-heartedness as an excuse, choosing security and parental protection over and above her own needy child.

Turner, she thought, might show backbone, perhaps till the end.

Moon would believe, when she woke from her chloroformed sleep, that she was being held for ransom, and when she found that her daddy was not going to be riding over from his stables to rescue his little girl, then Laurie would probably dissolve into a tear-sodden mess of cowardice.

Ralph wished she could be there.

Cursed her inadequate body and Rose Miller, who had stopped her forever from *playing* the game.

They could not play without her help, she sometimes comforted herself.

But so much could go wrong this time. One twist of bad luck, one chink in her not quite armoured planning. Nothing about this was truly safe.

She had told them that during the plan's conception, had cautioned them.

'This one could be dangerous for you,' she had said.

They had told her they accepted that, but Ralph knew they hadn't really believed it. That their faith in the game, in her, their talisman, was still intact.

By then, of course, they'd had no choice *but* to believe, she knew that too. Because without it, and without the ongoing possibility of the *next* game, whatever it might be, they would again be as they had perceived themselves long ago, before the book, before Wayland's Smithy, before she had come along and become Ralph.

They would be nothing again.

The Game

They brought Laurie into Caisleán, conscious but still dazed, and propelled her to one of the straight-backed dining chairs, which they turned away from the table, so that it faced the sofa and Kate.

'All right?' Roger asked the other three.

'Perfect,' answered Jack.

They pulled off the young woman's leather bomber jacket, left her gloves on, as they had with Kate, then tethered her wrists behind her back, and Kate saw her flinch – drugged, she thought, her reactions vague – as they pushed her down on to the chair and bandaged her ankles together.

Her own heart was pounding again and she was perspiring.

She knew that something very bad was happening.

She looked at her fellow prisoner. She was young, in her early twenties, pretty, with bobbed fair hair and blue eyes, wearing a poppy red pullover and blue jeans, like her own.

The young woman was clearly in shock, her skin clammy-looking, her whole body trembling as she stared back at Kate.

'Ready?' asked the female named Simon.

The man called Pig went to the front door, checked it was locked.

Kate was not certain, but she thought he might be trembling too.

'Get a move on, Pig.' Jack was impatient.

For *what*? If Kate's heart pounded any harder, she thought they would hear it.

They took up positions, their moves appearing almost rehearsed, Roger stepping to the right of the new captive, Pig to her left, Simon sitting on the sofa beside Kate.

Jack took up a central position, standing on the kilim rug.

He nodded at Simon. 'Right.'

Simon leaned across Kate and pulled the tape off her mouth.

Kate breathed in, smelled body odour.

Fear.

She swallowed hard, tried to moisten her mouth.

No one spoke.

'What's happening?' she asked.

'The game,' Roger answered.

Game.

She had learned by now not to waste questions.

'Who is she?' She looked at the other young woman.

Her fellow captive.

The answer came from Jack.

'She's your punishment,' he said.

Ralph

The waiting was becoming more agonizing as time went on, the lack of contact vital now. They could not afford any interruptions at this stage, time being of the essence.

The longer it took, the more chance for something to go wrong.

Ralph's part played, after all, for the moment.

She knew they'd need her again afterwards to take care of details.

Details were her specialities. Like finding out about Caisleán's excellent locks, presumably fitted because Rob Turner's insurers would have been mindful of intruders or squatters at the mostly unoccupied property. Like learning that Kate Turner – unbeknown to the insurers, perhaps even her husband – kept her spare keys buried beneath the wild primrose patch twenty-three feet from the front door.

Details, afterwards, would be crucial too.

Like Laurie Moon's car. Safe for now in the derelict cow byre Ralph had located well ahead of time, but as soon as possible that would need to be dealt with. Jack knew about things like that, but would probably want Ralph to arrange them; respraying the VW, changing its number plates and serial numbers.

Miss Moon would not be needing it any more, that was one certainty.

As for the rest, they'd all have to see how it played out.

You never knew with the game.

The Game

'**Y**ou should know,' Roger said to Kate and Laurie, 'why you were both nominated for this game.'

Kate heard the word that ordinarily had desirable connotations – people were 'nominated' for awards, weren't they, or for election – and thought how deadly a ring the calm-voiced terrorist had bestowed on it.

The second prisoner had been coming to gradually, had been given coffee to drink, before Jack, growing impatient, had thrown a glass of cold water into her face, making her gasp, bringing tears of new shock and fear into her eyes, and Kate had wanted to comfort her; had wished she could have turned back time, delayed her awakening.

Delayed *this*.

'You're doubly qualified, Turner,' Simon addressed her, 'because not many women get to be cruel to both their children and their mothers.'

Kate bit down a retort, saw the other captive's eyes dart suspiciously to her. No longer believing, perhaps, that they were in exactly the same boat, hoping therefore that maybe her own predicament might be less grim than the woman they'd taken prisoner before her.

'Your qualifications –' Pig informed Laurie – 'are simpler.'

'But your crime –' Roger took over – 'is every bit as bad.'

'Worse,' Pig said.

Kate saw that shred of hope die in the younger woman's eyes, felt pity for her.

'You put your kid in a *home*,' Jack said, 'when you didn't need to.'

'I—'

'Shut your mouth,' he cut her off, took a step closer to Laurie, who cringed.

'No breast feeding,' Simon said.

'No cuddles,' Pig joined in.

'No mum when he was ill,' Roger said.

'Probably better off without her,' said Simon.

Kate saw the young woman's face, saw a different kind of torment in her eyes, hated them more than ever for this new cruelty.

'No loss for Sam if he loses her now,' Jack said. 'That's for sure.'

The telephone – Caisleán's landline – began to ring.

Kate's heart hurtled into double speed. It could be her father or Fireman – she'd told them both she was coming here, after all. Anyone else failing to reach her at home would surely be ringing her mobile, which was in her bag on the floor near the door.

The landline went on ringing.

'If I don't answer,' she said.

'Shut up,' Jack told her.

There was no machine, no 1571 set up, so after a couple more rings, it stopped, and maybe it had been Rob trying to reach her, and maybe her mobile wasn't working and maybe he really—

'Pay attention, Turner,' Roger snapped.

Kate's eyes shot daggers into the woman's stocking-veiled eyes.

'We're keeping this nice and simple for you,' Roger went on, 'because we like our games to move snappily.'

Speed, Kate thought, couldn't be good news.

'Ready?' Jack looked from one captive to the other. 'Good.'

Not ready, Kate wanted to say, saw fresh wild fear in the other woman's face.

'The game is,' Roger said, 'usually—'

'We pick a Beast and punish it,' Jack said.

'But this time,' Pig said, 'we've got two Beasts.'

'Which is a first,' Simon said.

'So it took us a while,' Roger said, 'to decide how to deal with you.'

'Simple, in the end,' Pig said.

'You're going to punish each other,' Jack said.

* * *

The silence in the room seemed to last for minutes, until finally Kate said:

'No.' Her voice was clear, firm. 'We're not.'

'Shut it,' Jack told her.

'What do you mean by *punish*?' Laurie asked.

She had been beginning to wonder if she would ever find the strength or courage to speak again, and maybe it was because the stuff they'd knocked her out with was wearing off, or maybe she had just realized that if she didn't fight back now, *really* fight for once in her wasted life, she might never see Sam again.

Or anyone else for that matter.

Those thoughts made her want to cry, but she was *not* going to give in to that, because the other woman wasn't crying, and whatever these *monsters* had been saying about her, she had been so brave to stand up to them just now.

'Who *are* you?' Not knowing seemed almost the worst thing. 'How do you know anything about me?'

The other prisoner smiled at her, gave her strength.

In the same boat, after all.

'I'm Jack.' He answered her first question. 'All you need to know about me.'

'Roger,' said the woman on her right.

'I'm Pig.' The second masked man said it as if they were being introduced at a party.

'Simon.' The other woman.

Kate was watching Laurie, saw she'd made nothing of the names.

'Not their real names,' she said quickly. 'Picked from a book. And I'm Kate.'

'I'm Laurie.' Quick, too. 'Laurie Moon.'

Jack took three steps towards Kate and whacked her hard across the face.

'Do not speak again unless you're asked.' He turned to Laurie. 'You too, unless you want the same.'

'Careful,' Roger said to Jack.

Through the burning, reverberating after-effects of the slap, Kate remembered Simon saying the same thing after Jack had slapped her the first time, and maybe they didn't want her marked – though after that, Simon had hit her, and no one had told her to be careful; in fact Jack had seemed especially pleased.

Laurie stared at the flare marks on Kate's left cheek and wondered, with a curious mental departure, what time it was, if someone at Rudolf Mann House had phoned her parents, if—

'My car,' she said.

'Tucked up, safe and sound,' Jack said, 'just like you.'

Kate saw tears spring again into Laurie's eyes.

'It's OK,' she said. 'We'll be OK.'

'Depends what you mean by OK,' Jack said ironically.

'I don't *understand*.' Terrified as she was, Laurie had to know. 'You said I put Sam in a home when I didn't need to, but it wasn't like that.'

'Were you too ill to take care of him?' Simon was swift, sharp.

'Were you in prison?' Pig was harsh too.

'Were you bound and gagged?' Roger asked.

'Of course not,' Laurie protested, 'but—'

Jack pulled the roll of tape out of his pocket again, ripped off a length and smacked it over her mouth so hard that her head jerked back.

'You are now,' he said.

Laurie began to cry, giving in.

'Bastard.' The word escaped before Kate had time to think better of it.

'You want some more?' Jack turned to her.

'Let's get on,' Roger said.

'Right,' Simon said.

The air hung still and silent for a long second.

'Still want to know,' Jack asked Laurie, 'how you're going to punish each other?'

There was nothing now, in the whole world, that she wanted to know *less*.

'It's simple,' he said. 'Like we said.'

'You –' Roger spoke to Laurie – 'are going to punish *her* –' she nodded towards Kate – 'by being her victim.'

'And you,' Jack said to Kate, 'are going to punish her—'

'No,' Kate interrupted, steeling herself for another slap. 'I'm not.'

'By *executing* her,' Jack finished.

Laurie gave a small moan, turned chalky white and passed out, Roger just catching her before she fell sideways.

'Hold her steady,' Jack said.

Pig held her from the other side, her head slumped over her chest.

'I'm not going to do anything to her,' Kate said. 'Whatever you do to me.'

'What about,' Jack asked, 'if we do it to Emmie?'

Kate felt as if a klaxon had gone off inside her head.

Flashes danced across her mind's eye of Rob's sweet daughter. 'You—' She couldn't speak.

'That's right,' Roger said. 'We have Emily.'

'I don't believe you,' Kate said, at last.

Laurie was coming round again, her face ghostly white, but all Kate could think about now was Emmie and how much Rob loved her, and they *couldn't* have her, it was impossible.

No more impossible than this.

'I don't believe you,' she said again.

Less conviction in her tone this time.

'If we don't make a call —' Roger checked her watch — 'in fifteen minutes, to say we've finished here—'

'Then they'll finish little Emmie,' Jack said.

Laurie was listening, trying to take things in, not really *wanting* to.

Kate licked her lips. 'Prove you have her.'

'We don't have to prove anything,' Roger said. 'You have to do what we tell you to do.'

'Unless you don't give a damn about Emily,' said Jack.

'She might not,' said Simon, 'with her track record.'

'That's true,' Pig said.

'Doesn't make much difference,' Jack said. 'We can find other ways to *make* her do it anyway.'

Laurie let out a whimper, her eyes terrified.

'Even if you do have her . . .' It was a struggle for Kate to keep her mind working. 'If you're so pro-life, you won't hurt a child.'

'Won't be us *making* her be hurt though, will it?' Pig said. 'It'll be you.'

'Times-a-wasting,' Roger said.

'You're right,' Jack said. 'Let's do it.'

Laurie made a choking sound behind the tape over her mouth.

'She's going to puke,' Pig said, freaked.

'Don't,' Jack told Laurie. 'Pig doesn't like puke, and it's not in the game.'

'Jesus,' Kate said, disgusted. '*Jesus.*'

Jack struck her hard with the back of his hand.

'Careful,' Roger cautioned again.

Not her imagination then. They didn't want her hurt, at least not so it showed.

'Get up,' Jack told Kate.

She blinked away the involuntary tears of pain, didn't move.

'Come *on*, girls,' Jack said. 'Time to get up and play.'

He bent down, took hold of Kate's left arm, Simon taking her right, hauling her up off the sofa. Over by the table, Pig and Roger pulled Laurie to her feet, and she yelped with pain.

'Move,' Jack ordered Kate. '*Move*, bitch.'

'I can't,' Kate told him. 'My legs are numb. I need a moment.'

'I think,' Pig said, 'we're going to have to untie their ankles to get them upstairs.'

Kate stared up at the gallery where she and Rob had made their bedroom.

'No untying,' said Roger.

'Couldn't we make her do it down here?' asked Simon.

'That's not the game,' said Jack.

'OK.' Roger changed her mind. 'We'll untie their ankles.'

Laurie's eyes were fixed on Kate now, beseeching.

'I'm not going to hurt you, Laurie,' Kate said. 'We'll be all right.'

'You think?' Jack said.

He ripped off another length of tape and covered her mouth again.

'Let's play,' said Roger.

Teamwork.

Jack held Kate while Simon cut the bandages around her ankles, then gave the knife – which looked to Kate like one of their sharpest kitchen knives – to Jack, who tucked it into his belt; and Kate wanted to kick out, but her legs just weren't *working*, and Pig gripped Laurie while Roger freed her feet, but she was too weak to stand, and they had to drag her towards the spiral staircase.

'Move,' Jack told Kate again, while Simon's gloved fingers dug into her right forearm. 'Move, or have another kid on your conscience.'

Insanity, it was all too crazy to be *real*, but the other three were already halfway up the stairs, and Kate could feel the blood starting to flow again through her arms and legs, and oh, dear God, what if they *did* have Emmie? And they were frogmarching her now, Jack yanking her upward, Simon right behind her, and it was hopeless, there was nothing she could *do*.

She saw the others reach the top of the stairs, turn right, saw Roger and Pig dragging Laurie to the bedroom alcove, saw them push her on to the bed, turn her on to her back.

Laurie began to wail.

That new sound, of pure mortal terror, seemed to blow apart Kate's helplessness.

They, too, were at the top, the gallery narrow for three people moving together.

Now.

She kicked out violently, struck Simon's left leg with her right loafer, so hard that the other woman cried out, stumbled, let go of Kate's arm, and Kate *used* the instant, used every ounce of her pent-up inner rage, shoved at her with her right hip—

Saw it happen in slow motion.

Simon losing her balance, her arms flailing, hands clutching air then falling forward, her momentum sending her crashing through the wooden rail—

'Simon!' Pig's cry from the alcove was of purest horror.

'Go!' Roger took the initiative, swiftly knelt on Laurie's thighs, pinned her down. 'Pig, *go!*'

'She's *OK!*' Jack's harsh shout of laughter jarred them all, and he grabbed Kate's hair with one hand, her arms with the other, yanked her right to the edge. 'See what you *didn't* do, bitch.'

Kate stared down and saw that Simon's fall had been halted by one of the thick old iron hooks, its sharp point snaring her overalls and saving her life.

'Simon!' Pig was already halfway down the staircase, trying to reach her. 'She's not moving!'

'She's fine, Pig.' Jack began moving again, dragging Kate towards the alcove. 'We have to finish this!'

'*Simon!*' Pig was distraught. 'Jack, she's not answering!'

'For God's sake, Jack,' Roger called, 'let Pig see to her.'

Kate saw that she still had Laurie pinned down, the young woman still and silent again, immured now in her personal nightmare.

'Let's *go*, Jack!' Roger told him.

'All right.' Jack took the knife from his belt.

'Jack, come *on*,' Roger urged again.

'I said all *right*.'

He turned Kate around, his free arm tighter around her chest, and she let out a cry, waited for the blade in her back, then jumped as she felt first her right glove being pulled off her hand, then, swiftly and shockingly, the coldness of steel against her palm and fingers.

Jack turned her back again, so that she faced the bed.

Laurie's eyes were closed, and Kate hoped to God she'd passed out, and why had she *done* that to Simon? She'd made things even worse, accelerated them . . .

Jack was holding the knife out in front of himself, blade down.

He was hesitating, Kate could *feel* it, he was wavering.

'Jack?' Roger felt it too.

'This isn't how it's supposed to go.' He sounded odd. 'The game.'

Suddenly, with more horror swelling in her chest, Kate understood how the game *was* meant to go.

Her prints on the knife.

Execution.

'It's not going right.' Jack's grip on her was still tight. 'Not the Chief's great fucking plan, is it?'

'Careful, Jack,' Roger said.

In control now, yet *she* wasn't certain either, Kate sensed.

'I put the knife in her hands now and untie her, she'll stick it in me, not *her*, stands to reason,' Jack said. 'So I got no choice, do I?'

Kate kept her eyes on the surgical-gloved hand still holding out the knife.

'But it's a bit of a thing, right?' He still sounded odd. '*Doing* it.'

Something shifted between them.

Something *big* changing in the atmosphere.

Hope shot through Kate.

'You don't have to, Jack,' Roger said. 'We can change it.'

'We can't change the game,' he said.

'Why not?' Roger said. 'The Chief isn't here. If you don't feel right . . .'

She *cared* about him, Kate realized, could hear it in her voice, feel it. These four all cared for each other, they weren't just some gang of cold-hearted villains, they—

And then Pig let out a terrible howl.

'She's *gone!*'

Kate felt Jack go rigid.

'The hook's gone right through *her.*' Pig's voice was anguished. 'Simon's *dead.*'

Laurie opened her eyes.

Sam filled her mind: his birth, his being taken from her at the clinic, his lovely smiling face.

'You,' Jack said to Kate. '*You* did this.'

She felt it, literally *felt* the heat of his rage as he raised the knife.

She shut her eyes, thought about Rob, about wasting love.

The sound she heard as the warm spray hit her face was thinner than a baby's wail.

Droplets on her eyelids, on her nose, her cheeks.

She commanded herself not to look – if she kept her eyes closed, she would not have to *see.*

What Jack had done to Laurie.

But she had to look, knew she had no choice.

A necklace of blood.

Laurie already gone.

And now Kate was screaming inside.

Ralph

J ack had just called.

'I'm in the kitchen,' he said. 'Turner can't hear me.'

A thrill ran through Ralph.

'Is it done?' she asked, knowing from his voice that it was.

'Yeah,' Jack confirmed. 'But the game's not over, Chief.'

She heard him tell her about Simon, grief striking hard as a hammer blow.

Time passed, evaporated, ceased to register or matter.

Ralph remembered Simon as she had been in the early days, soft and fair and sweet and very young. The most innocent of them all, always.

'Chief?' Jack said at last. 'You OK?'

'No,' she answered. 'Of course not.'

'Me neither,' he said.

Ralph tried to assemble her thoughts, assemble *herself*.

'How's Pig?'

'Like you'd imagine,' Jack answered.

Something different was whipping up in her now, along with the grief.

Rage.

'So,' she said, 'it was her. She did that to Simon.'

'Fucking right she did,' Jack said.

Ralph knew that she needed to still her own emotions, at least for a time. To help her surviving children deal with this.

To finish this imperfect game.

'Right,' she said.

The Game

The first thing they had done after killing Laurie was to attend to Simon.

Jack's grasp on Kate's hair in those minutes had been so brutally tight she had felt the roots shrieking as he'd made her lean with him over the rail, watching Roger help Pig ascertain that their friend was truly dead.

There was no doubting that Pig was right. The hook had pierced Simon's left breast and probably her heart, impaling her.

Ending her life.

Kate had looked down and seen the glistening, horrifying, dark red pool on the stone floor directly below.

She thought, though the stocking over Roger's face made it hard to be sure, that the terrorist was weeping.

No such doubts about Pig.

'Right.' Jack had spoken at last, his voice low and choked and savage. 'Right.'

Roger had looked up at him. 'What do we do?'

'Call Ralph,' he had said.

Kate registered the name. Another from the Golding novel. The Chief's name.

'Shoes first,' Roger said.

Her weeping already over, her grief, at least for a time, contained.

'We need to check our soles,' she clarified. 'For blood.'

Kate had felt barely alive in the lull that had followed the killing.

Two killings, she supposed.

Supposed, too, that from their point of view she had killed Simon. Except she did not feel that pushing a person bent on murder qualified as *killing*.

They were responsible for Simon's death.

Not in their book, though.

Kate had found that she could not think about – knew she must not allow herself to think about – what had been done to Laurie Moon. A stranger, and yet her *sister*. About the unspeakable brutality of it.

Later she would think about it, find out about her.

If there was a later.

Back downstairs – after speaking, Kate presumed, to their Chief, to the newly named *'Ralph'* – Jack hog-tied her in the centre of the living room, ensuring that Simon's body was in her line of vision.

'Careful,' Roger said again as Jack tethered her wrists to her ankles, and he made a sound that was half grunt, half snarl, but the bandages were released just a little.

God, it *hurt*, caution or not, though the pain was almost welcome, helping to blot out the hideousness of the memory of Laurie Moon's killing – but then Kate's eyes fixed on the gory sight of the dead terrorist, and any relief was gone.

'We can't just *leave* her.' Pig sounded passionate, arguing with the other two about Simon. 'We have to get her down, we have to take her with us.'

'We can't,' Jack told him.

'You know we can't,' Roger backed him up.

'Why can't we at least take the stocking off her head?' Pig implored. 'I want to see her face, I want to say goodbye to her.'

'We can take off the stocking,' Jack granted. 'But that's it.'

'Is that what the Chief said?' Roger checked.

'It's what I'm saying,' Jack said.

Roger hesitated for a moment, then turned back to Pig. 'It's that or nothing,' she told him. 'We have to make this part of the game now.' She was gentle but firm. 'We have no choice, Pig, you know that.'

They began – Pig from above, kneeling at the jagged opening left by the broken rail, Jack from halfway up the spiral staircase – to ease the stocking as gently as they could from their friend's head.

Kate shut her eyes.

'Open your eyes, Turner,' Jack's voice rapped. 'See what you've done.'

Kate opened them, looked up again, saw a young woman with short fair hair messed up from sweat and the stocking's tightness, her face white and slack in death, grey eyes open. She looked, too, at Pig, whose shoulders shook with renewed weeping as he stretched out one gloved hand to stroke Simon's hair.

Love amongst killers.

'God.' Pig began to tug off his own mask.

'No.' Roger's voice was sharp, stopping him.

Maybe, Kate felt, that meant they still intended to let her live, after all.

And then she felt a scalding blast of shame, remembering poor Laurie Moon lying upstairs, her throat cut.

They moved rapidly for a while after that, their need to leave Caisleán as swiftly as possible; then forcing themselves to slow down again, urging caution on each other as they cleaned every trace they might have left.

And Lord, they were well prepared to do so, Kate could see from her increasingly agonizing best-seat position in their arena, armed with mini-vacuum cleaners, scrubbing brushes, torches, magnifiers and even tweezers, painstakingly picking up every suspect scrap and crumb and hair, depositing each item, like crime scene specialists, in plastic bags together with their disposable coffee cups and plastic spoons.

They went upstairs again, scouring the gallery, disappearing from sight for a time in the bedroom alcove – and it was good not to see them for a while, though Simon's body still hung there

like a monstrous reproach and Kate was starting to find it harder
to breathe, the position Jack had tied her in seeming to strain
her chest and constrict her throat.

They appeared again, came slowly down the staircase, cleaning
as they came.

And returned to Kate.

Fear filled every atom of her being.

They did not speak to her.

Roger took a penknife from one of her pockets and cut the
length of bandage that had attached Kate's ankles to her wrists,
and new, exquisite pain shot through her, searing her, making
her cry out through the tape still covering her mouth.

'Right,' Jack said.

What *now*?

Jack and Pig picked her up, and she cried out again.

'Shut it,' Jack said.

Roger went ahead of them into the bathroom, opened the door,
turned on the light.

The men set Kate down in the bath.

New panic soared, they were going to *drown* her.

Sitting her down, though, not lying, so maybe . . .

No one touched the taps.

'Here.' Jack fished out the bandage roll and gave it to Pig.

Pig bent, took off Kate's left glove, then placed the roll between
both her hands, pressed her fingertips and thumbs on the cut end
piece, then around the roll itself, before he straightened up and
placed the roll in her mirrored wall cabinet.

Kate felt her mind shut down again.

She sat there in her bath, a helpless lump, a *package*, while
Pig went through the same process with the unfinished roll of
adhesive tape, and then stood back.

Jack was the only one who spoke to her.

'I wish to God,' he said, 'I could kill you here and now.'

Kate sat very still and looked into space, not at him or the
others.

'Let's finish,' Roger said.

They cut the bandages from Kate's ankles and wrists, stuffed
them into one of their plastic bags.

'Lie down,' Pig ordered her.

She didn't move.

'On your back,' Roger told her.

'*Now*,' Pig commanded.

Oh, the *hate* in his voice.

Kate lay back, terror sweeping her again, and her feet and hands were free, but they were numb again, worse than before, and the pain was like hot needles from her neck and shoulders down to her calves.

Still no one turned on the water.

Roger knelt beside the bath, inspected her wrists, then rubbed her skin with her latex-covered fingers where the bonds had made indentations, lessening the furrows a little, then doing the same for Kate's ankles, rolling up the hems of her jeans a little to make her inspection, wiping away traces of cotton and gauze.

And all the while Kate half lay in the bath, panic receding again, her mind in a new, odd, fugue-like state, wondering what would happen next.

Which was simply that Roger peeled the tape from her mouth and placed it into the bag Pig held open for her.

And then, without another word, they left her.

They took their bags, looked carefully around the bathroom, scanning ceiling, walls, basin, toilet and floor – and the bath, too, as if *she* were not in it, as if she had become invisible.

And then they walked out of the room and closed the door behind them.

Locked it from the outside with a key, leaving the light switched on.

Several moments passed before Kate remembered that neither this door, nor any other in Caisleán – except the front door – had a lock.

Which meant that they had been here before, perhaps more than once.

Kate began to tremble, more violently and uncontrollably than at any time since the ordeal had begun, her teeth chattering and colliding, chills racking her.

Minutes passed.

Then came the sound of a door closing.

The front door.

And then nothing.

Kate

S he was still there, alone, still listening, ears straining.
Get up.

She felt too weak to move.

Have to.

She made the effort, finally, managed to haul herself up, clinging to the edge, stumbling as she clambered out, one foot striking the side of the bath with a clang.

She froze, afraid they might still be here after all, might come back.

Nothing.

They were gone.

Kate sat down on the edge of the lavatory, looked at her watch, saw that it was twenty-three minutes past twelve, wondered for an instant, overwhelmed by confusion, if it was day or night, then remembered that it had been morning, daylight, when they had brought her into this room.

She thought about Simon's body, wondered if they had, after all, left her.

Thought about Laurie, upstairs.

She turned around just in time to vomit, then, when she was done, she rinsed her mouth, caught sight of her reflection, saw Laurie's blood splattered on her face, and suppressed the urge to wash it off. She sank down on to the floor, huddling in the corner, shaking again.

Alone now, she told herself. *Safe.*

Perhaps.

She thought again about the lock that had not been there before.

She had not tried the door yet, had given no thought as to how she might get out, knew she would have to think about that soon, because the bathroom was small and windowless, and though there was comfort in being in here alone, without *them*, away from all the . . .

Death.

That word, even silent in the privacy of her thoughts, felt as shocking, as frightening, as if she had said it out loud. She waited again for repercussions, for them to come back to punish her, finish her off.

They would not, she knew that. They *had* gone and would not come back. They had clarified that much when they had argued over leaving Simon behind. And it had been implied, too, in those last words of Jack's to her:

'I wish to God I could kill you here and now.'

If not here and now, then where and when?

'Not now,' Kate said aloud.

All that counted.

The key was in the lock on the other side of the bathroom door, and Kate, remembering the old trick that even children knew, tore off the base of a tissue box, slid it under the door, then jiggled the key until it fell on to the torn piece of card and could be pulled into the bathroom.

Too easy. The key being there in the first place, its vertical position in the lock to facilitate pushing it out, enough space beneath the door . . .

Much too easy. Part of their game.

Kate felt sick again as she unlocked the door.

Opened it.

No one around.

Unless you counted two dead women.

She was trembling again as she reached the phone and picked it up.

No line.

Her heart began to thud harder.

Her bag was still on the floor near the door where it had been, but her mobile phone was missing, and her car key, too, and it was no great surprise to her to find the front door locked with no key in sight. The windows were locked, too, and those locks *were* their own handiwork, she and Rob had seen to them for insurance as well as peace of mind, but if the keys were here now, Kate couldn't find them.

Break a window.

She chose the kitchen pane, being the largest and, therefore, the easiest to climb out through. She found a heavy bottomed copper saucepan, hardly used till now, and, squeezing her eyes shut against flying fragments, swung it at the window, the violence of the act almost exhilarating.

She wound two tea towels around her hand and wrist and clambered painfully up on to the window ledge, knocked out as much of the glass as she could, and climbed out.

Cold fresh air, misty rain, the openness of the downs.

Purest heaven on earth for several seconds – and then fear returned with a vengeance, obliterating the pleasure, because she was, she suddenly realized, horribly exposed out here with no one for miles to run to for help—

And they might be watching, concealed by one of the copses of trees just beyond one of those benign-looking, softly rolling hills, they *might* be . . .

Kate moved carefully towards the Mini, her legs still weak, almost certain in any case of the pointlessness of the exercise, because they would hardly have taken the key just to unlock the car for her and ease her way now.

The doors were locked, but her key was in the ignition, her mobile in its hands-free cradle on the dashboard.

The game continuing.

Her hesitation was brief, her only other option a long and lonely walk.

She found a rock over by the stone wall, returned to the car, smashed the passenger window and reached into the car for the phone.

The signal was good, the battery charged, and what did *that* mean?

That they wanted her to be able to use the mobile, call for help.

Kate wavered again.

Paranoia. Of no use to her right now, even if she was entitled to it.

She brushed glass off the passenger seat, hunched over, kneeling so that she could reach across and open the driver's door, and then she shut the passenger door again, walked around to the other side, moving more quickly now, pulses racing, trying hard not to panic herself, got into the driver's side, shut and locked the doors again.

Realized the pointlessness of that, too, with one window smashed and open.

She turned the key in the ignition to see if it would start.
First time.

And then she keyed in 999, took a deep breath and waited.

'I've been held prisoner by a masked gang,' she said, when she was finally through, and it sounded mad even to herself as she spoke the words, told the woman at the other end where she was and that two people were *dead*.

'And I think the killers have gone, but I'm still so scared, and can you please *hurry*.'

She was asked to hold on.

'I want to phone someone else,' she said. 'My husband.'

She cut off the call, sat for another moment, trembling violently again, and then, when she could manage it, she called Rob.

He answered quickly.

'Is Emmie all right?' she asked, before anything.

She hadn't mentioned that threat to the police operator, had *forgotten*.

'Kate?' Rob sounded startled.

'Rob, tell me if Emmie's OK.'

'Of course she is,' he said. 'Kate, what's wrong?'

Speaking to the stranger coherently had been one thing, but telling Rob seemed suddenly impossible, as if layers of mud had suddenly caked her brain and larynx.

She told him, first, that she was at Caisleán.

'Something's happened,' she said. 'Something terrible.' Sticking to the bottom line, all that mattered now. 'I need you, Rob.'

'What's happened?' His voice was harsh with anxiety.

'Please,' she said, 'let me, or I won't get it out.' She took another breath. 'You have to come here, but you mustn't bring Emmie, you have to leave her with someone safe.'

'Kate, for God's—'

'Just *listen*, please.' Her throat hurt with the effort not to cry. 'You have to leave her with someone you trust completely, and tell them not to let her out of their sight for a second, and then you have to come here.'

'All right,' Rob said, bewildered.

'And you have to do it right now,' Kate said. 'You'll understand when you get here. The police are on their way, so I'm OK, so you can please drive carefully, but you have to *come*.'

She ended that call, too.
Went on waiting.
Nearly over now.

After

Kate

Kate knew, within a short space of time, that nothing was over and that she was still in trouble, albeit of a very different kind. Still, though, of *their* making.

The game continuing.

'I can see how odd it must all look,' she said to DCI Helen Newton and DS Ben Poulter in a shabby blue and grey interview room at the Oxford headquarters of the South Oxfordshire Major Investigation Team. 'From your point of view.'

Detective Chief Inspector Helen Newton of SOMIT was around thirty, Kate hazarded; a composed woman with jaw-length straight brown hair with a well-cut fringe, minimal make-up but fine skin and clear, candid light-brown eyes. Dressed in a charcoal trouser suit with plain white blouse; authoritative clothes.

'Odd not quite the word I'd use,' said the DCI wryly.

Two dead women, one tied up on Kate's own bed, her throat cut and the knife on the floor nearby – Kate, with Laurie's blood on her face, telling them they would find *her* prints on the handle. The second woman hanging bloodily off a hook, having crashed through a railing after being pushed.

By her.

Everyone had been kindly and considerate to her when they'd first talked to her at Caisleán – while around her an increasing number of men and women in white hooded suits and overshoes had set about transforming the former barn into what it had become, Kate realized, long before their arrival: a crime scene – a *murder* scene.

They had been gentle to her, both there and later, at SOMIT HQ, where paper chains and mistletoe glimpsed through open office doors reminded Kate that less than twenty-four hours had passed since she had been taken prisoner, and that life had gone on just as before outside Caisleán.

Gentle and apologetic too, as they photographed her, then
asked her to undress, took away her bloodstained blue sweater
and jeans, the Todds, even her bra and panties – which had
confused Kate, seeming to add to her already vulnerable, shocked
state – and issued her with a white suit of her own to wear. Still
considerate as they took scrapings from her face and beneath
her fingernails – even though Kate had told them she'd worn
gloves for most of the time and had never had a chance to scratch
any of the gang – and had a police surgeon examine her for
injuries and more trace evidence. All regularly offering her cups
of tea, telling her to take her time, telling her there was no hurry.

'But there *is*,' Kate had told them, had kept on telling them,
because with every minute that passed, Jack and Pig and Roger
were getting further away.

Not Simon, though, who she had killed.

All kindly to her, all gentle and patient.

Yet still, all the while, Kate had been conscious of their underlying doubts.

She had already volunteered as much as she'd been able, but
her thoughts were coming erratically and out of sequence and
sometimes repetitively, and she was finding it hard to work
through from the beginning, kept coming back to those final
details the gang had seen to in the bathroom.

'Part of their game,' she said.

She had mentioned the *game* several times already, had seen
their expressions.

Had felt she was not believed.

'Simon had a black stocking over her face,' she said. 'They all
did.'

'But *they* took it off her after the fall,' DS Poulter said. 'Not
you.'

The sergeant was a very tall, gangly man with narrow, angular
features and mousy, close-clipped hair. His wedding ring, Kate
noticed as he made notes, had a notch in it that looked almost
like a scar.

'Yes,' Kate said. 'But they made me watch.'

She looked down at her hands, trying not to go back *there*,
focusing for a moment on her own skin, on her fingers, on her
nails, and some of the pale varnish she'd painted on a few days
before was chipped, and that was OK, that was *real*.

'Did they take it off to try to help her?' Poulter dragged her back.

'No,' Kate said. 'I told you, she was already dead.'

The room smelt of stale cigarette smoke, and she'd seen No Smoking signs everywhere they'd taken her, but the smell, she supposed, was ingrained in the walls and in the old burn marks on the table between them.

'And they took the stocking away with them,' said DCI Newton.

There was no wedding band on her hand, no earrings, just a simple twisted gold ring on her right ring finger and a narrow black leather strap watch on her wrist.

'Along with everything else,' Kate said.

Which seemed to her one of the least significant things, yet they kept on about it, had asked her almost the same questions earlier, and she was doing her best to be patient, but it was getting harder.

'You do have people out looking for them, don't you?'

That was all *she* really wanted to know, that they would be caught.

'Depend on it,' Helen Newton said, 'though we don't have much to go on.'

Which was, of course, true. No vehicle to report on, not even the *sound* of one. Two men and a woman – probably separated by now – known only to Kate by aliases possibly plucked from a novel, carrying plastic bags filled with empty disposable coffee cups and spoons, discarded bandages, bits of sticky tape and sundry fragments of debris. Wearing red overalls and trainers and surgical-type gloves, all presumably shed long since – though the police did, at least, have Simon's clothes, which was something to start checking on . . .

'So,' Poulter said, 'they took everything, but left their colleague.'

Kate ignored what sounded like cynicism, forced herself to focus again on her own account. 'One of them – the man called Pig – was terribly upset – heartbroken, I thought – about leaving Simon, but the woman called Roger told him it was part of the game now.' She thought back. 'I think she said that after Jack had phoned their chief.'

'You didn't actually hear that call?' Poulter asked.

'No,' Kate said.

'So if leaving Simon was now part of this game,' Newton asked, 'do you think they might have planned her killing, too?'

'No.' Kate was clear on that. 'Definitely not. That was an accident. No one could have engineered it, and anyway, they were much too shocked, much too upset and angry.'

She had already told them about Jack saying he wanted to kill her.

'And you have no idea what this "game" is really about?' asked DS Poulter.

'I only know what they told us – me and Laurie.' The words came back to her with sickening clarity. 'They said – Jack said: "We pick a beast and punish it."'

'A "beast",' the detective sergeant echoed.

'Probably from the book I told you about,' Kate said. 'Same as the names.'

'*Lord of the Flies*.' The DCI nodded. 'The children in the story believe there's a dangerous beast they have to kill.'

Kate experienced a touch of relief, focused all her attention on the senior detective. 'And then the man named Pig said that *this* time – which I imagine means there must have been other games – they had *two* beasts, which he said was a first.'

'Meaning you and Laurie Moon,' Newton clarified.

Kate nodded. 'They said it was *simple*. They said we had to punish each other.' She took a breath. 'Jack said that Laurie was going to punish me by being my victim, and that I . . .'

'Go on.' The DCI was gentle.

Kate's shudder was involuntary. 'He said I was going to punish her by executing her.'

'And did he – this Jack – say what either of you were to be punished for?'

Kate felt her jaw tremble, dug her fingers into her thighs, then quickly stopped, hating the feel of the white suit that was not hers, and it reminded her too much of the overalls the gang had worn, and the next time she saw red overalls anywhere, she wasn't sure *how* she'd react, perhaps she'd run screaming through the streets . . .

'Mrs Turner?' DCI Newton nudged her gently again.

'Not exactly.' Kate dredged up more strength. 'Except that they were under the impression that I'd once had an abortion.'

'Had you?' Helen Newton asked. 'If you don't mind my asking.'

'I don't know if I mind or not.' Kate sighed. 'But no, as it happens, I had not, though I did have a miscarriage.' She paused.

'I have written a couple of pieces on abortion for my column, which they quoted from – I'm sorry, I can't remember if I've told you that already.'

DS Poulter consulted his notebook, raised both eyebrows. '*Diary of a Short-Fused Female.*'

'And Laurie Moon.' The DCI spoke again. 'What was she being punished for?'

Kate felt a great surge of sorrow and rage. 'They said she'd put her son in a home of some kind when she didn't have to.'

'And had she done that?' asked Poulter.

'I don't know,' Kate said. 'I've told you, I didn't know her.'

Neither detective said anything.

'It was insanity.' Emotion was starting to get the better of her now, was resonating in Kate's voice now, was in her face like a fever flush, she could feel it, building. 'All of it, from the moment it began. It was mad and it was *wicked*.'

'And did you?' asked Helen Newton.

'Did I what?' She was confused.

'Did you do what they – Jack – said you had to do?'

Kate stared at her. 'You're asking if I did *that* to her?'

'That is what I'm asking. Did you execute Laurie Moon?'

'No.' Kate was trembling now, with a different kind of anger. 'I did not. Of course I did not.'

'Even though they made threats against your husband's child?' asked Poulter.

'But it didn't come to that, did it?' Kate said. 'I told you, they put my fingerprints on the knife.' The words were coming quickly now, and she knew that the only way to put an end to this was to answer every question, however *stupid*. 'And then Jack said he couldn't trust me with it, with the *knife*, because I might stab him, and he said something about it not going right. "Not the Chief's great fucking plan" was what he said.' She stopped, breathing fast. 'Remember you have to find this *chief*, too, right? This Ralph.'

It had occurred to her a while ago that, bizarre as the idea was, she might perhaps need a lawyer, but that really did seem too mad, because she was the *victim*, and so what she needed most was for them to listen to and to believe her, so she was just going to go on giving them everything she could, just plunge on with the whole truth.

'I think he – Jack – was wavering for a moment,' she went on, 'but then, right after Pig shouted that Simon was dead, he just *did* it.' Her voice choked up for the first time. 'He just cut Laurie's throat.'

'How exactly did Jack do it?' asked Poulter.

'I don't know.' Kate looked hard at him. 'I shut my eyes because I thought he was going to stick the knife in me, to kill *me*, not Laurie, and then I heard this horrible little sound, and I opened my eyes, and the blood was . . .'

The two detectives gave her a moment.

'Why do you think they told you your husband's daughter was in danger,' Helen Newton asked, 'if they weren't even going to let you do the killing?'

'I can't answer that. Maybe it's what their *chief* planned, and they knew – or at least Jack knew – it wasn't going to work out.' Kate shook her head. 'I don't even know – I can't begin to imagine what I'd have done if Jack had put the knife in my hand.'

'Are you saying,' DS Poulter asked, 'that you might have killed Miss Moon?'

Kate's returning look was of pure disgust. 'I'm saying that I'm incredibly grateful that I didn't have to face that moment, and I have absolutely *no* intention of making this nightmare even more horrific by contemplating it now just to please you.'

Her anger and frustration spilling over, finally, for one reason above all others.

They did *not* believe her.

It was naïve of her not to have registered that cold hard truth right away. She was a journalist, after all, not a reporter, but still, this was textbook stuff. Two women dead, Kate the only witness. The surviving *victim*, but nothing solid to support her story.

In their eyes, first and foremost, she was a suspect.

Rob arrived, white-faced and growing ever more bewildered, but patently relieved to find her unharmed.

'Thank God you're all right,' he said. 'I've been imagining all sorts.'

'Where's Emmie?' Kate wanted to know.

'With your dad.' He shook his head. 'Kate, why did you say that about her?' His eyes were intense, almost fierce. 'What's been happening to you, and what in God's name does it have to do with Emmie?'

For the first time since walking into Caisleán the previous evening, Kate burst into tears, just let it all *go*, and Rob did what he always had on the comparatively rare occasions that had happened since he'd known and loved his emotional, but seldom histrionic wife. He put his arms around her and held her, and for just a few moments the sheer familiar physical comfort of the man pushed some of the horror away.

And then he drew back, held her at arm's length.

'I need to know everything, Kate,' he told her. 'Caisleán's cordoned off, and—'

'It's a crime scene,' Kate said bluntly through her tears. 'That's why I'm here.' She wiped her eyes with the back of her hand. 'I was beginning to think they might not let you see me.'

'I'd like to have seen them try and stop me,' said Rob.

'Good,' said Kate.

Ralph

R alph's isolation was greater than ever.

Everything now existing, it seemed to her, only in her imaginings.

The three leaving the barn together, in sorrowful silence, disposing of overalls and evidence and then parting – as had always been the plan – at separate points along the way.

One less stop than planned.

Then home. Roger and Pig to their homes in Reading and Swindon. Jack to his long-suffering wife and children in Newbury.

Simon's flat remaining empty.

Ralph wondered how long it would be until her body was identified.

It hurt just to think of her that way.

How long would it take before Simon's colleagues at school would become sufficiently concerned to query her absence, how long before an absent Oxford teaching assistant became linked to a violent death in an isolated converted barn in the Berkshire Downs?

Ralph wondered if a post-mortem might reveal any pre-birth internal scars caused by her desperate young mother, wondered if Simon's old hospital records were intact, if computer systems would be able to connect the dots; and if so, what difference it would make to the police investigation into the killing of Laurie Moon.

They had agreed, during their last, unhappy conversation, that there could be no further contact between them for the foreseeable future.

Safer that way for them all.

> *This game is over for our part. Now we can only observe, from afar, as other players pick up our balls and run with them. Nothing more to be done than to watch and wait to see where they fall.*
>
> *I wish, more than ever, that I could be with my children to comfort and grieve with them.*
>
> *None of us has said it, but we all know.*
>
> *We have played our last game.*

Kate

Rob had brought Kate back from Oxford that day to the cottage, and had not left.

Still paying rent on his flat in Coley Hill, though, both of them agreeing that the hideous shocks of unlawful imprisonment and murder might not be the soundest foundations for reconciliation and long-term happiness.

The police had not finished with Kate and were still putting her through interviews, the stresses of being pulled back and forth, being treated one moment as victim, the next as a potential suspect, all taxing her considerably. Laurie Moon and Simon preoccupied her constantly, her attempts to deny to herself her part in their deaths hopeless; the dead gang member exercising her conscience almost as much as Laurie, however irrational she knew that to be.

'Something monstrous was about to happen.' Rob had reiterated that in so many ways, as had her parents. 'You had to do something, you had to fight.'

'I know that,' Kate had told them all.

Except the fact was that *what* she had done had resulted in Simon's death. And Jack *had* been wavering about killing Laurie until Pig had told him Simon was dead.

'Which means that if I hadn't pushed Simon, Laurie might still be alive now.'

'You can't think like that,' Rob had said.

'You *mustn't* think like that.' Her father.

Her mother had not said that, for which Kate was grateful.

'If you are feeling it,' Bel had said last week, 'it's probably better to voice it than let it eat you alive.'

'But there's no justification to Kate feeing even a *shred* of guilt,' Michael had said with passion, 'when it's clear that if she hadn't fought back at that moment, she and Laurie might *both* be dead now.'

'No,' Kate had said. 'That wasn't the aim of the game.'

That was when she'd seen the flicker in her father's eyes.

Of doubt, or at least confusion.

She had seen it in his eyes before, and in Rob's, too, when she'd mentioned the *game*. Though not in Bel's, interestingly. From her often self-obsessed mother, she'd had nothing but support of the most unconditional and intelligent kind.

As, of course, she'd had around the time of her miscarriage.

'Mum's being amazing,' Kate had told Rob soon after the Caisleán weekend.

'She adores you,' he had said, simply. 'Couldn't bear to lose you.'

'But she's being so calm,' Kate said.

'Don't knock it,' Rob advised. 'Try cherishing it instead.'

They were both a little confused about their reconciliation. They knew they had been coming close to it before, when they'd argued shortly before the horrors; but they *had* argued, and their separation had come about in such an acutely painful way. Kate still remembered, all too clearly, longed to forget, the way Rob had changed then, the hardening of his attitude towards her –

and though the blue of his eyes was soft again now, the chastening fact remained that they were only together again now because Kate had come so close to death, and because she needed help.

And because Rob loved her. And she him.

Surely no better reason.

They all spoke of Laurie by her first name, as if they had known her.

They did know a little more by now.

She had been identified within twenty-four hours by her father, the Mann Children's Home having notified her parents of Laurie's no-show, and a missing person's report having been made by afternoon that same day.

The news story had made the national press by that Monday morning, local TV and radio news reporting it before that. Pictures of Caisleán surrounded by crime scene tape and looking somehow sordid; shots of Kate – including a honeymoon photo of her with Rob in Venice, no one having any idea how it might have been obtained – and of Laurie, Michele and Peter Moon, and of their young grandson, Sam. Quotes from Laurie's neighbours expressing shock and disbelief, all speaking of a lovely, friendly, quiet, talented young woman – and of their surprise, too, that she had a child.

'The boy is eight years old, and has Down's syndrome.'

Kate had heard this from Martin Blake, her new lawyer, a former colleague of her dad's. Having continued to insist for days that as a victim she did not need a lawyer, that bringing one in seemed tantamount to raising her very own question mark over her innocence, Kate had finally accepted that she probably needed all the help she could get.

'Even that word – *"innocence"* –' Bel had been incensed, had told Michael as much – 'implies she has something to prove.'

'No one's saying that,' Michael had tried to calm her. 'We all know Kate is completely blameless.'

'Of *course* she's blameless,' Bel had shouted at him. 'She's the *victim*.'

The fact that Sam Moon had Down's syndrome – Martin Blake agreed – lent weight to Kate's theory that the gang might be some kind of fanatical pro-life splinter or entirely independent group. He also said that, so far as he could ascertain, the general consensus of opinion, pending further investigation, was that the police did not exactly *dis*believe her.

'Not exactly,' Kate had echoed grimly.

'The problems lie, obviously, with all the physical evidence,' Blake said.

'All against me,' Kate said.

'It would be preposterous,' Michael said, 'if it weren't so tragic.'

'It's barking *mad*,' Bel said.

'It's their game,' Kate said.

Ψ

'The problem,' Martin Blake pointed out to Kate at their next meeting, a few days before Christmas, 'is that even the elements which seem to support your story can be explained away.' His expression was apologetic. 'Could even, theoretically, have been arranged by you.'

'God,' Kate said.

They were alone together in Blake's office, both feeling better able to proceed more effectively without family passions igniting every other minute.

The room, in a modern building in Banbury Road, Oxford, was well-ordered, if not overly tidy. Unlike the law offices her father had formerly practised from in Henley, this possessed, Kate felt, no elegance or even any atmosphere to speak of, yet in a curious sense that seemed of comfort to her at present, since normality, even the commonplace, was what she craved a return to.

The solicitor himself – a pleasant-looking, sandy-haired man in his late thirties with features that drooped in repose, but were all the more bright and pleasant when he became animated – was clearly a realist but on her side, which seemed to her what mattered most, especially since she hoped that ultimately there would be no need to prove his talent as a lawyer.

Blake went on to catalogue the problems.

The minor bruising – Kate's only injuries, caused by the slaps and hog-tying – could have happened as a result of her tussle with Simon.

'Though if it came to it,' Blake said, 'we'd have an expert witness to support our explanation and refute theirs.'

The tyre tracks found some way from the barn and probably left by a van, which tallied with her account of the gang's comings and goings, could have been left by *any* van, its driver perhaps altogether unconnected with the criminals or Kate, maybe lost and seeking an address.

'Or you might have set up the tracks yourself,' Blake said.

'Not very likely,' Kate said, 'surely.'

She was choosing, she was aware, not to face the incredible devastation of all that had happened and was still happening to her. Not just of being a victim and a witness to a most depraved brand of so-called 'justice' handed down in the name of the unborn and sinned-against mothers. In some ways, what was happening now seemed just as hard to believe; the very notion that someone might for a single moment believe that Kate could . . .

Too much to face.

Better, therefore, not to.

Her missing front door keys, Martin Blake continued, had been found buried beneath the wild primrose patch where Kate had told the police she always left a spare set, proving nothing in her favour.

'Likewise the kitchen window smashed by you from inside,' said Blake.

'May I ask a question?'

'As many as you wish.'

'Exactly *why* am I supposed to have set up this elaborate chamber of horrors?'

'I would presume,' the lawyer replied, 'that any basis for accusation would be on the assumption that you *were* taken prisoner, but that either you used excessive force against Simon . . .' He paused. 'Or, even more ludicrously – lest you doubt my opinion – that you killed both Simon and Laurie Moon.'

'And then set up all this evidence after they'd gone,' Kate continued the theme. 'Because I thought no one would believe me otherwise.'

'Unless someone comes up with some other motive,' Blake said, 'some link, perhaps, with either Laurie Moon or the other woman.'

'Which they won't,' Kate said, 'because it doesn't exist.'

'Quite,' Blake said.

The telephone, not working when Kate had tried to summon

help from inside Caisleán, had been functioning perfectly by the time the police had arrived. The distress in Kate's voice, recorded when she'd managed to make her report from outside, didn't count for much, since she might, of course, be a good actor.

'Can't they tell if a phone line's been cut off or tampered with?' asked Kate.

'Perhaps,' Blake answered. 'I have a colleague looking into that.' He saw her frustration. 'You must remember that you and I are playing our own game of worst case scenarios, which is an unusual approach, and one we've only begun because your family are getting so angry and upset on your behalf.'

'Can you blame them?' Kate asked hotly.

'Not at all,' Blake replied. 'That's why Michael approached me, because he thought I'd understand your collective anxieties and do my best to shoot down any seriously off-course wild geese before anyone tries to chase them.'

Kate laughed. 'If I ever want to seriously dement my editor, could I please come to you for some metaphor-mixing lessons?'

'Any time,' Blake said.

The lightness had already passed. 'Do you think DCI Newton believes me?'

'I'd say so, in all probability.' Blake paused. 'Though until she has more to go on, or at least some starting point in the hunt for the gang—'

'I'm the only game in town,' Kate said.

'More accurately,' the lawyer said, 'you're their only witness.'

'I suppose,' she said slowly, 'I need to keep my focus on that, rather than being so oversensitive. Concentrate on helping the police catch the bastards.'

'That's what we both need to focus on,' said Blake.

'Thank you,' Kate said. 'I think we've strayed from your list of problems.'

'It wouldn't do,' Blake said wryly, 'to be too upbeat.'

He returned to his notes.

'Miss Moon's car hasn't been found yet,' he said. 'Which only presents a problem in that the car might provide valuable evidence if they could locate it.'

'I'm surprised no one's suggested I've got it stashed away somewhere.'

'I thought you were going to be positive,' Blake said, 'and let me play devil's advocate.'

Kate nodded.

Her claim to have been locked in the bathroom, Blake went on, could not be proved because she'd got out so easily, and her insistence that there had been no lock – confirmed by Rob – was not provable since he had also had to admit that prior to the weekend of the killings he hadn't been to the barn for months, which meant that Kate might have had the lock fitted, or even have done it herself.

'I'm lousy at DIY,' she told Blake.

'So you say.' He grinned.

'Ask anyone,' she said.

'All people who love you,' he said. 'They don't count.'

'God,' she said again, humour gone.

'On the plus side—'

'Is there one?' Kate interrupted.

'Certainly,' Blake said. 'We've already touched on the fact that the police do appear to believe that you did not know Laurie Moon.'

'Hang out the flags.' Kate shrugged. 'Sorry.'

'Bizarrely enough,' Blake went on, 'the fact that there were *two* bodies in Caisleán works in our favour, since one would have been much easier to pin on you.'

'Tell that to the bodies,' said Kate.

'I do have something more,' Blake said.

'A third body?' Her irony splashed up like acid.

'Something rather better.'

'Go on,' Kate said. 'Please.'

'A possible precedent. In Oxford – in Summertown, to be precise – about a year ago, a primary school teacher named Alan Mitcham, charged with armed robbery, claimed he'd been forced to commit the crime by a gang of abductors wearing black stocking masks.'

'Goodness,' Kate said. 'What happened to him?'

'He was convicted.'

'Great.' Kate paused. 'I take it there's more.'

'I'm afraid Mr Mitcham was murdered in Oakwood Prison.'

'I thought this was meant to be a good precedent,' Kate said.

'It is good,' Blake said, 'because the police seem to be looking at Mitcham's story again with fresh eyes.' He rubbed the side of his nose with his thumb. 'It's also of very great interest for another reason.'

Kate waited.

'Mitcham claimed after his arrest,' Blake went on, 'that the gang had used false names taken from a novel.'

For the first time, Kate experienced a real kick of hope. 'The Golding?'

'The very same,' said Blake. 'Though he said there were three gang members, not four – but since their names were Jack, Roger and Pig, it's hardly likely to be a coincidence.'

'So Newton has to be starting to believe me,' Kate said.

'Let's say things are heading in the right direction,' Blake said.

Ralph

The knowledge that it was all over was even more painful than Ralph had ever anticipated it might be.

Knowing there would be no more games.

No more group.

Knowing that when the time came, none of them would be able to attend Simon's funeral, nor even, later, visit her grave in case the police were watching.

Her grief for Simon and her fears for the others grew daily. They were so scarred, so damaged, and now they would have to go on alone, and she wondered how they would manage.

Maybe they would be fine, maybe *better* than before.

More ordinary, their lives commonplace.

Better without her influence.

Better without *her*.

She hardly seemed to care about herself any more, felt unable to. If she didn't eat or sleep well, or didn't exercise, or didn't even get out more than was absolutely necessary, there was no one to bother about her. She had been managing to continue with her part-time job and a little telephone counselling – she had to pay her bills, after all – but there was no satisfaction in any of it, which reminded her of the way her life had been before that long-ago evening at Wayland's Smithy.

Before the group.

One of her great fears was that the other three might be bent on revenge. That Pig, in particular, might try to do something to avenge Simon, endangering himself and the other two. They'd agreed on as little contact as possible; not even so much as a Christmas card, and phone calls only if absolutely necessary and with great caution, but on the rare opportunity Ralph did find to communicate with any of them, she was determined to use it to discourage acts of retribution as well as she could.

Keeping her surviving children safe was the least she could do after all the harm she had already done them.

She knew that she would never forgive herself.

And her own hatred for Kate Turner grew stronger every day.

Kate

They were both beginning to accept, Kate felt, that they were truly together again, their reconciliation less tentative than it had at first been.

They'd done a few things to mark new permanence, bought new cushions and a couple of jacquard throws for the coffee-stained sofa and armchairs, gone to the garden centre and chosen plants, then dug them in together. Sharing their home again and their daily lives, through Christmas and into the New Year, felt better than right to them both.

She looked at herself sometimes in mirrors, assessing the damages of the past year. She'd gone to a hairdresser after Caislean, had her hair cut shorter, and it suited her well enough. Her hazel eyes gazed almost calmly back at her, the shadows beneath them less pronounced than they had been, though her face was still thinner.

Rob told her she was beautiful, and she told him he was hand-some, and that she'd even grown fond of his beard. But then he'd startled her, early one morning, by inviting her to shave it off for him.

'Are you quite sure?' She'd felt tentative.

'It reminds you, I think,' he said, 'of our bad times, so I want it gone.'

'But you like it.'

'I love you more.'

It had been an extraordinarily intimate experience, leading to love-making, and that too was better than it had ever been, though the new bond between them seemed far more important than physical pleasure. Kate thought, perhaps, that it was she who felt that so much more, the sheer relief of coming together, the sense of safe harbour she experienced being closer than close, Rob deep inside her.

'God, no,' Rob told her. 'Same for me, because I thought I'd lost you forever.'

Not quite the same, then, Kate realized, because her craving for safety stemmed from those twenty or so hours spent in the company of monsters, with a masked killer who'd thrust a condom in her face and told her how he would have liked to *'educate'* her, a man who had cut a young woman's throat . . .

Not quite the same.

Not *all* roses, either.

The Caisleán 'incident', as some called it, had given Rob's ex-wife a maddeningly rational excuse to keep Emmie from her father. They couldn't possibly imagine, Penny said, that she would take any more risks with her daughter.

'Not with those people still out there.'

Kate would have liked to strangle Penny just for the reminder, then do it all over again for her unkindness to Rob. Strangle her *figuratively*, that was, she amended even to herself, the reality of physical violence still too bloodily fresh in her memory.

She felt deeply altered by the Caisleán weekend in many ways.

'You're post-traumatic,' she had been told by just about everyone from DS Ben Poulter to Richard Fireman – who had been amazingly patient about her inability to string together a decent *Short-Fuse* since her ordeal.

Guest writers filling her slot for now, which ought, she supposed, to be worrying her more than it was. Not exactly hard to replace, after all, a hack who'd struck lucky with a provincial paper.

'Out of work soon, if I don't get my act together,' Kate said to Rob.

'You will,' he told her. 'Got to give yourself time.'

Kate supposed he was right, that they were all on the mark too about the post-traumatic thing. She was displaying all the symptoms: anxiety, nerviness, flashbacks, nightmares and periods of depression (not at all like her PMS black moods, these were quite different, affecting her physically as well as emotionally, often making her feel ill, wanting to sleep rather than lash out). Yet at the same time, she seemed to have a desire to be kinder, was less impatient and generally less verbally antagonistic with those people she loved.

She was also more suspicious of strangers, whether they came a little too close out in the streets, or rang the doorbell at the cottage because they wanted to read a meter or make a delivery; and with those people she'd never wholly trusted – like Delia and Sandi – she was more prickly than ever, and she thought she'd have liked to have recovered from that, like flu, but her hackles continued to rise when they met. Yet despite those abiding dislikes, her family seemed more united than at any time she could remember.

'I still can't quite imagine Delia and I ever being friends,' she had told Michael a couple of weeks ago, 'but she does seem to make you happy, so I'm going to promise to try and do better around her.'

'That's all I can ask for,' her father had said.

It was hard, though, for Kate to forget that Delia had been sufficiently sceptical of her account of events to suggest that she see a therapist.

'I'm not saying I mightn't need some therapy,' Kate had said after that to Rob, 'and maybe I'll think about it when I'm good and ready. But I don't think Delia likes the fact that I'm still occupying centre stage in Dad's life.'

'He's not really spending much more time with you than before,' Rob said.

'But I think perhaps I spend more time in his mind,' Kate had told him. 'Delia knows she probably can't do much about that, but I don't think she'd mind shrinking my credibility a bit more.'

'I'd better not hint at paranoia then,' Rob said.

'Oh, God,' Kate had said. 'Maybe I do need therapy.'

But Rob had just smiled and kissed her, and she'd left it.

She found it harder to leave things alone where Sandi West was concerned.

'She's still so shocked by what happened,' Bel told Kate in mid-January.

'I wish,' Kate said, 'you wouldn't talk to Sandi about me.'

'And I wish you'd understand that even if she can be tactless, she's not your enemy,' Bel replied. 'You know what a very good friend she's been to me.'

'And you to her,' said Kate.

'I still have trouble understanding what's wrong with that,' Bel said reasonably.

So reasonably, in fact, that Kate began to feel that perhaps her mother's friendship with Sandi was another area she should try reassessing while putting her character in order.

'Very admirable,' Rob said to her later, when she told him.

'Why so wry?' Kate asked.

'Because however much you may try, for Bel's sake, I can't imagine you're ever going to change your mind about someone you dislike as much as Sandi.'

'But you've said in the past that I ought to make more effort,' Kate said. 'Are you saying you were wrong?'

'I think what I'm saying,' Rob said, 'is that, for the most part, I've learned to trust your instincts.'

That warmed her in a way that few compliments ever had.

And then the phone rang, and it was Martin Blake, telling her that DCI Helen Newton had requested that she come back to Oxford.

A real turning point, at last.

Blake was already at the SOMIT offices, waiting for her.

'Don't look so worried,' he told her quietly. 'It seems they've made a little progress, and they're doing us the courtesy of keeping us informed.'

They were shown, moments later, into one of the interview rooms.

Getting too familiar, Kate thought, looking around.

DCI Newton and DS Poulter both present.

Usual suspects, Kate thought.

'We're telling you this in confidence,' Helen Newton said.

'Of course,' Blake said.

'We identified Simon,' the DCI said, 'ten days ago.'

Kate's pulse rate increased.

'Her real name was Carol Marsh.' Newton looked directly

at Kate. 'She was a teacher's aide at an Oxford primary school.'

'Twenty-four years old,' added Poulter.

'Bit of a loner, so far as we can make out.' Helen Newton referred to notes. 'No partner or notable social life, according to the neighbours. Marsh's teenage mother battered herself to try to get rid of her, then committed suicide after Carol was born. Father unknown, so the little girl was raised in a children's home.' The DCI looked up. 'The home's records state that she was prone to bouts of depression.'

'Poor little cow,' Ben Poulter said.

Which might, Kate thought, have described the mother or Carol Marsh.

Simon.

The image of her hanging from the hook in Caisleán flew into her mind, and she pushed it away.

'Did she, by chance,' Blake asked, 'work at the same school as Alan Mitcham?'

'Summertown Primary,' Newton answered. 'Yes, she did.'

Which was the reason, presumably, for Simon not having been part of the attack on Mitcham; he might have recognized her as a colleague.

Relief hit Kate first, for several sweet seconds, then renewed anger.

'So now you believe me,' she said.

'I don't recall telling you that we didn't believe you, Mrs Turner,' Newton said.

'But you've known all this for ten days.'

'Not all of it,' Newton said.

Frustrated, Kate glanced sideways at Martin Blake, who gave a gentle shrug.

'Before I share one more thing with you,' the DCI went on, 'I must impress on you both again that this information is strictly confidential.'

'You already told us that,' Kate said, still crisply, though her anger was fading.

'We appreciate everything you feel you can share with us,' said Blake.

Kate flashed him another look, which he returned with a smile.

'I rather think,' Helen Newton said, 'that you will appreciate this.' She nodded at the detective sergeant.

'Marsh's flat in Cowley wasn't much to write home about,' Poulter took over. 'Sparsely furnished and a bit sad, really.' He paused. 'Being in the teaching game, though, there were quite a lot of books, as you'd expect.'

Kate felt skin creep at the base of her spine.

'What you might *not* expect, however –' Newton's eyes were fixed on Kate's face – 'was that there were five editions of one novel.'

'*Lord of the Flies*?' Martin Blake asked.

'Yes, indeed,' Newton confirmed.

Kate remained silent for a long moment, then said: 'You start to wonder, after a while, if perhaps you imagined it all.' She paused. 'If maybe you are a little mad.'

Helen Newton smiled at her.

'Not even a little, Mrs Turner,' she said.

Ψ

Surprise of a different kind two days later.

'Sandi and I have fallen out,' Bel told Kate on the phone.

'I'm sorry,' Kate said.

'Don't be silly,' Bel said. 'Of course you're not sorry.'

'She's your friend. You've been very close.' Kate felt her cheeks warm with guilt. 'So, yes, I think I really am sorry.'

Her mother made a wry sound.

'What happened?' Kate asked. 'If you don't mind telling me.'

'Sandi said one spiteful thing too many about you,' Bel said.

'I don't understand.'

'It's not complicated,' her mother said. 'And I think it's better this way. Which has nothing whatever to do with the fact that you disliked Sandi so much.'

'I'm glad to hear it,' Kate said.

It was still troubling her later when Rob came home from school.

'God knows Mum's hardly overrun by friends,' she told him. 'I feel guilty.'

'I can't see why you should,' he said. 'Bel broke up with Sandi for a perfectly good reason.'

'Me,' said Kate.

'Her choice, though. Nothing you said.'

'I suppose.'

'You've never been able to stand Sandi. If Bel had taken any notice of that, she'd have ditched the friendship long ago.'

'You said "broke up" before,' Kate said. 'Makes them sound like lovers.'

Which thought made her feel even sadder for Bel.

'Is your mother all right?' her father asked Kate the following week.

'A bit low, I think,' she said. 'About Sandi.'

They'd already talked once about that issue.

'I hope she's OK,' Michael said. 'She seems – I don't know – a bit distant.'

'You're divorced, Dad,' Kate said. 'You're meant to be distant.'

'I still worry about her,' Michael said.

'Me too,' Kate said.

'I don't think she's been drinking,' Michael said. 'Would you say?'

'I'd say not,' Kate consoled him. 'But I'll keep an eye on her, if that's what you're asking me to do.'

'I suppose I am.' He paused. 'Any further developments in the case?'

'If there have been,' Kate said, 'no one's telling me.'

'It'll come,' Michael said.

There were times when Kate found herself wishing that it would *never* come, that the police would never find the rest of the gang, so that maybe eventually the memories would just fade and she might be able to move forward, be fully herself again.

Rob and her father, she knew, would never be happy until the killers had been locked up for the duration.

'Whoever the fuck they are,' Michael had said, quite violently, one day.

To Kate, of course, they were and would remain two men and a woman – faceless, but distinctive – named Jack, Roger and Pig.

Easier not knowing their identities.

'I don't think I want them humanized,' Kate said to Rob.

'Like Carol Marsh,' he said, understanding.

'Before I knew about her,' Kate said, 'she was just Simon, dead terrorist.'

'Easier to hate,' Rob said.

'Maybe even to forget,' she said. 'One day.'

'Are you still having nightmares?' Bel asked her on the first Tuesday of February over a little late lunch at Caffè Nero in Henley.

They had been doing more mother-and-daughter things since it happened – and even more since Sandi had moved out of Bel's life – which meant that there were *two* things, Kate supposed, that had come out of the horror for which she could be grateful: her ever-improving relationships with both Rob and her mother.

'Not every night,' she answered now.

'I was wondering,' Bel said, 'if you'd consider . . .'

Kate looked at her, had thought since they'd sat down that her mother had something on her mind, decided now that she was not going to like whatever was coming next.

'Well?' she said.

'My self-help group,' Bel said. 'There's a meeting this Thursday. I haven't been for a while, and I know that ordinarily it's not your kind of thing . . .'

'No, Mum,' Kate said quickly. 'It's not.'

'I think you'd be surprised,' Bel said, 'by what a mixed bunch they are.'

Kate thought of Sandi, then of her mother at her worst, and cringed at the very idea of a roomful of kindred spirits.

'It sounds,' she said, 'like hell.'

'I wouldn't ask –' clearly Bel had prepared for this conversation and for her refusal – 'if I didn't feel I so badly need to go.'

'So why haven't you gone?' Kate paused. 'Is it because of Sandi?'

'She's not going any more,' Bel said, 'so it's nothing to do with her. But I do seem to be just a bit nervous of going back on my own.'

'I can't believe you agreed,' Rob said. 'Are you sure this is a good idea for you?'

'I'm not going for me,' Kate said. 'Strictly to give Mum moral support.'

Rob looked dubious.

'And I did promise Dad I was going to keep an eye out for her.'

'And you think there's no hidden agenda?' Rob asked.

'So long as Sandi isn't there,' Kate said, 'I can't imagine one.'

'I'm just picturing you in a room full of well-meaning therapy pushers.' Rob shook his head. 'I hope Bel doesn't think they could be what you need.'

'I don't think so,' Kate said. 'Though I was thinking I might possibly get a column out of it.'

'Would that be OK with Bel?'

Simon's taunt about cruelty to mothers flashed suddenly back at Kate.

'I don't know.' She realized how tired she felt.

'You OK?' Rob was gentle.

'Not really.'

He was silent for a moment, and then he said: 'You don't need to change yourself, you know. You're fine just the way you are, the way you've always been.'

'So fine you couldn't bear living with me any more,' Kate said softly.

'That was the pair of us,' Rob said, 'both being fools.'

Kate sighed. 'I don't think doing this one small thing for my mother's going to constitute a major character reform.'

'And it might even be therapeutic, I suppose,' Rob pondered. 'So long as you don't take them too seriously.'

'Feel like joining us?' Kate asked.

'Poking needles into eyes comes to mind,' he said.

Ralph

Ralph could hardly recall a time when she had still thought of Simon by her real name.

Like the other three, Carol Marsh had been of no particular significance to her in her official capacity at Challow Hall. They had been just four more luckless kids with little hope for their futures. She'd encountered them periodically, a part of the mass, had known them better on paper than in reality.

Until the evening at the Smithy, when she had become entranced by them.

After that, Carol Marsh had ceased almost entirely to exist for Ralph.

Simon until the day she died.

She wondered how long the police had known Simon's identity before releasing her name. How much time they had spent digging around in Carol's life, presumably hoping to dislodge the others?

Jack had been the first to phone her after the name had hit the news.

Ralph had known she should rebuke him for breaking their no-contact rule, should forbid him from doing it again for all their sakes, but she had been so overwhelmingly glad to hear his voice that she'd said it more mildly than was wise.

'We mustn't do this, Jack.'

'I reckon we'll know,' he had said, 'if they find out about any of us.'

'They may be cleverer than that,' Ralph said.

'Not all that bright,' Jack said, 'in my experience.'

'That's your experience,' Ralph had said, 'as a burglar.'

She had not used the word 'killer', nor had either of them mentioned the game or any of the other's names. Just in case someone was listening – Pig's talents had made them too alert to the possibilities of phone tapping.

'How's he doing?' Ralph had asked. 'Do you know?'

'I thought you said we're not to get in touch,' Jack said.

'And I meant it,' Ralph said. 'But I know you.'

'I did take a drive just the other day, over to Swindon, saw him coming out of his place,' Jack admitted. 'He didn't see me, but he looked pretty bad, I thought. Can't say I was surprised.'

'Do you think he'll stay away from the funeral?'

It had been on her mind constantly, a gnawing worry.

'I bloody well hope so,' Jack said. 'I don't think he's that much of an idiot.'

Ralph had said she hoped not, too, and then she'd told Jack how good it had been to hear his voice, but that he mustn't do it again.

'Only in a real emergency,' she had said.

Giving them both the get-out they had wanted.

*   *   *

She had known all along that none of them would be able to stop completely.

Not just because they were addicted, both to the group and the game. Not even just because they all loved each other.

It was what they had all known, deep down, since Simon had died.

That this game simply was not yet over.

Kate

'I'm only coming this once,' Kate reminded her mother on the phone at lunchtime on Thursday, 'to support you, right?'

'I know,' Bel said, 'and I'm properly grateful.'

'Just so long as they know I'm not going to talk about myself.'

'I've told the organizer,' Bel said, 'but why don't you see how you feel about it when you're there?'

Kate knew there and then that she should have backed out.

The meeting was in a sitting room in a Victorian terraced house in East Reading, the room filled with a variety of unmatched chairs and stools, and an equally motley group of about twenty men and women, most of them helping themselves to polystyrene cups of strong tea from an old, sturdy urn and custard creams from two large paper plates before sitting down and beginning, one at a time, to unburden themselves.

All perfectly tolerable, Kate found, to her surprise, and actually more interesting than depressing because it was plain, from the start, that these people were relieved to be there, that perhaps this might be their first chance to unload since the last meeting.

Until twenty minutes into the meeting, when the door opened.

'Apologies,' Sandi West said, entering the room.

Kate shot an accusing look at Bel, saw that her mother's cheeks were flushed.

'I had no idea,' Bel whispered. 'Do you want to leave?'

Kate shook her head, irritated, but unwilling to give Sandi that satisfaction.

Her mother's former friend was leaning more heavily on her walking stick than Kate recalled from past encounters, looking decidedly weary, her pale face quite haggard and her eyes reacting to Bel's discomfort with unmistakable sadness.

Kate felt a pang of pity, then a twinge or two of shame.

All of which disappeared when, within moments of having wedged herself on to an already fully laden sofa, Sandi got back to her feet with a groan – definitely over-egging, Kate decided – and addressed a question to her.

'Are you starting to recover, do you feel, Kate,' Sandi asked, 'after your terrible experience?'

Kate felt her face grow warm, but maintained her composure.

'Yes, thank you, Sandi,' she said. 'Though I really don't want to speak about it.'

Another member of the group rose, ready to speak about his own depression following the loss, five months earlier, of his sister.

Kate began to relax again.

Until the speaker sat down.

'Another question for Kate.' This time, Sandi remained seated. 'I was wondering if you're planning on going to Laurie Moon's funeral?'

Kate could hardly believe her ears.

'I don't think –' her voice was shaky with anger – 'that's any of your business.'

'I hope you're not experiencing much guilt over her death,' Sandi persisted.

'Didn't you hear Kate's answer?' asked Bel clearly and crisply.

Kate managed a swift sideways smile at her mother.

'Do you know yet –' Sandi was like the worst kind of bludgeoning reporter, the sort that gave Kate's own profession a bad name – 'why those people picked on you?'

'Are you deaf and stupid,' Kate asked, 'as well as insensitive?'

Composure gone now.

'Change of subject, please,' someone said.

It was the organizer, a woman named Mary, to whom Bel had introduced her earlier, and now Kate cast her an appreciative glance as the older woman deftly and firmly turned the focus away from Kate, silencing Sandi and setting in motion a general group discussion on the pros and cons of cognitive therapy. Which rolled along quite engrossingly until another minor skirmish occurred between two other members, and a white-haired man named Charles brought that under control.

Sandi waited for the next pause.

'Too many chiefs,' she said and smiled, looking straight at Kate again.

The word sent a sharp ice sliver through Kate's head.

Bel saw her reaction. 'Darling? Are you all right?'

'Fine,' Kate answered mechanically.

Not fine at all.

'Want to leave?' asked Bel.

'Sorry,' Kate said, 'but I think I do.'

Not wishing to be party to another murder.

'If it didn't mean anything,' Kate said later to Rob, 'why did she look at me that way when she said it?'

'Probably just miffed because you'd had a go at her,' he said.

'Don't you think I was entitled?'

'Very much so.'

'Are you placating me?' Kate was starting to bristle again.

'Not at all,' Rob said. 'I think Sandi was incredibly out of order.'

'But you do think I read too much into that last remark.'

'I do,' he said unequivocally.

Which calmed her, almost settled her, certainly enough to leave it alone, telling herself that Rob was probably right. 'Too many chiefs' was a perfectly ordinary phrase, nothing whatever to do with what had happened to her.

And face it, if she was going to start playing her own hare-brained 'game', imagining gang members around every corner, she'd have to come up with someone a damned sight more probable than Sandi West.

Ψ

The following Monday, four days after the meeting, she was coming home after a sandwich and chat with Fireman at the paper when she heard it – less than a second after the front door had closed behind her.

Coming from the living room – from the telly.

A voice so horribly familiar it gave her chills.

She flew into the room, and there was Rob, work spread across the table in front of him, holding out the remote control, channel hopping.

'The woman just speaking –' Kate's voice rapped out sharply – 'did you see her?'

'Who?' Rob looked blank.

'The woman who was just *speaking*, about a second ago.' She knew she must seem mad to him. 'On the TV.'

'You OK?' Rob put down the remote, stood up. 'Problem at the paper? How was Fireman?'

'He was fine.' Kate fought against impatience. 'Rob, this is terribly important. I heard a voice as I was coming through the front door – I have to know who it belonged to.'

'I'm sorry,' Rob said. 'I can't help you.'

'Try,' Kate insisted. 'What was on?'

He shrugged. 'Ads, maybe. I wasn't listening, just taking a break, trying to find something halfway decent to watch.'

Kate looked at the homework strewn over the table and sat down heavily in an armchair, feeling sick.

'It was Roger,' she said.

Comprehension dawned on Rob. 'You mean it sounded like Roger.'

Bloody *teacher*.

'It was her,' Kate said.

'OK,' Rob said. 'Maybe. What was she saying?' He sat down on the sofa, facing her. 'Maybe I heard it without registering. Was it an ad, do you think, or a programme or a continuity thing? Can you remember what she was saying, selling maybe?'

Kate closed her eyes, felt the world spin, fought to remember, could not.

'Shit.' She opened her eyes again. '*Shit.*'

Rob said nothing, giving her time.

'You don't even know what channel it was?' Kate asked.

'Sorry,' he said again. 'Chances are it wasn't her at all, you know.'

'I think it was,' she said.

'Then the best approach has to be to try not to dwell on it,' Rob said rationally. 'That way it's more likely to come back to you later.'

'If it was an ad,' Kate said, 'we could track her down.'
'If,' Rob said.

Over the next month, Kate became obsessed, aware on one
level of the probable futility of her search, but wholly unable
to stop. If she could just *hear* the voice again, she told herself,
even for a moment, just long enough to note the time or the
commercial or programme, she could stop listening, stop
tormenting herself, just pass it on to Helen Newton, leave it to
the police, whose job it was, and once they had Roger, it would
be only a matter of time till the other two were locked away
as well.

She watched as much TV as was humanly possible, and a
great deal more than was tolerable. She became angry with
herself at times for watching instead of just *listening*, for losing
concentration or even, on occasions, for falling asleep, because
this wasn't just for her, it was for Laurie and her family. Rob
became seriously concerned and spoke to her father about what
was happening. Kate knew this, because Michael began
phoning her more than usual, and when she visited him one
morning, Delia switched on the television and passed a remark
about keeping the volume turned up so Kate wouldn't miss a
second.

'I don't care,' Kate said, 'if you all think I'm losing it.'
'We don't think that at all,' Michael said.

'I suppose you can't even just tape everything so you could
whip through,' Delia said, 'because then you wouldn't hear the
voices, obviously.'

'Obviously,' Kate snapped.

She was beginning to wonder, in fact, if she might actually be
losing the plot, knew that the fact that Laurie Moon's funeral
was now imminent and preying on her mind was not helping.

Roger's voice perhaps a kind of distraction from that.

Bel had suggested just the other day that, since she'd heard
the suspect voice at around five on a Monday afternoon, she
might as well restrict her listening to that same daily time slot.

'They seem to run the same programmes and ads over and
over again on some of those channels, don't they?'

Sensible advice, Kate had agreed and meant to heed, but she
had not stuck to it, and now she'd even taken to having the radio

on in the bathroom and in the car, concentrating on voices instead of the road.

'If I'd been through your ordeal,' Delia said now, 'I'd be a wreck too.'

'Gee,' said Kate, 'thanks for that.'

'Take it easy,' Michael intervened. 'She's only being sympathetic.'

'I don't need sympathy,' Kate told him. 'I need to find Roger.'

'You need to relax,' Delia said. 'Have some camomile tea.'

'And you,' Kate said, 'need to mind your own business.'

So much for trying her best around her dad's partner.

Laurie

'I wish to God,' Shelly said to Pete on the last Saturday morning of February, the day of their daughter's funeral, 'she would stay away.'

Pete knew, of course, who she was talking about. Felt the same way.

Kate Turner.

Without whom, they both believed – however often they had been told otherwise – Laurie would still be with them. Would not be dead and, within a matter of hours, soon to be lowered into her grave.

It had taken long and incredibly painful weeks to arrive at this day. Forever, and yet fast as the blink of an eye. Or a drop of lifeblood. The world going on, yet seeming to have remained almost motionless around them. Every damnable cliché in the world, many of them true.

They knew, in their more rational moments, that they were probably being unfair to the journalist, their daughter's fellow victim, but they could not seem to help themselves. It had happened in *her* home. *She* had been taken first by those people. *Her* sin – according to her own bizarre account – a million miles worse than Laurie's.

Which was, of course, *their* sin, not hers at all, but that was another story, one too unbearable for them to cope with now, if ever.

Easier – if anything could be easy – to blame Kate Turner.

When Shelly remembered her final conversation with Laurie, she wanted to die. Those foolish, petty recriminations against her daughter about not mopping up their kitchen, followed by stony silence. Her very last chance, and she'd wasted it, had thrown away her final opportunity to hug her child and tell her that she loved her.

Pete had told her about his late-night visit to Laurie's room, about their brief conversation and the small warming between them that had become his most precious memory, something to hold on to. Shelly had been so jealous when he'd told her, that for a time she had literally hated him; but then she'd come to see that he had only shared it with her because he'd wanted her to know that Laurie had left home more happily than she might otherwise have thought.

'Not your fault you were asleep, Shelly,' he had said.

'Not that, perhaps. But everything else.'

'Mine too,' Pete had said.

Their shaming had been abject enough before Angela had arrived from Provence and made it absolute.

Grieving alongside them without condemnation until, with a few choice words, Shelly's sister had targeted their hearts with perfect and vicious accuracy.

'Whatever you decide to tell people about Sam, I'll back you up.'

They had looked at each other and said nothing.

'If you want to pretend it was Laurie who couldn't cope, I won't tell anyone different,' Angela said. 'It'll make no odds to her now, after all, poor little love.'

Leaving them no real choice at all, not with nine years of guilt rising up to choke them anyway. Growing worse with every passing day.

'What are you going to do about Sam now?' Angela had asked a day later.

'We've been thinking,' Pete had said.

'I thought you might,' Angela said.

Andrew, their son, losing his hair, gaining weight instead, was present but silent as usual on this subject. Angela had asked him once, long ago, for his feelings on the subject of the enforced separation of his sister and her son, and he'd fobbed her off, leaving his aunt uncertain if he was simply a chip off Pete's block or too mortified to share the truth with her.

'We were wondering,' Shelly had said, 'if we should bring him home.'

'Should,' Angela had echoed. 'Bit late for *should*, don't you think?'

The look in her eyes had crucified them both.

'We want to do what Laurie would have wanted,' Pete said.

'What Laurie *wanted*,' Angie said, 'was to have Sam with her while she was here, while she was *alive*.'

'Still, for him, we thought,' Shelly said wretchedly, 'maybe better late than never.'

'You really are a pair of tossers, aren't you?' said Angie.

'Stop it, Aunty Angie,' Andrew had said, flushed. 'There's no need for—'

'It's all right,' Pete had said.

'I suppose what Angie's saying –' Shelly had tried not to start crying again – 'is Sam might be better off staying at the Mann, now he's used to it.'

'Better off there than with you two, is what I'm saying,' said Laurie's aunt.

She remembered all the days and nights of her sweet niece's exiled pregnancy too well, her unforgiving impulse now to be cruel to the two people who had decreed it.

The crueller the better, so far as she was concerned.

Shelly wasn't sure which had been more unbearable, seeing Laurie in the mortuary two months ago, or this.

Her daughter's coffin going down into the ground.

At least in the mortuary she'd been able to *see* her. Laurie had been there, just feet away, appearing to be still in the world. Not in a box, with the terrible sound of earth thudding on to its lid.

She looked up, abruptly, and saw Kate Turner, standing a decent distance away, as if she realized that her presence might be hurtful to them.

She didn't have a *clue*.

Sam was there, standing between Pete and a woman from the Mann who had one arm around his shoulders, which he seemed to like.

He wept for a few minutes when they began to lower his mother's coffin into the grave, as if he understood what was happening, and the woman gave him a hanky and he blew his nose with it.

The woman spoke to them afterwards.

'We all love your grandson at the Mann,' she said.

Sam gave Shelly a lovely smile, but she knew there was nothing meaningful in that, not for her as his grandma, and how could there be? If he ever learnt the real truth about what his grandparents had done to him and his mum, and if he had the capacity for hate, he would despise them forever.

Shelly was conscious of people watching them with Sam, felt vaguely surprised by the fact that she did not seem to care, after all, what they thought. Which made her hate herself even more because if that was true, it meant they could have let Laurie bring him home years ago, and it might have been difficult, but they would have been a proper family.

And Laurie would be alive.

Would not have suffered for years, or died in terror.

'Do you like horses, Sam?' Pete asked his grandson.

Sam looked at the woman with him, as if she could supply the answer.

Which she did: 'You love horses, Sam, don't you?'

'Perhaps,' Pete went on, 'you might like to come to the stables then?'

'That's where we keep horses,' Shelly said.

'I know,' Sam said.

Putting his grandmother in her place.

'I couldn't really grieve,' Kate said to Rob later, 'because, of course, I didn't know Laurie. All I could think about was how terrified she was that day, which I'm sure she would hate.'

'You went out of respect,' Rob had said. 'It was the right thing to do.'

'Her parents blame me.'

'I imagine they associate you with it,' he said, 'rather than blame you.'

'I wanted to speak to them,' Kate said, 'but I thought it might make it worse.' She'd written to them some weeks back, a letter of condolence, trying to say something of comfort, but had found nothing, and then her failure to find Roger's voice again had seemed to load her with extra guilt.

'At least,' Rob said, thinking of the funeral, 'it's over.'

'I wish,' Kate said.

Kate

The decision to put Caisleán up for sale had been something that Kate and Rob had both agreed on unequivocally. When it came to showing it to a couple of local estate agents at the end of March, however, Rob tried hard to convince Kate to let him go alone, hoping to spare her, but she felt compelled to go back.

'I think I need to face it,' she said. 'It'll be fine with you there anyway.'

'If you're quite sure,' Rob said.

Not sure at all.

It was no better than she'd thought it would be.

'It's strange, though,' she said. 'It feels so unreal.'

She felt unreal, disconnected.

'None of it happened to me,' Rob said, 'but even I don't want to spend one minute more than necessary here.'

'All your hard work. Such a waste.'

Kate tried to look around without remembering that last day, but in her mind Simon's body still hung from the hook and Laurie still lay, freshly murdered, on their bed. And the truth was, she wasn't sure now that she'd feel even a glimmer of sorrow if she heard that the barn had burned to ashes.

'We can always do it again,' Rob said, 'somewhere else.'

'Maybe we should stick to hotels when we want a break.'

Kate said that lightly, so that maybe he wouldn't realize quite how terrified she felt at the prospect of staying in any weekend cottage anywhere, ever again.

'You don't have to pretend with me.' Rob was gentle. 'About anything.'

'No,' Kate said, with relief. 'I know I don't.'

They took their time on the way home, enjoying the sight of a few early lambs in the fields, then taking a detour to the west for a long lunch at a restaurant near Pangbourne. The food was delicious and the room relaxing, but Kate felt that even if they'd stopped for a sandwich at a pub on that particular day, they'd probably have felt the same special pleasure.

Closer now, the two of them, than ever before.

Contentment still lapping over her as they drove towards their cottage.

Still in place as Rob unlocked their front door.

Gone in an instant, as they both realized they'd been burgled.

Nowhere safe, after all.

Just another statistic.

Not the worst kind of robbery by any means, in that they had not been home at the time, and the intruders had not been vandals; they had, in fact, been methodical about removing two televisions, the DVD, the PC and laptop computers, and had made minimal mess as they'd apparently searched for jewellery and cash in wardrobes and drawers.

'They're sending a locksmith,' Rob told Kate a little later.

'Right,' she said.

He knew what she had to be thinking.

'I've talked to Helen Newton,' he told her. 'She's certain there's no link because there's been a rash of burglaries in the area.'

'OK.' Kate found she could believe in that. 'Good.'

'I think we should consider an alarm,' Rob said. 'Or maybe a big dog.'

'I'm not sure,' Kate said, 'if that kind of thing wouldn't just emphasize what I'm trying so hard to forget.'

'Let's give it some thought, OK?' Rob said gently.

'Sure,' she said.

The burglary notwithstanding, it had all seemed to get just a little better for Kate once Caisleán was on the market. It troubled neither of them greatly that no one had yet made an offer, nor that many of those calling the agents for viewings might be doing so out of morbid curiosity.

'No rush,' Rob said.

'So long as the agents deal with it all,' Kate said.

'You won't ever have to see it again,' Rob told her.

'Suits me,' she said.

She was beginning, she supposed, to heal a little, with time passing and the horror receding. People told her how much better she was looking, which always made her feel guilty about Laurie, which was patently foolish, but thankfully the attacks of shame never lasted too long because Kate was not that much of a fool, and she did, in truth, feel lucky to be alive.

And then it happened again.

On a Saturday night at the end of April, when she was home alone because Rob had been invited by Penny to stay for the weekend up in Manchester to talk over their daughter's education – and Rob must have wanted to leap at the prospect of extra time with Emmie, but he'd felt doubtful about leaving Kate alone just yet.

'Don't be silly,' she'd reassured him. 'I'll be fine.'

She heard nothing while it was happening, slept undisturbed, oblivious until Sunday morning when she found the garden door ajar and knew, with an awful, sickening blow, that someone had been in the cottage overnight.

'The creepiest thing,' she told Rob on the phone, with the local police already looking around and Michael on his way, 'apart from the fact that they were here while I was sleeping, is that the only thing they seem to have taken is food. Every single thing that was in the fridge.'

'Hungry burglars?' Rob said.

'Maybe.' Kate was still jittery. 'Or maybe they weren't real burglars at all.'

'Kate, we don't—'

'I think they just wanted us to know, for sure, that they've been here.'

More than jittery.

Rob told her to make sure someone stayed with her till he got back.

'I'm leaving immediately,' he promised. 'And this time, we're definitely getting the alarm, no arguments.'

'None from me,' Kate said.

*   *   *

Three weeks passed before she discovered that something else was missing.

An ultrasound picture of their lost son.

'I wasn't looking for it,' she told Rob, 'but I took out our wedding album – had this nostalgic fancy – and it was always tucked in the back, remember, in its little envelope, and I thought it must have fallen out, but it's nowhere.'

'Let's have one more look together,' he said, 'and if we don't find it, we'll call Newton.'

'I was hoping you'd think I was overreacting,' Kate said.

'I hope we both are,' said Rob.

Helen Newton did not think either of them was overreacting, and dispatched a SOMIT technical team to place the cottage under a virtual microscope, hunting for anything that might previously have been missed.

'Not a thing,' she reported back later to Rob.

'Nothing to send away for testing?' he asked, disappointed.

'You've cleaned the house from top to bottom since the break-in,' Newton said. 'More than once, I imagine.' She paused. 'It was obviously going to be a long shot.'

'So what now?' he asked. 'Can you put a watch on the house?'

'I've already got the local patrols keeping an eye on things.'

'Is that all?'

'Don't forget,' Newton said, 'we're only looking at a slim possibility.'

'Don't you think it might be time,' Rob asked, 'to err on the side of caution? Kate's never been a nervy type, but this is really starting to get to her.'

'You are both certain the picture was there?'

'Kate doesn't invent dramas either.' Rob was firm.

'I wasn't suggesting for a moment,' Newton said, 'that she was.'

Ralph

'No more break-ins possible now.' Ralph had phoned Jack. 'You can't risk it now they've got the alarm.'

'Maybe not,' he said.

'Definitely not,' she told him. 'The police are sniffing around too.'

'I know,' Jack said.

'So you are listening to me,' Ralph said.

'I'm bloody good at what I do,' Jack said.

'And you want to be able to go on doing it, don't you?'

'Yes, Chief,' he said.

Oh, but it was just so *good* to be speaking again.

Playing again.

Kate

Kate heard a clicking sound on the phone while she was speaking to Bel on the last Monday of May.

'Can't you hear it, Mum?'

'Not a thing,' her mother said.

She heard it again the following evening, when her father called.

'Dad, can you hear those sounds?' If Rob hadn't been upstairs taking a shower, she'd have asked him to listen too.

'Maybe,' Michael answered, 'but then again, I'm always hearing things these days. Delia says it's probably old age.' He paused. 'How's the column coming along?'

She had been doing better, getting back on track, until the second break-in.

'Not too bad,' she said, lying.

'Better get back to it then,' Michael told her, 'and stop procrastinating.'

Kate did as he advised, and forgot about the sounds.

Ralph

'S erves two purposes,' Pig told Ralph. 'Listening, and freaking her out a bit.'

Ralph was glad to hear of something giving him pleasure, though she wished it were something more substantial and infinitely happier.

'Please,' she said, 'be careful.'

'I always am,' Pig said. 'I don't want to lose my job, Chief.'

'That won't be all you lose,' she reminded him, 'if you get caught.'

'Never have yet,' Pig said.

'No reason to get cocky,' said Ralph.

'I don't think I really do cocky,' he said.

Ψ

Pride and falls.
        Ralph heard the news from Roger.

The worst kind.

Not the very worst, of course. Not as bad as losing Simon. But awful enough.

Jack had been on a job in Princes Risborough on an early June evening when he'd tripped over a potted plant on his way out of the house. Which had given a vigilant Neighbourhood Watch type the chance to have a go with a cricket bat – which had pissed Jack off enough to give the bloke a severe kicking – which might have given him time to escape if the man's wife hadn't been *another* 'have-a-go' type.

'So now it's burglary *and* GBH,' Roger reported.

This was what Ralph had dreaded for so long. It was little short of miraculous that their boy had stayed out of prison for so many years, and however often she'd heard Jack brag about his ability to 'do the time' if it came to it, she could not help but fear for him now.

'Another one gone then,' Roger said. 'He's on remand.'

Ralph heard the sorrow in her voice. 'Where?'

'Tayton Park, over in—'

'You mustn't *think* of visiting him,' Ralph broke in, urgently. 'Officially or otherwise.'

'I won't,' said Roger.

'However much you want to,' Ralph pressed.

'I'm not daft,' Roger said.

'I know you're not,' Ralph said. 'But I don't want to lose you too.'

Kate

'That's her!'

It was a late June Saturday afternoon in the cottage, and Rob was marking essays at the table while Kate was lounging on the sofa reading Jon Henley in the *Guardian*, paying no particular attention to the ads rolling on television, and it had been a relief to find herself becoming less obsessive about listening in the past few weeks.

But now, there it *was*.

'Rob, that's Roger!'

'Jesus.' He'd already stopped marking, knew immediately that this was for *real*, was scrabbling for paper, pen poised.

Kate was staring galvanized at the TV screen, the newspaper dropped on the floor, not a grain of doubt in her mind about the voice, not even greatly chilled by it this time, simply bent on nailing the commercial, which was for a cheap household cleaning product.

'*Got* it.' Rob checked his watch and wrote it down. 'And time and station.'

The ad was over, and Kate got up and threw her arms around him.

'Thank you – oh, Rob, *thank* you!'

'My pleasure,' he said. 'Do you want to call Newton, or d'you want me to?'

'You,' she said, and handed him the phone.

Martin Blake called her two mornings later.

'You have to give the police a little time on this, Kate.'

'How much time? I've chewed off most of my nails already.'

'And made just a few too many calls to DCI Newton's office.'

'I'm sorry,' Kate said, not feeling in the least apologetic, 'but I don't even know if they've arrested her.'

'They're interviewing a suspect as we speak,' Blake said.

'Right.' Kate felt an adrenaline rush. 'So what's next? An ID parade?'

'Yes,' Blake said, 'though it might not be quite such plain sailing.'

'Because of the stocking masks,' Kate said. 'That's why I've been phoning, because I need Helen Newton to realize how much more I remember about Roger than her voice. The way she moved, the shape of her head—'

'Kate, haven't you heard of VIPER?' Blake interrupted. 'I thought, being a journalist, you would have. It's an acronym for—'

'Video Identification Parades Electronic Recording.' Her turn to break in, and of course she'd heard about VIPER, but she hadn't, until now, considered its impact on her case. 'No real parade, just video clips from some database. Head-and-shoulders, no movement.'

'A little movement,' Blake amended. 'The suspect and volunteers move their heads from side to side.'

'And no speaking.' Anger flashed in her. '*Worse* than useless to me.'

'Not necessarily,' Blake said. 'Your powers of recall may be very strong, and if this woman is Roger, she may stand out in some particular way.'

'What about the stocking masks? Can they arrange that, at least?'

'Probably not,' Blake said.

'I've tried not to let myself imagine them with faces.'

'Maybe that'll help you come to this with a clearer mind.'

'What if I pick the wrong person?' The thought appalled her.

'If it's one of the volunteers, it won't matter to them,' Blake said. 'It'll simply mean you've been unable to pick out the suspect.'

Kate took a moment, tried toughening up. 'Worth a try, I suppose.'

Blake hesitated. 'There is another potential problem, I'm afraid, raised by the guidelines that cover such things. The time lapse between offence and identification.'

In her case, almost six months.

'Oh, bloody hell,' Kate said. 'They'll say I've forgotten, won't they?'

'Certainly in a trial, the length of time would be pointed out to a jury, and a decent defence would almost certainly object to an ID.' Blake paused. 'But the same guidelines also refer to the amount of time a suspect was under observation by the witness – which in your case was exceptionally long.'

Kate thought. 'I'm sure I've read about voice identifications.'

'They'd only rely on that if, say, a ransom call had been recorded for comparison,' Blake said. 'Also, in a sense you've already identified Roger's voice, and if Newton were to try to push for something more formal, I expect they'd fuss even more about the time frame.' He paused again. 'As it is, there's the possible question of familiarity because of the television connection.'

Kate understood immediately. 'They'll say that if I heard Roger twice on TV, I could have heard her more often before that and be confused.'

'It won't come to that,' Blake said, 'if they can put together a good case.'

'So what does happen next?' she asked.

'More waiting, I'm afraid.'

'I don't suppose they've told you Roger's real name?'

'Not yet,' Blake said.

Something else occurred to Kate. 'What if she doesn't consent to the video parade? It's her right, isn't it?'

'In that event the police would have to use her mug shot, and the whole parade would be done using stills rather than moving images.'

'Wonderful,' Kate said sourly.

'I doubt that she will refuse.'

'Because she'll be confident I won't be able to pick her out.'

'Let's hope you can prove her wrong,' Blake said.

IT was arranged in a viewing suite at SOMIT headquarters.

No one present with any involvement in the investigation.

'To avoid suggestions of impropriety,' Martin Blake had advised her.

The suspect, he'd added, would not be there, though her solicitor would be.

'And you?' Kate had asked. 'Will you be there?'

'Fortunately,' Blake had replied, 'you don't need a lawyer.'

A good thing, of course, she realized, yet she felt, already, abandoned.

And intensely afraid, all over again.

'Try not to let them do that to you,' Rob told her down in SOMIT reception, just before her escort arrived to take her to the suite.

She squeezed his hand, told him she'd be fine.

Lying through her teeth.

She was shown to the viewing room and introduced to the Identification Officer, a pleasant man who told her that the viewing and her reactions would be recorded, told her that she should not feel under pressure, that she should relax and take all the time she needed.

Relax. With so much riding on this, not just for her, but for the Moon family.

Kate thanked the officer.

Flashes of memory already assaulting her.

The four of them coming at her in their eerie dark masks.

Roger holding her face down on the sofa, almost suffocating her.

Kneeling on Laurie's thighs, pinning her down for Jack to cut her throat.

Relax.

The officer read her a formal explanation of the procedure, told her that the suspect might or might not appear on the film she was to see; that Kate was to view the entire film at least twice; that she could, if she wished, see all or any part of the film more often and that if she could not make a positive identification, she should say so.

Panic ignited, made her feel ill, made her want to run. Without masks, it would be impossible to recognize her – the whole thing was a travesty because Roger would go *free*, they would all stay out in the world knowing they'd won.

But then it began.

Nine images, one after another, on a screen, each image numbered.

Nine strangers.

But she *knew* her.

She half-closed her eyes as she had earlier decided she would to make the line-up fuzz a little, and her heart hammered and prickles of gooseflesh sprang up on her arms, and each time she was shown the film, they had moved Roger's image to a different place in the parade, her face looking into the camera, turning her face first to one side, then to the other.

A monster brought to life.

It was strange beyond all Kate's imaginings to see how attractive she was, her eyes dark and clear, betraying nothing, her neck slender as a model's. Remembering that they were recording her reactions, her mind working well now, her fear gone, determined that nothing be allowed to undermine this identification, Kate opened her own eyes fully, examined each image carefully, took her time, though there was no need.

Because she knew her.

Knew which of those women was no stranger, which of them had dragged her to the bathroom and pulled down her panties so she could pee, which of them had recited the savageries of late abortion.

Which of them had helped Jack to kill Laurie Moon.

She knew her without a shadow of doubt.

And told them her number.

Ψ

One of the most significant outcomes of having Roger in custody, charged with the kidnapping and murder of Laurie Moon, as well as Kate's unlawful imprisonment, was that her detention had swiftly led them to Jack.

Karen Frost was the name of the actress who had been Roger.

Not just an actress. Also an official prison visitor who had not long since approached the chaplain at HM Prison Tayton

Park – because every voluntary OPV had to apply to each new prison they wanted to visit, to go through all channels each time, including Home Office checking. Frost had given her changed address as her reason, having lately moved from Reading to a flat less than five miles from Tayton Park, and her request had been granted.

After which she was documented as having paid special attention to one male prisoner by the name of Paul Wilson, presently on remand, charged with burglary from a dwelling and grievous bodily harm.

Kate and Rob invited Michael and Bel to the cottage, swore them to secrecy and brought them up to date with the developments.

'Tayton Park wasn't where the teacher was murdered, was it?' asked Michael.

Kate shook her head. 'Different prison – Oakwood.'

'They're checking in case Karen Frost was ever a visitor there,' Rob said.

'Nothing yet to link her to Alan Mitcham,' Kate said.

'It's still promising news, though, surely,' Bel said.

'The main point for now,' Kate said, 'is that Helen Newton thinks Wilson is almost certainly either Jack or Pig.'

'We already know he's definitely our burglar,' Rob continued. 'They went through items found in his home after his arrest, and found our ultrasound picture.'

'Goodness,' said Bel, and took a large swallow of red wine.

'Wilson tried claiming it was from one of his own children's scans,' Kate said, 'but his wife let him down, said it wasn't.'

'Good for her,' Michael said.

'Anyway, the picture had a date on it,' said Kate.

'And by that time,' Rob went on, 'they had a warrant to search Karen Frost's home too – and guess what they both had in common.'

'The book,' Bel guessed.

Kate nodded. 'Not many novels in Wilson's place, according to Newton.'

'Is that enough?' Michael, the former lawyer, was wary.

'Of course not.' Rob's smile was grim. 'But there's more.'

'Carol Marsh, Paul Wilson and Karen Frost were all at the same children's home,' Kate explained. 'A place called Challow

Hall.' She paused. 'About five miles from Swindon, a little way off the Ridgeway Path.'

'And not a million miles from Caislean,' Rob finished.

'Bloody hell,' said Bel.

'I'm betting Wilson is Jack,' Kate said.

'Why not Pig?' asked Michael.

'No solid, stand-up-in-court reason.' She shrugged. 'I just don't feel that Pig was the type to be a burglar – which could be complete nonsense – but Jack was definitely more obviously violent, so the GBH seems more likely to be his thing.'

'How are you coping with all this?' Michael asked her.

'Bit nervous,' Kate said.

'She's very brave,' Rob said.

'Another identification?' her mother asked.

'I suppose,' Kate nodded, her stomach already in knots.

Ralph

R alph had known in her heart, however much Roger had denied it, that the younger woman would be unable to resist visiting Jack, but she had also known that she was as helpless to prevent that as she had been to halt the disastrous chain of events that had since come to pass.

All down to Kate Turner.

All of it.

Kate

It was almost the same as it had been with Roger.

They were all tough looking in different ways, but only one was *him*.

Jack, as she had believed, not Pig, who had, even in red overalls, looked thinner, seemed altogether weaker.

This man had flame red hair and pale skin, and green eyes that were sharp and hard. And a straight, uncompromising mouth.

A cruel mouth, Kate thought.

Don't choose him for that.

But she had stood so close to Jack, had been slapped by him, menaced by him, dragged around by him, hog-tied by him.

Threatened by him.

'I wish to God I could kill you here and now.'

Words she would never forget, any more than she'd ever manage to blot out the memory of the man who'd spoken them, the man who'd murdered Laurie Moon.

Besides, something else was making it almost easy for her now.

The way he had looked into the camera when they'd made their recording.

As if he was looking at *her*, not into the lens.

Looking at Kate, at the woman who had killed his friend, with pure hate.

It seemed to her like a challenge, as if he wanted to be chosen.

Kate watched the film right through three times.

Knew she was making no mistake.

Told them his number, and that it was the man she had known as Jack.

And prayed with all her might that he would be found guilty, given life.

He had been named Paul, they learned later, after the man who'd found him as an abandoned newborn in a supermarket car park, and Wilson after one of the nurses on duty at the Bristol Royal Infirmary to which he'd been taken.

Sad stories, unlucky beginnings, for Wilson, Marsh and Frost. Probably for Pig, too, whoever and wherever he was.

It began to appear likely, too, given their use of the same aliases with Alan Mitcham, that the gang's obsession with the book and perhaps their bizarre game-playing, too, might have begun back in their years in the children's home.

'Maybe,' Kate said, 'they just liked being fictitious characters better than themselves.'

She used their real names now, of course, whenever she spoke to the police or to Martin Blake, but she never thought of them that way.

To her they were still Jack, Roger and Simon.

Ralph

Both charged now, awaiting trial. Roger in HM Prison Stonebridge, Jack still in Tayton Park, his court date for GBH and burglary imminent.

More than a hundred miles apart but both locked up, out of Ralph's reach for heaven knew how long.

Forever, it seemed to her.

'What can we *do*?' Pig asked her on the phone, despair in his voice.

'Nothing,' Ralph answered. 'Not a single thing.'

'I'm not much for violence, as you know,' said Pig, 'but I think I could kill *her*.'

'Promise me,' Ralph said with passion, 'you won't do anything stupid.'

'I won't,' he said.

'If something happens to you, too,' said Ralph, 'I'll have no one.'

'It's all right,' Pig told her. 'You don't have to worry about losing me. I just can't stop thinking about how they'll be standing it in those places.'

'They'll stand it because they have to,' Ralph said.

Kate

The whereabouts of Pig began to consume Kate.

Newton's team had tried to find staff who had worked at Challow Hall in those days who might remember a fourth child, or maybe even a fifth, remembering their 'chief' – any other children especially close to Marsh, Wilson and Frost – but as yet no one had come up with an answer.

No one caring enough to notice, perhaps, Kate thought.

They had cared, she knew that, about each other.

She remembered Pig stroking Simon's hair after he'd removed the stocking from her head, remembered feeling that he loved her, felt now therefore that *she*, Carol Marsh, was most likely to prove his Achilles heel.

'Which is why I'm so sure,' she said to Helen Newton in July, 'that he's bound to visit her grave one of these days.'

There was nothing, Newton responded, to say he hadn't already done so, since there were no CCTV cameras at the cemetery, nor was there any feasibility of keeping a physical presence there.

'It's almost as if they've lost interest,' Kate fretted on the phone to Martin Blake afterwards, 'now they've got the other two.'

'I don't think that for a minute,' Blake disagreed. 'Especially as they'll have Laurie Moon's parents on their backs too.'

'Do you suppose Newton thinks Jack or Roger are going to give up Pig's identity?' she asked the lawyer. 'Maybe as part of some kind of plea bargain?'

'It could happen,' Blake said. 'Possibly.'

'He's no real help at all,' Kate complained to Rob over dinner that night.

'Not a lot he can do, I imagine,' Rob said.

He took a forkful of pasta, saw that she wasn't eating, put it down again.

'All down to interrogation, then,' he said, 'or deal-making with the other two.'

'They won't give Pig up,' Kate said definitely.

'You can't be certain of that,' Rob said.

'I can,' Kate said. 'I'm not sure why, exactly, and I know it sounds odd, but I just feel they won't ever betray each other.'

'Honour among thieves,' Rob said.

'Murderers,' Kate amended.

'I'm glad you said that.' Rob picked up the bottle and poured more red wine into both their glasses. 'You were beginning to sound as if you almost admired them.'

'Not if I live to be a thousand,' Kate said.

Laurie Moon's death before her eyes again.

Ψ

The situation, Kate had come to accept, was probably as good as it was going to get, at least for now.

Jack having been found guilty of GBH and burglary, serving ten years.

So, one dead, two facing trial.

Life, in the meantime, going on for her.

Her column, on the other hand, she realized, might not have that much longer to live. The Caisleán nightmare had made it not only emotionally difficult, but also legally impossible to share as many of her day-to-day thought processes with her readers as she had in the past. The strain had shown in *Diary of a Short-Fused Female*, and Kate felt sure it was only a matter of time until Fireman was forced to junk it.

Which was why she had told him, in late July, that she'd decided to write a biography of Claude Duval, the French highwayman said to have owned a house in Sonning-on-Thames – where Dick Turpin's aunt had also lived.

'Curious in a way,' Fireman said, 'that you should be attracted to villainy now.'

'On the contrary,' Kate told him. 'Seductive and charming as he might have been, Duval went around terrorizing travellers, so I can assure you I won't be painting him as a gallant romantic.'

Rob, too, had come upon a new interest, sparked by a colleague working in his school's office, Marie Coates, a long-time paraplegic

who spent her time off helping disabled children to ride ponies at
Lambsmoor Farm, south of Blewbury.

'It's a small, independent scheme,' Rob told Kate. 'She's
suggested I might like to come along one Saturday to take a look.'

It was near the Ridgeway, Kate thought, not far from Caisleán.

'Lovely idea,' she said.

Not far enough.

'Do you really think so?' Rob checked.

'Of course.' She saw his doubt, knew it was because he disliked
leaving her alone for too long these days, decided that was ridiculous, something she needed to stop before it got out of hand.
'Rob, I'm fine with this, truly.'

'If you liked riding, it would—'

'But I don't.' Kate smiled. 'And I certainly don't want you turning
down something you're so incredibly suited to, just for me.'

'I'd do anything for you,' he said.

She read the intensity in his eyes and knew that now, after
the journey they'd travelled, both together and apart, it was true.

'I'm hardly short of things to do,' she said. 'I'm behind on
Short-Fuse, as usual, and I really need to get into my research
for Duval. And the fact is, we have to get back to normal, at
least until the trial.'

No real normality so long as that was in the offing.

Ψ

It was while she was in London in August, paying a visit to Claude
Duval's gravestone in Covent Garden Church, that Kate, glancing
at the date of the highwayman's birth, felt her mind drift to an
entirely unconnected set of dates she appeared to have memorized,
and realized that they were just two days away from another birthday.

She phoned Helen Newton, was put through to Ben Poulter
instead.

'It's Carol Marsh's birthday on Wednesday,' she told him.

'We know,' Poulter said.

'So does that mean you'll be watching in case Pig visits
Simon's grave?'

'We'll be doing what we can,' the detective-sergeant said.

'But what does that *mean*?' Kate wanted to know. 'You've
got to be there the whole day, waiting, not just having some car
drive past every hour.'

'As I've said, Mrs Turner –' Poulter was not to be budged – 'we'll be doing everything we can.'

'Newton never called me back,' Kate told Rob the next evening, pacing in their bedroom, 'and I just *know* they're not going to handle this properly.'

'I think they might.' Rob paused. 'In fact, I know they will.'

Kate stopped pacing. 'How do you know?'

'Because Helen Newton phoned me this afternoon—'

'You didn't tell me,' she accused.

'She phoned to ask me –' Rob remained steady – 'to keep you occupied tomorrow, in case you've been having any crazy notions of keeping watch yourself.'

'But did she actually say they'll be keeping watch?'

'She wasn't specific on details,' Rob said. 'But she asked me to have a little faith.'

'Really?' Kate was surprised.

'It's what she said.'

Kate took a moment.

'Better occupy me then,' she said.

And sat down on the bed.

Wednesday grew harder as it progressed.

'Couldn't we just drive by?' Kate suggested at around eleven.

'No, we couldn't,' Rob said. 'For one thing, it's exactly what Newton told us not to do. And supposing we pick just the moment when Pig's arriving, and he sees you and takes fright.'

Kate raised a sceptical eyebrow.

'Faith,' he reminded her.

He was paying household bills at the table after lunch, believing her to be in the office working on Duval, when he saw her through the open doorway coming down the staircase, car keys in hand.

'I could lie,' she said. 'Tell you I'm going to get some milk.'

'Kate, please.' Rob got up, came into the hallway. 'Give me the keys.'

She shook her head. 'Just once round the cemetery, to see if they're there at all.'

He looked at her furrowed brow and intent eyes.

'We'll take my car,' he said.

* * *

There was a junction with traffic lights near the gated entrance.

'Good,' Kate said as the lights changed to red and Rob slowed the Saab to a halt.

A man was walking in their direction, a bunch of flowers in one hand.

'Don't stare,' Rob said.

'Doesn't matter if I do,' Kate told him. 'It's not Pig.' She looked around, craned her neck, shook her head. 'I don't think the police are here at all.'

'What about him?' Rob said about the man with flowers.

Kate made a sound of derision.

The lights began to change.

'Round the block one more time,' she said.

'You said just once.'

'Please.'

Rob sighed, began to move away slowly. 'Once more, and that's it.'

His mobile phone rang.

'In my pocket,' he told Kate.

She fished it out, hit the receive button. 'Rob Turner's phone.'

'Kate, this is Helen Newton.'

'Newton,' Kate mouthed at Rob.

'Shit,' he said.

'Which is where you'll both be,' Newton told Kate, 'if you don't stop behaving like idiot children right now and go home.'

'Tell her we're leaving,' Rob said.

'Now, please,' Newton said sharply.

'She's watching us,' Kate said.

Rob sped up a little, moving away from the cemetery.

'But what if he shows up?' Kate said. 'You'll need me to identify him.'

'If someone shows up who might possibly be your man,' Newton said, 'we'll handle it, Kate, in the appropriate manner.' She paused. 'Tell Rob to turn left, please.'

Kate told him.

'Good,' Newton said. 'I'll call you when we're done.'

'But when—?'

Kate was talking to a dead phone.

The cemetery had been closed for over five hours, Rob had made dinner, watched his wife unable to eat or settle, and had resigned

himself to a sleepless night because Kate had pointed out earlier
that a man who'd been part of that gang might not let a little
thing like a locked gate or stone wall stop him.

'It's not going to happen, is it?' she said quietly, just after eleven.

'I don't know,' Rob said. 'It's still Simon's birthday for another
hour.'

'Do you think the police are still watching?'

'Perhaps.' He shrugged. 'Easier for them to be unnoticed in
the dark.'

'Maybe just one poor PC now,' Kate said, 'hiding in the bushes
near the grave.'

'Maybe,' Rob said. 'And no, we can't take them a thermos of
coffee.'

She smiled. 'I know we can't.'

They were in bed, awake, when the phone rang at one fifteen.

Rob answered, listened for a moment, then said: 'I'll pass you
to Kate.'

Her hand trembled slightly as she took the phone.

'He came,' Newton said.

Rob turned on his bedside light, his eyes glinting with excitement.

'Tell me.' Kate's heart was thumping hard.

'At twenty to midnight,' the DCI expanded. 'He came over
the west wall, made straight for Marsh's grave, got down on
both knees and began weeping.'

Kate found she couldn't speak.

'He's already said enough for us to be fairly certain it's your
man.'

'You mean he's confessed?'

Rob was out of bed, watching Kate expectantly.

'Nothing quite so cut and dried,' Newton said.

Kate shook her head, saw Rob's face fall.

'I'd say we'll be talking to him for some considerable time
before I have much more to tell you,' Newton said, 'but I wanted
to let you know.'

'Thank you,' Kate said. 'So much.'

'It's my pleasure.' Newton paused. 'So, more patience needed.
I know it's hard, but it's the safest way.'

'We're getting there,' Kate said. 'That's the main thing.'

*   *   *

'One more to go,' she said an hour or so later, after she and Rob had got back into bed with a bottle of red and a pizza from the freezer because suddenly they'd realized they were both famished. 'The Chief.'

'I reckon the others will give him up,' Rob said.

'You still think it's a man,' Kate said.

He'd told her once that he thought a person who sent others to do their dirty work was probably fundamentally cowardly.

'I still think women, on the whole, are braver than men,' he said now.

Kate shrugged, snuggled closer.

'Right this minute,' he went on, 'we have more important things to think about.'

'Like our pizza getting cold,' she said.

'Fuck the pizza,' Rob said.

And began to kiss her breasts.

Ralph

R alph had known that Pig would not be able to resist much longer.

She had made him promise, last time they spoke, not to do anything stupid, had even mentioned Simon's birthday, and he had told her not to worry.

Foolish, loving man.

Edward Booth, as *they* would be calling him.

She had always known how much Pig had loved Simon, wondered now, suddenly, if maybe he'd known they would catch him, if maybe it might even have been what he'd wanted.

She was all alone now. All her children lost to her.

Only her hate left to warm her.

To keep her going.

Kate

The end of Kate's world came in a phone call.

At five forty-three on an early September afternoon.

Rob's first Saturday as a volunteer, though he'd visited Lambsmoor Farm twice before as a spectator.

'I might not get to do any riding,' he'd said that morning before leaving. 'Each child has one helper to lead their pony, and at least one – sometimes two more – to walk by their side to avoid accidents.'

Kate had liked the sound of that.

'Perhaps this is something,' she said now, 'that I could do with you sometime. So long as I don't have to get up on the horse.'

'You wouldn't,' Rob had said, real pleasure in his face. 'I'd love that.'

It had not happened during the children's ride, the organizer told her on the phone.

His name was Mack, and his own shock and distress were clear in his voice.

'It was later,' he told Kate, 'while Rob and another helper were riding together on Lambsmoor Hill.'

In the kitchen, Kate sat down at the table, laid her left hand on the surface.

'His colleague's horse was acting up, and your husband went to help,' Mack went on. 'His mare lost her footing and fell.'

She stared at her wedding ring, then at the veins beneath her skin.

'Is Rob all right?'

She could hear calm in her voice.

Knew, already, that in another moment it would be gone.

Everything would be gone.

'Please,' she said. 'Tell me.'

'I'm afraid your husband was crushed by the horse,' Mack said.

Blood rushed through arteries, roared in her head and through her soul.

Her hand moved off the tabletop and gripped the edge, to keep her from falling from her chair.

'Is he alive?' Kate asked, at last.

'I'm afraid not,' Mack answered. 'I am so very sorry, Mrs Turner.'

His face was unmarked. Calm and peaceful.

Sleeping. None of it true, after all.

Kate's father was holding her right hand tightly while she fought to keep the inevitable at bay for just a few more seconds. *Please.*

Michael began to weep, his tears confirming what her eyes had refused to register: that it was true. Yet still it was not real to her even then, with Rob before her.

And her tears, like her mind, seemed frozen.

They gave her time, were all very kind.

Someone came, after a while, to speak to her about tissue donation.

A woman in a dark suit with ash blond hair and sad eyes.

Kate heard the word 'tissue' and stopped her.

'What about his organs?' she asked. 'Rob carried a donor card.'

She comprehended what the other woman was speaking about, but it seemed to be happening at a strange and inaccessible level, as if they were talking about someone else entirely.

'Your husband's heart,' the woman explained to Kate and Michael, 'stopped beating too long before the paramedics reached him, which means, unfortunately, that his organs are unusable. Tissue and bone, however, can be donated for up to twenty-four hours after death.'

'Right,' Kate said. 'OK.'

And then, with a shudder of deep shock, it came to her what they would have to do to Rob to grant that final wish, and though his death was still not real to her, the picture of scalpels cutting into his flesh was suddenly so *acutely* real she wanted to scream.

'Now, please,' she said to Michael, her voice harsh. 'We have to go now.'

'But don't you want to—'

'*Now.*'

Ψ

T he days blurred, one into the next.

People around her all the time. Her parents, other people, Abby Wells flying over from Brussels where she'd been working, other friends and colleagues. Richard Fireman, the police, Martin Blake, neighbours she scarcely remembered meeting. All wanting to help her, treading gently.

She hated them all, longed for them to go.

To leave her alone with what was left of Rob.

They had been together again for what seemed such a short time, yet it had begun to feel as if he had never gone away; his essence had been infused back into their cottage, which was why she needed them all to be *gone*, so that she could hold on to it for as long as it remained.

Hold on to *him*.

Bel was there all the time, sleeping there, making her breakfasts and lunches and suppers, feeding her in a way Kate could not recall her ever having done during her childhood.

'I'd rather do it myself,' she told her repeatedly.

'Plenty of time for that,' her mother said.

'It's helping Bel,' her father told Kate. 'If you can stand it.'

'Yes,' Kate said. 'Of course.'

Why not let them do it for her, she decided dully, the way all her thoughts came and went now. Why not let them make her food that she couldn't eat, and see to it that she went to bed and not sleep, and sit with visitors and not listen to the kind things they said about Rob?

Bel and Michael scarcely pushed her, until it came to the funeral arrangements.

'Do what you think,' Kate told them.

'You need to be involved with this,' Bel said.

'We want this to be right for you,' Michael said. 'For Rob.'

'He won't know,' Kate said.

The essence she'd wanted to cling on to, to wrap herself in, be *alone* with, was ebbing steadily away, was already almost gone, being rubbed out by these other loving, well-meaning people. And when that was finally erased, there would be nothing left of him.

The funeral arrangements meant nothing to her.

Rituals.

Ψ

Marie Coates, the woman from Rob's school who'd first suggested he volunteer at Lambsmoor Farm, came to visit Kate one week after the funeral.

It was late September and Kate was alone, Bel having gone home to Henley at last, two days earlier.

'I didn't want to intrude before,' Marie Coates said, after Kate had helped her ease her wheelchair over the threshold and into the sitting room.

She was, Kate thought, in her late forties or perhaps early fifties, had short salt-and-pepper hair and keen grey-blue eyes, wore a cornflower blue pullover over an old-fashioned tweed skirt that covered her knees.

'No intrusion,' Kate said, politely.

She was still on automatic, going through the motions. Not allowing herself to think about her loss, about the months wasted in their last year. Visitors came but soon left again, unnerved, Kate realized, by the invisible but solid wall they encountered, perhaps afraid of being the ones to finally penetrate the force field and release the grief dammed up behind it.

'I didn't come to the funeral,' Marie Coates went on, 'because I felt I might be the last person you'd want there.'

'Why?' Kate asked. 'You and Rob were friends.'

'But it was my doing,' the other woman said. 'Which is why I've come now. To ask for your forgiveness.'

'It was an accident,' Kate said.

'But Rob wouldn't have been there,' Marie Coates said, 'if I hadn't talked him into it.'

Which was true.

'He wanted to go,' Kate said.

Because being unkind would not bring him back, and anyway, it was true, he had wanted it.

'Have they told you,' the older woman asked, 'that it was me Rob was trying to help when it happened?'

Kate wished now that she would not go on, because her own courtesy was, in fact, utterly sham. Because ever since she had heard that Rob's body had been crushed because of his courage, she'd wished with all her strength that this woman had died instead of him.

'You mustn't blame yourself,' she managed to say.

Hauling up the last dregs of her own kindness.

And then, abruptly, she realized that Marie Coates seemed familiar.

'Have we met before?' she asked.

At school, perhaps, though she'd seldom gone there, had not been in the habit of meeting Rob after work. And in any case, since Rob had said Marie Coates worked in the school office, she'd probably kept different hours, so Kate was even more unlikely to have met her there, and yet . . .

'Briefly,' the other woman answered her question. 'At a self-help group meeting in Reading some months back.'

Kate remembered. 'You were the organizer, when—'

'When one of our members behaved very badly towards you.'

'And you intervened,' Kate said. 'I don't think I ever thanked you.'

'It was my job,' Marie Coates said. 'It was nothing.'

It came to Kate then – for she hadn't given it a thought till that moment – that Sandi West had come to the funeral and spoken to her, just a few trite words, kindly meant, she supposed, and she recalled now, with mild surprise, that she'd felt no animosity towards her – nor towards Delia, who had, of course, been there. Though then again, feelings of any kind had been at a premium that day, and any that had slipped through had been, in any case, for Rob.

She offered tea, finally, politely, realizing that for some reason she no longer needed this woman to be quite so swiftly gone.

'I thought my mother told me,' she said, 'your name was Mary.'

'That's how Bel knows me,' Marie Coates explained. 'Another member called me Mary my first time there, and I didn't like to correct her, so that's who I remained.' She smiled. 'It didn't seem important.'

Kate found, despite herself, that she liked her, understood why Rob had admired her. Her deftness with her wheelchair and her attitude was such that her disability seemed almost invisible most of the time, certainly irrelevant. She seemed calm, a woman of common sense and candour, which had, Kate presumed, to make her especially effective with children.

'Your volunteer work must be rewarding,' she said.

'Very,' Marie said. 'Rob told me you don't like horses.'

'I like them well enough from a distance, but getting on board scares me.'

'You're not alone there,' the older woman said.

'If that weren't the case,' Kate said, 'I might have been with Rob that day.'

'And he might not have been riding with me.'

Kate shook her head. 'There's no point to that.'

'None at all,' Marie agreed.

They spoke for a while about Rob, and Kate could tell how much this woman had liked him, which warmed her. Their cottage had been full lately of people who'd both liked and respected Rob, none of them managing to reach Kate's penned up senses; but there was, as he had expressed, something special about Marie Coates.

'I hope you know,' the older woman said, with great gentleness, 'how very happy you made him.'

Others had told her that too, yet now the words seemed to rip at Kate's insides, brought tears to the surface.

'I'm sorry.' She wiped at her eyes.

'Nonsense,' said Marie Coates.

'I've hardly cried,' Kate said, which was true.

'Then let it out,' Marie said, softly. 'You won't lose him.'

Kate wondered, even as she wept, how this stranger could know that was one of the reasons she'd been holding herself together so tightly; because of her irrational fear that by opening up too much, a little more of Rob's essence – the last, most precious stuff of all hoarded inside her – might escape through the cracks.

There was something else that Kate had been holding on to tightly.

A secret, hers and Rob's, though he hadn't known about it *before*.

He knew now, if he was anywhere at all, for she had whispered it to him a thousand times or more.

It confused Kate that she should be on the verge of telling

this woman, this *stranger*, something she hadn't yet shared with her own parents. Perhaps it was because Marie Coates had been Rob's friend, or perhaps because she was the last person he had spoken to in his life.

'I'm pregnant,' Kate said.

Fifteen weeks, give or take.

She'd had not even the slightest suspicion, before Rob's death, that she might be pregnant. Her periods, ever since Caisleán, had been erratic, her body confused by shock, she had assumed, still settling down into her new life back with Rob.

The recent absence of PMS ought, she eventually realized, to have flagged some kind of alert, but it was, she supposed, a little like removal of pain; once you were free of it, you didn't go in search of it, didn't ask for trouble.

Her regret that Rob had not known was vast and all-consuming.

'I don't want any special tests,' she had instructed her GP and midwife. 'No AFP test – or at least, if you have to do anything like that, please don't tell me if anything's wrong – and *definitely* no amniocentesis.'

She was adamant. Everything necessary to protect the baby, but no deliberate hunt for problems, because nothing and no one would persuade her to consider termination under any circumstances, and she wanted no negative thoughts to scar their child's growing processes.

None of that had anything to do with what the Caisleán gang had claimed to stand for. She spat on their brand of fanaticism, whatever might ultimately be claimed by some defence lawyer to have been their fundamental motivation.

This was the one and only thing she could still do for Rob.

Their baby, due in mid-March.

Their *baby*.

Ψ

The inquest, in November – opened soon after Rob's death and then adjourned for reports – seemed to hit Kate harder than the funeral had.

Keeping her grief so rigidly locked down had been a semi-subconscious act. Initially, for self-protection, and because the events at Caisleán had taught her that it was possible to block out horror, to pick oneself up and skate over the surface rather than delve into what lay beneath. Then, once she'd learned about the pregnancy, she had hung on to that same mechanism because of the new life growing inside her, because now all that mattered was protecting their child.

'Better to let it out.'

She'd lost count of how many people had said that.

She did not believe it.

When it came to the Coroner's Court, however, with the protective numbing of early shock long gone, Kate found that, when Marie Coates and one of the attending paramedics gave their accounts of the accident and Rob's injuries, she felt as if she was hearing the horrifying description of his death for the first time.

'Be over soon,' Michael, beside her, told her softly.

Only if she blotted it out again, buried it deep.

The verdict, as had been anticipated, was straightforward.

Accidental death. No one to blame.

Kate's emotions were far more complicated. Not least those relating to Marie Coates, for whose new friendship she found she felt grateful, despite her part in Rob's accident. As sociable as she could be in the right frame of mind, Kate had never been a chummy person, had, she supposed, many more acquaintances than real friends.

'Never underestimate the value of a good woman friend,' Bel had once told her.

Another sample, Kate thought now, of her mother's wisdom.

And felt, some twenty-two weeks into her own pregnancy, quite overwhelmed by a suddenly intense gratitude for her, too.

Ψ

The call from Martin Blake came first – at nine thirty in the morning a week after the inquest – to let Kate know that the trial was scheduled to begin on the eleventh February, but to reassure her that she did not, at this early stage, need to concern herself with any preparations.

Bel telephoned, five minutes later, to ask if Kate had heard Marie's bad news.

'There was a terrible fire,' she said. 'Her flat's been completely gutted.'

'Is she all right?' Kate was dismayed.

'She's fine,' Bel told her. 'She was out, thank God, but still, you can imagine.'

Certainly Kate could imagine. The ramifications for anyone would be dreadful enough, but for a disabled person who must, presumably, have had special equipment fitted in her home, who'd probably taken years to get everything just *so* for her safety and comfort . . . And such a loss was bound to be an added burden for a woman as independent as Marie Coates.

'I wonder,' she said, on impulse, 'if she might like to come and stay here.'

'Goodness,' Bel said. 'You need to think about an offer like that.'

'I know,' Kate agreed. 'But we do have a sofa bed in the office.' Conscious of the *'we'*, she moved swiftly on. 'And the shower's downstairs, isn't it, so it should work in theory.'

'I thought,' Bel said, 'you wanted space.'

Said with remarkably little irony, Kate thought, considering how often her offers to come and stay through her daughter's pregnancy had been rejected.

'This does sound like an emergency,' she said.

'And it's very kind of you to offer,' Bel said. 'But you have to be absolutely sure you could stand it. Having a disabled person to stay could be complicated, though clearly you're already considering that.'

'It's quite likely,' Kate said, 'that Marie might hate the idea.'

'Knowing how well she thinks of you,' Bel said, 'I rather doubt that.'

Ψ

As another, infinitely bleaker, Christmas came and then merci-fully departed, Kate sensed that some of the illusory calm she'd just about been managing to keep wrapped around herself, was beginning to disintegrate.

Grief, pregnancy and apprehension about the trial – now less than a month and a half away – were still preventing her from working properly. Her research for the Duval biography had all but ground to a halt, and in mid-December Fireman had told her that he could no longer put off the decision to bring in another columnist.

'I wish to Christ I could have held on a bit longer, Kate, and I wish I could say this is temporary.' His youthful face had been regretful. 'But the fact is, I think we both know that circumstances aside, you're not really the *Short-Fused Female* any more.'

'So who am I exactly, do you think?' Kate enquired.

She felt no shock, nor even sadness, certainly no resentment.

'I think you're a been-through-hell, not-quite-back, bloody brave mother-to-be.'

'Do you think I'm ever going to be able to write again?'

'You won't be able *not* to,' Fireman said. 'Once the hormones have settled, or probably before, who knows? You're a good writer, Kate. It's just time to move on.'

Nicest sacking she'd ever had.

Marie, who had been staying with her by then for almost a month and from whom Kate had refused to take rent, said it was high time she started paying her way.

'Not necessary,' Kate had told her.

'It would only be for as long as you want me here, of course,' Marie said. 'After the baby's born, you'll probably want Bel or a nanny.'

'I shouldn't think I'll want either,' Kate had said.

The fact was that then, and still now, with the festive season over and with Martin Blake telling her she needed to meet with a barrister to discuss her evidence, Kate couldn't seem to really think about the birth at all, could scarcely even seem, for the moment, to relate properly to the tiny girl growing inside her – healthily, thank God, they kept reassuring her.

'Anyway,' she'd told Marie, 'money's not a problem yet.'

Rob's life insurance policy was cushioning her, along with his pension fund, and to date Kate had been managing to keep at least that side of her life ticking over, paying bills and dealing with Rob's estate, though each successive stage of that was another harsh reminder, rocking her with fresh sorrow and intense bitterness, seeming to leave her a little weaker rather than stronger.

Marie had been an easy house guest, taking care of herself as much as possible, taking pains not to get in Kate's way more than necessary; three days a week she drove herself to Rob's old school in her modified Nissan, then spent hours at a time seeing friends, running errands, monitoring progress on the restoration of her flat and, for the most part, refusing offers of help.

'You've given me a home,' Marie said. 'No one could do more.'

An almost perfect house guest, in fact. Yet still, Kate had begun to wonder if she might not start feeling just a little more like a mother-to-be if she had the cottage back to herself again for the remaining weeks before the birth.

'You mustn't feel you can't leave when your place is ready,' she'd said to Marie between Christmas and New Year, 'because you think I won't be able to manage alone. Any time you're ready to move back, I'll be happy for you and absolutely fine.' She'd paused. 'As it is, for the moment, I can't seem to see beyond this damned trial.'

'Hardly surprising,' Marie said. 'And if you can stand having me around for a while longer—'

'It's not that at all,' Kate jumped in. 'You're a pleasure to have around.'

'In that case,' Marie said, 'I would like to be here for you through to the end of that dreadfulness, whatever the outcome.'

No one else, except Martin Blake, had been honest enough to raise with Kate the possibility of a negative outcome to the case.

After so much time having passed since the crime, the *Flies* trial (the name bestowed by the media) seemed suddenly to be closing in with alarming rapidity. The eleventh of February, the scheduled date, was just inside the custody time limit appertaining to the charging of Edward Booth – Pig – the last of the trio to have been arrested; the prosecution having managed to circumvent the rules to a degree because all three defendants were to come to Crown Court in one trial.

CPS approval notwithstanding, Kate and Blake were still aware of the prosecution's continuing misgivings over the burden of proving beyond reasonable doubt that the three accused, together with the late Carol Marsh – allegedly directed by an unseen leader – were guilty. Kate's identifications and statement having been enough to result in charges, certainly, but still potentially shakeable by sharp cross-examination.

'I didn't go through all that,' she told Blake, 'to let them unnerve me in court.'

'I don't doubt that,' the solicitor said.

Fine words, they both knew, cloaking her ever-rising nervousness.

There was still too little conclusive evidence for their liking. A few copies of a famous book owned by each of the accused was not irrefutable proof of anything. Nor even their time together at the same children's home.

The Summertown newsagent's robbery, though helpful, was no huge booster either, with Mitcham dead.

Only one of the gang could be proven conclusively to have been at Caisleán, and that only because she had died there.

Kate's parents, Blake and Marie all strove to buoy up her spirits.

'They wouldn't be continuing with the prosecution,' Michael maintained, 'if they weren't fairly certain of a good outcome.'

Fairly.

'For myself,' Kate said to Marie one evening in the first week of January, 'I still sometimes wish there didn't have to be a trial at all.'

'Let them get off scot-free, you mean?' Marie shook her greying head. 'I don't think I could be as generous in your place.'

'Nothing to do with generosity,' Kate told her. 'More to do with cowardice. Having to see them, go through it all again.'

'But you are an exceptionally forgiving person,' Marie said. 'Having me here.'

This was one of the reasons Kate thought she wouldn't mind when Marie left.

'Please,' she said. 'Stop.'

She had told her repeatedly that she did not blame her for Rob's death, but that talking about it was almost unbearably painful and draining, which troubled her for the baby's sake more than her own.

'I do worry,' she said now, 'about not being able to get justice for Laurie.'

'So is that the real crux of the trial for you?' Marie asked. 'What happened to Laurie Moon, rather than to you?'

Kate felt a surge of irritation, the question seeming to her intensely stupid. 'It's both, obviously. But Laurie is dead, and her son has no mother.'

'Though it seems he never did have much of one.'

'Please don't.' Kate was sharp. 'I suspect Laurie may have suffered more than enough of that while she was alive, poor girl.'

'I'm sorry,' Marie said. 'I seem to be upsetting you tonight.'

'It's upsetting stuff,' Kate said.

'I know how much you hate me nagging,' Bel said next day, after she'd turned up at the cottage bearing lunch, 'but you're not eating properly, whatever you say, and you don't look very well, and I'm frankly worried about you.'

Kate didn't answer, an attack of bleakness threatening to engulf her.

'Do you think, perhaps,' Bel said, after a moment, 'it might be time for you to ask Marie to move out, especially since her place seems almost ready?' She paused. 'You know you could stay with me for a little while – I promise I'd leave you in peace. Or I could come back here, give you a little TLC.'

'I'm sure I'll manage perfectly well on my own when Marie does go.' Kate sighed. 'I just don't want to seem ungrateful to her, especially since she seems so keen to keep me company till after the trial.'

'Even so,' Bel said, 'it does occur to me that you might not be doing Marie the greatest of favours by letting her become too dependent.'

'She hardly lets me do anything for her,' Kate said. 'On the contrary.'

'I meant dependent on your company.'

Kate managed a smile. 'You mustn't worry about me.'

'Comes with the job,' Bel said.

'How often do you think about the fifth gang member?'

Marie's question, that same evening, startled Kate, jangling her nerves.

'As seldom as possible,' she answered.

'I can imagine,' Marie said. 'Because it could, of course, be anyone.'

'One of my reasons for not thinking about it,' Kate said pointedly.

'It's all a bit of a mystery, isn't it?' the other woman persisted. 'Why their leader wasn't there with them?'

Kate bit down her irritation. 'Rob's theory was that he might be a coward.'

'He?' Marie queried.

'Rob thought so.'

'And you?'

'I don't want to think about it at all,' Kate said. 'As I've told you, repeatedly.'

'You'd like me to shut up now.' Marie was good-humoured.

'On this subject, yes,' Kate said. 'Definitely.'

'Of course,' Marie said. 'No problem.'

The time really was coming, Kate knew, for her to ask her to go.

Those questions about the fifth member had felt almost deliberately provocative, which seemed strange given the nature of their friendship till recently; a calm, restful kind of companionship, just what Kate had needed in the early weeks after losing Rob.

Something else, too, had been nagging at her.

An incident a couple of weeks ago that she'd neglected to mention to Bel or Michael – that she had, in fact, been trying hard not to dwell on.

She'd gone to the cemetery with a pot of budding white Christmas roses, and been startled to find Marie there, sitting in her wheelchair on the gravel path close to Rob's grave.

Tears in her eyes.

'I'm sorry.' Marie had brushed them swiftly away. 'I hope you don't mind.'

'Of course not,' Kate had said, not quite truthfully, for she had found, perhaps oddly, that she did mind.

'I just feel so guilty,' Marie had explained.

Which Kate had certainly believed. Yet finding her there, so visibly upset, had made her wonder suddenly if perhaps Marie might have been a little in love with Rob. Which was, despite the age difference, not so improbable, since Rob had been an attractive man, and plainly fond of Marie.

Admiration on his part, Kate had no doubt, but on hers . . .

Which would make Marie's drawing close to Rob's widow quite sad.

And a little disturbing.

Ψ

Martin Blake telephoned on the eighth of January with news of a breakthrough.

'They found Laurie's car,' he said, 'some time ago.'

'Why didn't you tell me?' Kate asked.

'Because no one told me,' Blake said. 'There's more.'

Anticipation sent a prickling down Kate's spine.

'Whoever drove her car and hid it was not quite as meticulous as they were, later, at Caisleán.' Blake paused. 'Kate, they have a DNA match for Carol Marsh.' He noted her silence. 'Which proves, at least, that "Simon" was party to Laurie's kidnap.'

'But doesn't necessarily help convict the others,' Kate said.

'Patience,' Blake said, gently.

Ψ

An unwelcome visitor arrived, without warning, three days later. Sandi West, coming to call on Kate.

Just what she needed, after a night of crazy dreams that had seemed, so far as Kate could recall, to have included everything from being tied up in the bath at Caisleán to breastfeeding an unnaturally large baby.

'I've come now,' Sandi said, 'because I know it's a school morning for Mary.'

Having no real alternative, Kate invited her in and offered her coffee.

'I don't want you to put yourself out,' Sandi said.

'It's no problem,' Kate said.

'All the same,' Sandi said. 'No, thank you.'

Her disability was plainly causing her more pain than ever, Kate saw, as her mother's friend made her way into the living room. She was using two sticks now, manoeuvring herself with difficulty towards one of the armchairs.

'I've come,' she said, settling down at last, 'because I have something to tell you.'

'All right.' Kate sat on the sofa in the centre of the jacquard throw she and Rob had bought together in the brief golden months of their reconciliation.

'I've tried talking to Bel about this,' Sandi said, 'but she doesn't really listen to me these days, and I accept that's out of loyalty to you, which is fair enough. But I've decided this is something you really do have to know.'

Kate had been tired before Sandi came, the baby's kicking wearing her out.

'It's about Mary,' Sandi said.

'Her name is Marie.' Kate hadn't bothered to correct her the first time, but now it irritated her. 'What about her?'

'I know she's been living here,' Sandi said, 'which is not my business, of course, except I feel you should know what a great interest she's always shown in you.'

'And isn't that a good thing?' Kate asked.

'It's a peculiar thing, I'd say,' Sandi answered. 'I'm talking about long before you met her, Kate. When Bel was still coming with me to the group, and Mary always used to pick out people to be especially interested in. When it came to you, I can tell you she often used to pump me for information.'

For just a moment or two, Kate had found herself starting to listen with a degree of real curiosity, but then she remembered Sandi's appalling insensitivity at the group meeting she'd attended, and recalled, too, Marie's intervention – and Sandi West was most definitely the type of woman to bear a grudge, of that she was certain.

'I think, perhaps, you're overreacting,' Kate said.

'I don't think so,' Sandi disagreed. 'I've thought about this long and hard, Kate, and I know we've never got along, so I expect you think this is sour grapes. But don't you think, given what those terrible people were saying to you about your poor dead baby before they killed Laurie Moon—'

'Sandi, I'm not allowed to speak about the case.'

'I'm not asking you to,' Sandi said. 'Just to listen when I tell you that what Mary Coates seemed most interested in about you was your *miscarriage*.'

'For God's sake.' Kate stood up, trembling with anger, one hand covering her abdomen. 'I'd like you to go, please, Sandi.'

'Mary kept her questions low-key, but there was no mistaking her curiosity.' Sandi had always been tenacious. 'The fact is, your mum used to bring her problems to the group, and in those days, let's face it, you were often one of her biggest problems.'

'I want you to go *now*,' said Kate.

'All right,' Sandi said, 'but—'

'*Now.*'

'Just don't say I didn't warn you,' Sandi said.

Of what, exactly, Kate wondered afterwards, had Sandi been warning her? If any of that rambling unpleasantness had been true, what had she been suggesting it meant?

That Marie was a much nosier creature than one might believe.

Which might be cause for annoyance, but hardly constituted a capital offence. Especially considering that disability might, for some, lead to an unhealthy interest in other people's lives.

Except that Marie Coates was an active woman, and even though she hadn't wanted to return to the disabled children's riding group since Rob's accident, she still worked at the school three days each week. Hardly the personality to sit and feed off the misfortunes or joys of others.

There was one other possibility, too ludicrous even to consider, and it had only flashed up in Kate's mind because of Sandi's melodramatic 'warning'.

Could she, by any insane chance, have been implying something else altogether? That Marie – or Mary, as Sandi persisted in calling her – might have been somehow connected to the gang?

Had perhaps even *been* the fifth member? The Chief?

That was laughable. Truly mad. Although not much more so, Kate reminded herself, than the time after that meeting when she had briefly entertained a wild suspicion that Sandi West herself might have been involved.

'Too many chiefs.' The remark Sandi had made then that had sparked the suspicion. Looking right at Kate as she'd said it.

And that had happened, now she thought about it again, immediately after Marie had stopped Sandi from harassing her.

Which only meant that, as Kate already knew, Sandi was a mixer, nothing more sinister than that. And that Marie was an occasionally irritating, but wholly innocent, bystander.

Who might have been in love with Rob, Kate reflected again. Who was now living with her because of her friendship with Rob.

Because of Rob's death.

Who had been with him when he had died. The only person with him.

Their tiny daughter kicked inside her, coinciding with another entirely new possibility.

Was it remotely possible that Marie might have made some kind of overture to Rob that day on Lambsmoor Hill, and that he might have rejected her?

Kate thought again about those tears at the cemetery.

If there was anything at all *wrong* about Marie, then it had nothing whatever to do with Caisleán. And if she was going to consider this rationally, Kate knew suddenly that she needed to forget, for the time being, about everything except Rob.

His accidental death.

The only account of it Marie's.

Ψ

S andi turned up again two days later, while Marie was at work. Kate spotted her parking her aged Morris Oxford outside the cottage, ducked inside, well away from the window, and turned off her CD player.

She'd had another restless night's sleep, punctuated by hideous nightmares about babies being aborted with kitchen knives.

She did not respond to the bell.

Which rang three times.

'I know you're in there,' Sandi's voice called.

She sounded even more insistent than the last time.

'You can't ignore me forever, Kate.'

Now she sounded belligerent.

'You've already as good as taken away the best friend I ever had.'

Aggressive.

'I hope you know I can never forgive you for that.'

'Are you feeling all right?' Marie asked that evening, after Kate had cooked dinner but hardly touched it.

'I'm fine,' Kate said.

'If you're unwell, you mustn't put on a brave face.'

'I wouldn't do that to the baby,' Kate said.

'You're allowed to take care of yourself too, you know,' Marie said. 'Don't forget you have to be mother and father to this one.'

'Thank you for reminding me,' Kate said.

Marie broached the subject first next morning, as Kate was making tea.

'I was very tactless last night. I'm sorry.'

'It's all right,' Kate said. 'Forget it.'

'I know you're not as comfortable as you were, having me here.'

'I wouldn't say that,' Kate said.

'No,' Marie said. 'You probably wouldn't, being a kind person.'

Kate felt embarrassed. 'I'm not sure I qualify as kind, much of the time.'

She brought two mugs to the table as Marie wheeled herself into position, then went back to butter toast and slip two more slices into the toaster. Things that weren't possible for the disabled woman to do here as she would have in her own adapted home; things she would, undoubtedly, be relieved to be able to do for herself again.

'I've been thinking about something else,' Marie said after a moment, 'and I know you don't like talking about it, but I would like to ask you something.'

'Go on,' Kate said.

'I know that if I were you,' Marie said, 'I would never have let the woman who caused my husband's death—'

'Please.' Kate's stomach began to knot. 'Don't.'

'Hear me out, please.' Marie saw Kate shake her head, turn away. 'It's simply that I was wondering if it might help, just a little, if I was to show you where it happened.'

Kate had not been up to the Ridgeway Path since Rob had died.

An insane picture grew suddenly in her mind, of the disabled woman rising from her wheelchair to push her over the edge of Lambsmoor Hill.

She turned around to face Marie.

'Yes,' she said. 'I think it might.'

They went in the modified Nissan, Marie driving further than cars were officially permitted, bumping along a narrow track until they were part-way up the hill, as close as possible to the place where it had happened, and then Kate stood by while the other woman worked herself from vehicle to wheelchair.

'I wish you'd let me help,' Kate said.

'I prefer to do it myself,' said Marie, her breath steaming in the winter air.

'I know you do.'

Remarkable person in general, no question about it.

Rob had been right.

Not a bad place to die, Kate thought, standing on the pathway on the curve of the hill in the freezing January wind, the Ridgeway in sight to the south. And Caisleán was just a handful of miles away, yet the clamour in her mind of those wicked memories was silenced now, their images smashed by the realization of what had happened *here*.

She raised her eyes, looked towards the winter bleak summit of the hill, the sounds and smells of the downs whipping up around her, the beginnings of a sleet shower lashing her cheeks and ears, stinging her eyes, enveloping her as she waited.

For something. She wasn't quite certain what.

The baby, their daughter, kicked her vigorously, as if she was trying to bring her mother to her senses, to remind her that she had to live for *her* now.

'I can't come with you all the way,' Marie said. 'It was different on horseback.'

'Of course,' Kate said.

Marie raised her right arm and pointed, indicated the spot. 'There,' she said.

Kate climbed the hill and stood there, all alone, near a solitary birch tree, leafless and bending in the wind.

She shut her eyes.

The disabled woman down below did not rise from her chair.

Kate imagined her husband falling from the horse, the crushing of his body.

They had told her it had happened swiftly, and she had chosen to believe that, wanting to think of Rob in the kind of rural place he loved, perhaps fearing for his horse more than for himself; then simply, painlessly, gone.

And since then, much of the time, she had *chosen*, with an iron will, to think of his absence as little different from the period of their separation. Something survivable.

But now, here on this hill, it was all terribly different.

Suddenly she could *feel* Rob's death, and knew it had not been painless at all, but fires of agony instead. His ribs pounded by the massive weight, bones being smashed, his poor lungs exploding, his knowledge that it was all about to end.

Kate *felt* it.

And began to scream.

Ψ

They told her, much later, that Marie had dragged her back, somehow, into the car. Which had been, of course, all but impossible, except, they said, that her upper body strength was extraordinary, that *she* was extraordinary, that she had torn a shoulder muscle and wrenched her back, but had ignored her own pain, taking care of Kate.

Without Marie Coates, they all said, Kate would have had her baby right there on that cold, windswept hill, and there would have been no hope for her scrap of a daughter.

In the Special Care Baby Unit in Swindon's Great Western Hospital, Roberta Turner – born in the early hours of the fifteenth of January, and to be known as Bobbi – lay and wriggled and fed and peed and slept in an incubator, but was, her mother was assured, doing very well.

At thirty-one weeks, Bobbi was frighteningly small, Kate thought, but she watched her incredibly tiny, dark-haired daughter each and every minute she was allowed to, and felt love in ways she had never known before.

The connection with her child was all there now, almost miraculously, love filling her, spilling over, making her feel both deeply afraid and joyously happy; though for a time after Marie had brought her to hospital and phoned her parents, they had feared that the belated hurricane of grief that had slammed through Kate up on Lambsmoor Hill might have ushered in a deeper depression, built up some terrible, new and impenetrable wall around her.

Birth itself had shattered all barriers.

And the infant had taken care of the rest.

Kate's gratitude to Marie seemed too vast to articulate.

'I wish you wouldn't try,' the older woman told her.

'I have to,' Kate said. 'I need to.'

'I should never have taken you there,' Marie said.

'Yes, you should,' Kate said. 'I had to be there, to feel it.'

Her parents had mixed feelings about going to the hill, but felt the same deep gratitude towards the woman who had saved their daughter and grandchild.

'I can never begin to tell you what I feel,' Michael said. 'We owe you so much.'

'Love is what I feel,' Bel told Marie warmly. 'From the bottom of my heart.'

'I did nothing more than anyone else would have,' said Marie.

'I'll just never understand how you found the strength,' Michael said.

'I don't care how,' said Bel. 'They're both here, and that's all that matters.'

Ψ

Sandi West was dead.

Bel heard the news three days after Kate had left hospital – forced to leave Bobbi behind, hating every minute of separation – from another member of their self-help group.

'An overdose,' Bel told Michael and Delia, her shock palpable. 'A whole week ago, and I didn't even know.'

Michael was gentle with her, and even Delia, seeing his ex-wife looking suddenly so much older, wanted to reach out to her.

'I know you'd fallen out,' she said, 'but that doesn't make it easier, does it?'

Michael shot her a look.

'Sorry,' Delia said. 'I didn't mean to sound so tactless.'

'I know you didn't,' Bel said. 'It's all right.'

'Had you seen her lately,' Michael asked, 'at the group?'

'Sandi stopped coming again a while ago,' Bel said.

Because her best friend had abandoned her, she thought, but did not say.

Because she had been criticized in front of the group.

Because Bel had rejected her.

'I wouldn't let Sandi in,' Kate said to Marie, after hearing the news, 'last time she came.'

She had not told either her mother or Marie what Sandi had said to her on her previous visit, had not intended even to mention that she had come, but now the words just slipped out.

'You probably had your reasons,' Marie said, comfortingly.

'She knew I was here,' Kate said, 'but I pretended not to be.'

Guilt tore at her, as it had at Bel.

'Best thing for you to do right now,' Marie said, 'is to go and pick up your mum and take her to see your beautiful little girl.'

Kate knew she was right.

Dried her crocodile tears and went on her way.

Ψ

M artin Blake telephoned on the first of February, three days after Kate had brought Bobbi home.

Chaos and joy and sadness in the cottage, all mingling.

'I need to see you,' Blake told Kate.

'What's happened?' she asked.

'I'd rather speak to you in person,' he said.

He came to the cottage, looked awkward because Marie was there.

'You can speak freely,' Kate told him.

No more secrets from the woman who had saved Bobbi's life.

'They're not going to trial,' Martin said.

His words hung in the air, stark and irrefutable.

'What's happened?' Marie asked the question for Kate.

'It seems,' Blake said, 'that the evidence from Laurie Moon's car is tainted.'

'How, in God's name?' asked Kate.

'I don't know the full story.' The lawyer looked upset and frustrated. 'Helen Newton's spitting feathers – I know she's going to call you when she can bear to.'

'And this is enough to bring down the whole case?' Marie asked.

'On top of the growing doubts over Kate's identifications,' Blake said.

'That's outrageous,' Marie said. 'For that other poor family, too.'

Kate sat quite still, a curious flatness descending on her.

'We always knew it was touch and go,' she said after a moment. 'So long after the crime, and not being able to hear them speak or move around.'

'Still, you recognized them,' Blake said. 'No one on our side's disputing that.'

'They're cowards,' Marie said contemptuously. 'Not even to try to win the case.'

'They're afraid, these days,' Blake said, 'of unsafe convictions.'

They were all silent for a moment or two.

'So does that mean they're going to be released?' Kate asked quietly.

She felt almost calm, knew that it was, of course, spurious.

There was a slight flush on Martin Blake's cheeks.

'As we speak, except for Wilson,' he said. 'I'm so sorry, Kate.'

Jack, at least, still locked away for years for the crimes he'd been jailed for before she'd identified him.

*   *   *

She offered Blake lunch, going through the motions again, chan-
nelling all her feelings into her baby daughter.

The lawyer refused lunch but stayed for a while, concerned
about Kate, taking time to admire Bobbi, marvelling at the tiny
perfection of her.

'I'm very glad they have you,' he said to Marie, quietly, before
he left.

'For as long as Kate wants me,' Marie said.

Michael went to see Helen Newton next day at SOMIT.

'How do we know Booth and Frost won't come after Kate?'

'We don't,' the DCI admitted.

'What about protection?'

'I'm doing all I can,' Newton told him.

'Meaning what?' Michael was sharp. 'The odd patrol car
driving past?'

The detective was sympathetic. 'I'll arrange for a security
advice visit.'

'Kate already has an alarm,' Michael pointed out. 'She and
Rob had it installed after Wilson burgled them for the second
time.'

'I promise you –' Helen Newton was gentle – 'we'll be helping
all we can.'

'And will you be watching *them*?' Michael paused. 'Off the
record?'

'Off the record,' Newton answered, 'depend on it.'

Ralph

R alph telephoned Roger first.

She had dreamed of this, had hardly dared to hope.

Two of her children, free again.

'How are you?' Such a prosaic question, but there would be
time to talk now, plenty of time.

'Getting better,' Roger said.

The voice was still beautiful, but strained.

'Was it very bad?' Ralph asked.

'What do you think?' Roger said.

Ralph asked if she was alone, hoping that company might explain the coldness.

'Just me,' Roger said.

Ralph was getting a bad feeling.

'When can we meet?' she asked.

'I don't know,' Roger said. 'We have to be careful.'

'Of course,' Ralph agreed. 'I was hoping, when the dust's settled a little, maybe we could all manage to meet at the Smithy again.'

'Not all,' Roger said.

'I know,' Ralph said. 'But still, it would be so good, when the time's right.'

'I'm not sure,' Roger said, 'that the time's ever going to be right for that.'

Ralph phoned Pig's number.

'The number you have dialled has not been recognized.'

She tried it again, heard the same robotic voice.

She called Roger again.

An answering machine picked up.

'This is Karen Frost's machine. I can't pick up right now, but I'm available for work, so please leave me a number so I can get back to you.'

Ralph hesitated, abruptly aware that they might be monitoring Roger's calls, wondering if she'd said too much in the last conversation.

'It's me,' she said. 'Please call my mobile.'

She waited for twenty-four hours before she tried again.

Both numbers.

Pig's still unobtainable.

She left a second message for Roger.

Who did not return her call.

Kate

On the fourteenth of February, Martin Blake telephoned Michael to tell him that Wilson was appealing against his sentence, his lawyer claiming that the fairness of his GBH trial had been prejudiced by the adverse *Flies* publicity.

'Does he have a chance?' Michael asked, newly appalled.

'You know as well as I do it's a possibility,' Blake said. 'And there was always the question about the neighbour going for him first with the bat.'

'I'm not sure I want Kate to know,' Michael said, after a moment.

'The Moons are already beside themselves about the spoiled evidence, talking about suing,' the lawyer said. 'Kate's going to hear. Better coming from you, I'd say.'

'Damn and blast him to hell,' Michael said.

'Delia and I have been thinking,' he said to Kate, a few days after he'd broken the news to her, 'that it might be best, just for a while, if you and Bobbi were to move in with us.'

Kate laughed, then felt bad.

'I'm sorry,' she said. 'Truly.'

He'd come for Bobbi's bath, currently his favourite pastime, but even while he held his tiny granddaughter snugly wrapped in her towel he'd had no peace, his mind filled with images of evil roaming free again to target his own child.

'Delia's fine about it,' he said now, downstairs in the kitchen as Kate made him a coffee, 'if that's what you're thinking.'

'And I thank her for that – I thank you both,' Kate said. 'But I really can't see it working out, can you?'

It was hard to know if the thought made her want to laugh again, or cry.

'If it's a space thing,' Michael said, 'we could move to a bigger place.'

'That's more than kind, Dad,' Kate said, 'but it's not just space, and you know it. I'd probably turn into a queen bitch in no time, and I'd really hate that to happen now.'

Which was true, in fact, because Delia had been lovely about Bobbi and kind about Rob, genuinely so, and Kate acknowledged that and was glad of it.

'You already know –' Michael wasn't giving up easily – 'how much Bel would love it if you went to her.'

Kate handed him his mug, and they both sat at the table.

'Same difference,' she said. 'Mum and I get on so wonderfully these days. I'm not sure if I could bear it if that changed, and it would if we tried living together again.' She paused. 'And there's no point you saying "for a while", when we both know you're talking about *them* being out there, which makes this a long-term situation.'

'Forgive me if I find that prospect very hard to take,' Michael said.

'I'm OK, Dad,' Kate said 'all things considered. And don't forget I'm far from being alone.'

A newborn baby and a woman in a wheelchair.

'Not exactly a pair of bodyguards,' Michael said.

'And Mum would be?' Kate asked.

Her father took the point.

'Besides,' Kate reminded him, 'Jack might not win his appeal.'

'I wish to God I could kill you here and now.'

The words still haunted her from time to time.

Michael took a sip of coffee. 'Have you done anything about the panic button?'

'Installed last week.' Kate reached for his hand. 'You and Mum really need to stop spending every minute worrying about us.'

'Not quite every minute,' her father said.

Kate watched him for a moment. 'What else, Dad?'

'Just about Marie.' He paused. 'She is out, isn't she?'

Kate nodded. 'At some meeting.'

'You know how we feel about her saving you and Bobbi, of course.'

'But?'

'Only that before that,' Michael went on, 'your mother and I had the impression you weren't too keen on her staying much longer.'

'That was then,' Kate said. 'Pregnancy and everything else making me ratty. All very different now.' She smiled. 'And let's face it, it is nice having someone else around, at least for the time being.'

'You could get a nanny,' Michael said.

'I don't want anyone else to take care of Bobbi.'

'Or a lodger,' he persisted.

'I have a lodger,' Kate said. 'Who's insisted on paying rent, and who seems to be turning out to be one of the best friends I've ever had.'

Ralph's Children

They met at Wayland's Smithy in the second week of May. Just the three of them.

It was breezy but mild and dry, the place filled with memories. Ghosts.

'I've brought champagne,' Roger said.

'Lovely,' said Pig.

'Nice one,' said Jack.

Roger pulled the bottle and three plastic tulip glasses from a black cool-bag.

'Thanks,' said Pig. 'Though I still feel bad about dumping the Chief.'

'I thought I might,' Jack said, 'but I don't.'

'Let's face it,' Roger said, 'if we'd gone down, it'd all have been her fault.'

'From the word go,' Jack agreed.

'I don't know,' Pig said.

'You're such a fucking softie,' said Jack.

'Can't help it,' Pig said.

Roger opened the bottle and poured, not spilling a drop.

'A toast, don't you think?' she said. 'To freedom.'

'And Simon,' Pig said.

'To Simon,' Jack echoed.

They all drank deeply, drained their glasses.

'She'd still be here,' Pig allowed, 'if it hadn't been for the Chief's plan.'

'There you are then,' Jack said, as Roger poured again. 'So no more feeling bad about her, right?'

'Yes,' Pig said. 'OK.'

'So,' Roger said, 'how long before we can play again?'

'I don't know how that'll go,' Pig said. 'Without the Chief.'

'It won't *be* without the Chief, will it,' Roger said. 'Or have you forgotten?'

'You mean like in the book,' Pig said.

In which Jack, the character, had overthrown Ralph as the children's leader.

'Obviously,' Roger said.

'I think,' Jack said, 'we need to be careful, wait a while.'

'You're right,' said Roger.

For the time being, they drank.

Kate

On a warm, sunny afternoon in late June, Kate was standing in her kitchen looking out into the garden at Marie, who was sitting in her chair beside the playpen in which Bobbi was lying on a blanket, kicking her little feet.

Kate felt almost content.

She still missed Rob every single day, but their daughter was healthy.

The first rough draft of her biography of Claude Duval was half written, and she understood from her new London-based agent that an editor at a firm of publishers was keen to see it on completion.

Bel was dating a landscape gardener, a man named David Miles who everyone seemed to like. Much more to the point, her mother seemed happier than Kate could recall seeing her in a great many years.

Michael and Delia were getting married, and Kate had never

imagined that could make her feel remotely glad, yet it had done exactly that, and she thought that if Rob were here, he might be proud of her for it.

Never too old, it seemed, to grow up.

Bobbi, she supposed, was responsible for that.

Kate looked out at Marie, at her sensible, increasingly grey-haired, very good friend, and wondered if the time was ever going to come when she might want to leave, and how she would feel about that when it happened.

How she would feel about it if it never happened.

Fine, she decided, for now.

Which was, after all, the most that anyone could wish for.

Ralph

R alph sat in the Beast's garden, promises of early summer all around her, the child on the ground beside her.

Ralph was thinking about *them*.

Her lost children.

She knew now that she would never see them again.

All her fault.

The Beast's.

She thought about them all the time, wondered if they would ever forgive her. Wondered if they would ever play the game again; if maybe they already had.

As for her, she'd done what she had to, had gone on with it, played it on her own, one step at a time.

The husband first.

The fire next.

Then the simple good luck of Sandi West's death wish.

No need for intervention there, not a scrap of trouble for her.

Not much luck in her life before her children.

Taken from her now.

Ralph looked towards the cottage, saw *her* in her kitchen, making their tea.

On the ground, the chestnut-haired, blue-eyed baby girl kicked her little legs and smiled up at her.

The Beast trusted her completely now with her child.

So Ralph could take her time. As long as she wanted.

Biding her time.

Planning her own game.

The best and most important game ever.

Motherhood.